Trouble Ahead

Rob Lofthouse

D1634334

Quercus

First published in Great Britain in 2017
This paperback edition published in 2018

Quercus Editions Ltd
Carmelite House
50 Victoria Embankment
London EC4Y 0DZ

An Hachette UK company

A CIP catalogue record for this book is available
from the British Library

EB ISBN 978 1 78429 355 0
PB ISBN 978 1 78429 356 7

10 9 8 7 6 5 4 3 2

Typeset by Jouve (UK), Milton Keynes

Printed and bound in Great Britain by Clays Ltd, St Ives plc

Robert Lofthouse was born in Twickenham and joined his local county infantry regiment (1 PWRR) straight from school at the age of sixteen. After serving twenty years, in locations such as Poland, Germany, Kenya, Canada, the Falkland Islands, Iraq, Northern Ireland and Kosovo, he retired in the rank of Sergeant.

He now works as a defence consultant and lives in Portsmouth with his wife and three children.

Also by Rob Lofthouse

A Cold Night in June
Bazooka Town
Trouble at Zero Hour: The Complete Zero Hour Trilogy

We ought to have a corps of at least 5,000 parachute troops, including a proportion of Australians, New Zealanders and Canadians, together with some trustworthy people from Norway and France.

Winston Churchill, June 1940

Prologue:
Battle of Greece, April 1941

From a large tent surrounded by a few buildings, the soft inviting glow of dawn creeping over the Greek horizon was a welcome sight for Bentley Paine. It marked the penultimate hour of his watch-keeper shift at Regimental Headquarters. As the sun crept up, he rubbed his tired grainy eyes and continued to sip at the foul sweet tea which he had been nursing for a while.

Life for an infantry officer seconded to a cavalry regiment like the 4th Hussars was certainly testing Paine's sense of humour. Drafted in as a liaison officer, he had the unenviable job of keeping a degree of harmony between two constituents of a rather ad hoc battle group: the 4th Queen's Own Hussars, a senior British regiment, whose officers boasted that their forefathers had sat on their chargers next to Wellington himself, and a rough and ready New Zealand infantry battalion. Meetings between the two respective command groups were heated to say the least, since the Kiwi officers were from broad-backed farming stock and unaccustomed to being told what to do by what they claimed were jumped-up, over-priced, silver-spoon-sucking halfwits. They gave Paine no quarter either, concluding rather quickly that he was cut from the same cloth, infantry or not. Bentley didn't have much time for the Kiwis but had to choose his words carefully when in their company, not to mention with the cavalry, who had no time for their infantry bretheren. Not accustomed to street fighting, Bentley had already had to prove his worth by physically stepping in, keeping the New Zealand officers out of arm's reach of their opposite numbers. The young officer would now and then end up with a shiner for his efforts at mediating.

The colonel in command of the battle group was continually phoning Brigade Headquarters, demanding that the troublesome Kiwis be replaced by more reserved, measured men. His demands fell on deaf ears. Unsurprisingly, the command group of the 4th Hussars had been nominated to lead the battle group, and so the Kiwis just had to suck it up and get on with it. In order for there to be some kind of civilized communication between the two, the powers that be had felt it wise to ship in Paine: British enough to understand the intentions and sensitivities of the gentry, yet rough enough to empathize with the New Zealanders.

There was a silver lining to his appointment: to add to his clout while seconded to the cavalry, his own regiment had seen fit to promote him to captain for the duration. This was wonderful news for both Paine and his family. The extra pay made a big difference, even though he was ultimately destined to inherit the Richmond Furlong Company of Richmond, North Yorkshire, an equestrian retail empire that his great-grandfather had carved out of nothing long ago. So once Paine's brief stint in the army was over, everything would eventually be all right, regardless of who won. The Paine family business was convinced that even the German equestrian community needed a company to service its needs, so the war wouldn't ruin their business model. Indeed, in the back of Paine's mind the war was the last thing the family needed to worry about. But his promotion had also unnerved him a little, since he had yet to even serve as a lieutenant commanding a platoon. It was only when he graduated from the military college at Sandhurst that it came to light that no suitable infantry platoon vacancy could be identified, hence the swift secondment to Greece. It just showed Paine that the British Army could indeed think on its feet and find jobs for anyone.

Paine's personal position with 4th Hussars wasn't without issues. The Regimental Headquarters staff made it clear that infanteers were very much outsiders, British or not – ironic, given his family's equestrian business. The adjutant made no apologies for putting Paine on the graveyard shift as watch-keeper, while he and his chums would stroll off into Corinth to sample what was on offer. Corinth was a coastal town, almost eighty kilometres west of the Greek capital Athens. Paine had to settle for the company of corporals and a few troopers who knew how to operate the radios and run the light tanks when their batteries required recharging. He was looking forward to the end of his attachment.

Paine's own unit, the 2nd Battalion of the Yorkshire and Lancashire Regiment, otherwise known as 2 Yorks and Lancs, was stationed on Crete, which did not look too dissimilar to the terrain that flanked the high banks of the Corinth Canal: arid and dusty, with sparse vegetation that varied from green olive groves to harsh clusters of dried grass with spiteful, thorny, lifeless bushes. Regimental Headquarters was situated in among a group of off-white dwellings with flat, roughly tiled roofs. The light tanks were dispersed among the buildings and draped in tatty hessian netting, which served two purposes: it offered shade from the crushing Greek heat and hid the tanks from German aircraft. The main buildings served as billets for the headquarters staff including the commanding officer, whose large, olive drab canvas tent was established in the centre, complete with its own camouflage netting to hide it from the air.

Paine looked around the tent. The radio operators had handsets attached to telephone lines running from the tanks' junction boxes. This allowed the radios to be powered from the vehicles, giving them greater range, which was useful, since Paine and the headquarters staff had to communicate with all the units from the Hussars and the New Zealand battalion; units which included an anti-aircraft location of four 20-millimetre Bofors flak guns and tank squadrons dispersed to the south. The tent was also furnished with folding canvas chairs and a couple of six-foot wooden tables, along with maps neatly pinned to wooden crate lids marking where the battle group were dug in.

Paine's routine of running headquarters in the silent hours was interrupted by a gluttonous belch behind him. In his peripheral vision Paine could identify the arrival of his batman, Corporal John Hallmark. Hallmark stood, one hand down the front of his trousers, adjusting himself, his other hand running through his dark, dry and stiff hair. 'You won't find this view in Blackpool, that's for sure,' he remarked. Paine was not in the mood for conversation with the oaf. Hallmark had given him enough grief, ever since being assigned to him by the adjutant of their battalion back in Egypt. Hallmark, dragged up from the rougher side of the Pennines, specifically Preston in Lancashire, was not to officers' liking at all. Rude, abrasive, it was amazing to think that the man had even received one chevron, let alone three to make him sergeant, prior to his demotion to corporal before sailing to Greece.

Hallmark took a few paces forward to ruin what was left of Paine's morning view, not to mention his mood. The corporal, who was six foot if not an inch more, went out through the open canvas door for his morning piss in the dirt without a care in the world. Paine had passed the point of being bashful; Hallmark went out of his way to try and shock him and whoever else was about. Unshaven, with boots undone, and his trousers and braces hanging over his backside, Hallmark sported an off-white vest that had not been laundered in a while. His arms and shoulders, coated in thick dark hair, were large, powerful, bronzed by the Greek sun. Indecent tattoos covered the majority of his bare skin. He was as strong as an ox and had the sprint power of a prop forward. A good few men back in their parent battalion feared him, and rightly so. Quick to resort to his fists, even quicker when full of ale, the former sergeant gave no quarter to those who he felt to be inferior, officers included, a failing which had facilitated his demotion, and which in turn had led him to his current assignment.

Paine could not bring himself to finish his umpteenth cup of tea of the night and walked outside, tipping its contents onto the dusty ground. He re-entered the gloom of the olive drab tent quickly, anything to put distance between himself and Hallmark. The light breeze coming through brought its fair share of dust, but it was a welcome relief for the lads who were manning the radios. Their job was not all that challenging; most were reading books. The main task for them was just to stay awake. The night had passed without incident. The troops had nothing to report when the operators called them, and that suited Paine just fine, given the chaotic withdrawals of recent days. The Germans were pushing hard into Greece, but British and Commonwealth forces were making it tough going for them. Greece was a harsh mistress to both invader and defender. Both sides were struggling for a decisive advantage, while their political and military masters made increasingly unrealistic demands. It just so happened that the panzers needed fuel more than they needed ammunition, which had given the battle group the chance to withdraw and regroup, and get their affairs and troops in order. And since they had dug in around the canal to the north and its bridge, the Corinth area had been rather settled.

As Paine took note of which officers required early calls, a handset perched on the shoulder of one of the operators crackled into life. The sudden flurry of information caused the operator to flinch and grab for the handset as it slipped towards the floor. Placing his book on the table, he calmly returned the call. 'Hotel Zero Alpha say again. Over.'

Paine moved close to the radio man. The call was from the Kiwis: something was going on. 'Alpha Zero Bravo,' spouted from the headset, 'we have aircraft engines getting louder from the north-east – no, wait . . . We can now see aircraft, twenty plus escorts, over.' As the call cut out, Paine looked at a map pinned to a board. Aircraft from the north-east didn't appear too out of the ordinary. The next incoming call was frantic however. 'Stukas, wait. Out.' Bentley looked up at the roof of the tent. He was suddenly very aware that the flimsy canvas tent would do little to protect them from anything the Germans could throw.

Those who, like Hallmark, were getting up, suddenly moved with a purpose, rushing out to wake their commanders. There would be no lie-in this morning. Paine strode out of the tent and went to where he could see the north side of the canal. He could see the German dive-bombers beginning to work on the forward company, the concussion of their bombs rippling through the area. A commotion behind him caught his attention. Officers in various states of undress were coming out of the buildings and making their way into the tent.

It was chaos. Paine's cavalry colleagues demanded to know what was happening to their companies and squadrons, while the radio operators were fighting the din in the tent, trying to get in touch with the units in the field.

Paine could hear a rumbling noise. As it got louder, so did the voices in the tent. He noticed Hallmark standing just inside the tent flap. Hallmark's hand was slowly rising, as if to ask a question. 'Shut up, all of you!' he bellowed. The corporal was never one for etiquette.

Not used to being shouted at, certainly not by a lowly corporal, the headquarters staff turned, some on the verge of protesting to Paine about his batman's outburst. Paine held up a finger for them to keep mute, for he could also hear the noise building above. 'Listen.'

Everyone stood stock still. The wailing drone got louder; it then became a high-pitched scream. The commanding officer suddenly dashed inside the tent. 'Take cover,' he roared. All of the radio operators and commanders hit the floor, some diving under the tables.

The sudden crash of bombs thundered all around, along with the bass drum concussions of cannon as Stukas strafed the area. Their screaming engines faded instantly as they pulled out of their dive.

As the cacophony subsided, cannon fire could be heard in the distance, with more bomb blasts. As the commanders and operators began to clamber to their feet, it quickly dawned on Paine that he had remained standing throughout the attack, as had Hallmark, who was pulling men up, helping to dust them down. Standing hadn't been stubbornness on Paine's part; it had all been over before he had a chance to pick his own piece of suitable cover. Not that anything in the tent qualified as suitable.

Radio operators went back to being harassed by their officers for status updates on the state of play among the companies and squadrons. Then the growing drone of aircraft dominated the air again. 'Paine,' blurted the commanding officer, 'make yourself bloody useful, and find out what on earth is going on with our flak guns.'

Paine looked down at the Webley revolver attached to his hip by a dusty canvas holster; it was all that most of the officers in the Regimental Headquarters were issued. He eyed the Lee-Enfield rifles sat in a rack next to a table and decided to help himself. Hallmark read his mind, getting there before Paine, grabbing two rifles. Paine pestered one of the radio operators for his clips of ammunition and then headed outside. Far less diplomatic, Hallmark was already plundering his way through the webbing of the other operators. Some stared in challenge at him, but he returned a menacing glare, as if to invite them to take a swing. 'You can go out there and fight, or let me do it. What's it gonna be, girls?' The operators backed off, returning their attention to the headsets.

Paine's plan to commandeer the colonel's staff car was short-lived. It had been punctured by a number of high-explosive cannon rounds and was burned out. The first flak position was a good fifteen hundred metres in the direction of the canal bridge, and to run there was really going to burn on the lungs. Before setting off, Hallmark spotted a few Kiwis who just so happened to be moving around the headquarters in fighting gear. 'You men, follow me. We have to get to the nearby flak position.'

The New Zealanders looked at him as if he had just demanded blood. He was about to reinforce his order when they looked beyond him, pointing north. Both Hallmark and Paine turned to see what had captured their attention.

In the sky above what would have been the forward Kiwi company position was a vast formation of German Junkers 88 transport aircraft. Before Paine could register what was taking place before him, flickering pink, green and white parachutes began to fill the air between the Junkers and the ground. The *Fallschirmjäger*, Germany's elite paratroopers, were attacking. Suddenly, it didn't take much effort for Hallmark to recruit the Kiwi infanteers to his cause; they were very enthusiastic about taking care of the new airborne threat.

Paine concluded that to make a direct dash to the flak guns would be suicide, for the Stukas were still marauding about. He chose a covered route through the olive groves. The best pace Paine and his small force could manage in such close country was a shuffle, with the Kiwi section puffing and panting not far behind him. The sweat running down his temples reminded him that he was without a helmet and probably not dressed as the cavalry would have liked, but given the circumstances that was the least of his worries.

When they finally broke cover out of the groves, the situation at the flak gun emplacement was dire. One gun was burning, a second abandoned, but the other two were giving it all they were worth at the aircraft and parachutes descending north of the canal. Some of the Junkers had dark oily smoke tailing behind them as the gunners found their mark. One of the aircraft burst into flames and then plummeted down out of sight behind a large rocky outcrop. Seconds later, a huge black mushroom cloud billowed skywards. Transfixed, Paine could do nothing but admire the skill of the flak gun crews. As their guns thundered away, he observed their tracer knocking pieces of fuselage from aircraft, occasionally adjusting lower to perforate the Fallschirmjäger as they drifted down under their canopies.

A tap on the shoulder from a Kiwi non-commissioned officer snapped Paine out of his trance, and he began to lead the group over to the battling gun teams.

With the din of battle overwhelming their senses, Paine and his small force were oblivious to the Junkers formation arriving over Regimental Headquarters behind them.

2

Despite the refreshing draught coming through the side door of the Junkers 88, Captain Martin Bassom and his men sweated like beasts. Volumes of equipment were strapped to each man, as well as their personal parachutes, and it had all combined not only to make boarding very cumbersome, but also to make the journey hot and uncomfortable. Only the jump master, who knelt close to the door, had any real freedom of movement. Between the jump master and Bassom were two supply containers, each with its own parachute attached to one end. Bassom despised the containers; they took up too much room, and there was always the hassle of having to recover them on the ground.

Earlier airborne successes had highlighted the need for the men to have their weapons attached to them, so they were fit to fight even before they were out of their parachute harnesses. But even after the victorious missions carried out the year before in the Low Countries, and the reports made by the officers who conducted them, the powers that be still insisted that containers carrying extra weapon bundles be deployed. Officers, including Major Taugen, Bassom's company commander, had managed to lobby the case hard enough for MP 40 sub-machine guns to be issued and attached to those who wished to jump with them. Taugen had conceded that the containers could deliver machine guns, ammunition and other specialist equipment to the battlefield, but argued that if MP 40s were carried on the person rather than in the containers, companies including his own would at least have the means to fight their way to the containers; knives, Luger pistols and grenades were not enough. The negotiated improvement in what weapons could be carried during a jump was still far from ideal, but Bassom knew that you could only demand so much, before being told to remember your place in the command chain.

Bassom adjusted his MP 40 under his chest harness as the jump master nodded in response to a message in his headset. The jump master rose to his feet, bellowing orders at the hot, sweaty paratroopers, but the wind hurtling past and the engine noise rendered him almost mute. However, they were all practised enough to know it was time to jump. 'Action stations,' came the call from the jump master.

With that, a dozen overladen men grunted and cursed as they fought to get to their feet. Bassom had the honour of helping the jump master invert the heavy containers, so they could be shoved out of the door when the order came. Everyone clipped their static lines to the cable that ran the length of the fuselage roof. When they dived from the Junkers, the static line would deploy their chutes for them. Once clipped on, they inspected the chute of the man in front of them, ensuring there was nothing untoward about its fitting and packing. When content, each slapped the shoulder of the man in front, confirming he was ready to dive into battle. At the front, Bassom was inspected by the jump master, the slap on the shoulder coming a few seconds later. Everyone was ready. Bassom acknowledged a thumbs-up from Sergeant Werner, who would be the last man to jump, and was Bassom's right-hand man for the time being. Bassom's wave was casual; nothing to indicate he considered Werner a Nazi upstart, nothing to indicate he was appearing friendlier than he actually felt.

Through the door Bassom could see the other half of his company under canopy as they drifted towards the ground, north of the canal. Some of the aircraft were spilling dark smoke from their engines, random licks of flame indicating some planes had more pressing issues than others. Soot-like shell bursts amid his drifting comrades informed him they would be landing under fire. The two containers prevented him from getting a view of what awaited them on the south side of the canal. But he would soon find out what was there.

The jump master tipped the first container out of the door, the slipstream ripping it rearwards. The second went out the door with the same ferocity. Then he took Bassom by the shoulder and manhandled him into the open aperture. Hands gripping the rails on either side,

Bassom fought the slipstream that tried its hardest to pull him out. It would only be for a few seconds, but to the young captain it felt like a lifetime. Then came the slap on the shoulder, to which he responded as he had been trained. He pushed as hard as he could with his legs to clear the aircraft door, diving down like the eagle printed on the side of his helmet.

As Bassom's canopy filled with air, the harness straps that went between his legs snapped up into his groin, causing him to grunt out loud as his gut began to burn. The din of slipstream and engine faded as he composed himself while drifting down. His company were all around him under mottled green silk. Down to his left, the two containers hit the ground in bursts of dust and arid brush, their pink and white canopies enveloping them; pink indicating medical supplies, white indicating means to wage war. He was heading towards what appeared to be a cluster of drab white flat-roofed dwellings with people running about, pointing up at him. Between the buildings was flapping material, which failed miserably to hide British armour; one of the light tanks appeared to be burning, a plume of smoke drifting lazily skywards. To his right on the ground, near a canal bank, was a smouldering dusty position, its flak guns pounding a steady drumbeat, the gun crews seemingly unaware of his men's impending arrival. He spotted a few men running from the sparse, sorry-looking olive groves towards the guns, but then his attention became consumed by the ground rushing up to greet him.

Cursing and grunting from his landing, which hurt, as they all did, Bassom fought like a man possessed to free himself from his harness. Once clear, he cocked his MP 40, ready for action, and began to move. His radio operator, Corporal Stolz, was swearing his head off as he fought to get free of his rigging lines, but was getting nowhere. Bassom knelt, cutting Stolz's lines as he spoke. 'We need those containers. I know where they are. Follow me.'

Stolz quickly knelt up, ready to fight with his MP 40. 'Yes, sir.' Other paratroopers began appearing all around as Bassom headed off down a slope towards white fabric caught in some bushes. The movement of all the paratroopers was swift and well rehearsed, even though some were limping. Parachuting wasn't without its hazards.

Bassom quickly located both containers, which looked a little battered after their brief flight. His captain's group had now assembled around him, and he stood guard with half of them while the other half attempted to fight their way inside. Within a few minutes they were all armed with extra ammunition, rifles, an MG 34 machine gun and radios. Having got his bearings, Bassom intended to move on the cluster of buildings and poorly concealed vehicles. He could identify the column of smoke from the burning tank he had spotted from the air. But his attention was diverted by fighting which erupted to the right of his group. Elsewhere, some of the paratroopers had gone straight into action, so there was no time to waste; shock was the key to success in seizing the bridge over the Corinth Canal.

'Has anyone got into the medical container?' Bassom asked, removing his helmet and running his hand through his ash-blonde hair. All he got in return was a chorus of 'Not sure' and 'Don't know, sir.'

Bassom addressed Stolz, who had quickly confirmed his radio set had survived its rough landing in the weapons container. 'Can you raise anyone yet?'

Stolz shook his head. 'Not yet, sir. Maybe no one has their radios running yet.'

Bassom nodded, for Stolz had a point. Bassom reminded himself that they had to get a move on. He waved his NCOs forward, for they would take the lead in the advance towards the buildings. The MG 34 crew were ordered to advance on the right side, so they could provide instant fire support if required. Bassom's group, despite its sprains, was now on the attack.

Corporal Muller, Bassom's lead NCO, was first to move from the low ground, and into a position where he could properly observe the buildings. He got down onto his belly, waving and hissing for Bassom to come to him.

Bassom crawled up next to Muller, fishing binoculars from his jump smock as he reached him. Muller whispered in his ear, 'I'm sure I saw men pointing at us, before we landed.'

'Yeah, I thought that too.' They continued to watch until they saw movement around the buildings and what appeared to be a large tent between the structures. But nothing about the movement showed hostile intent. Bassom decided to seize the opportunity. He would take the fight to the enemy. 'I want the MG 34 to remain in this position, and we will flank them from the left. Call the gun team up here.'

In hushed tones, Muller called for the MG 34 team to move up. Privates Kounter and Bernhard were skilled men on the machine gun and extremely fit, hence able to lug the heavy weapon around. They crawled in beside Bassom, once Muller made room. 'Set up here,' Bassom instructed the team. 'We will flank them from the left. Kill anything that runs away to the right, understood?'

The remainder of the group moved up to Bassom's position. After Muller briefed them, he led them at a sprint to the far-left building, Bassom following in the rear. Not because he was reluctant to get into the fight, but because close combat was corporals' work.

With chests heaving and lungs burning, the group made it to the first building without incident, but Bassom then heard commotion and foreign voices. Engines attempted to splutter into life. He had to act quickly; the light tanks could not be allowed to commit to the battle. At a crouch he brushed past his group as they composed themselves after the hot, dusty sprint. Carefully, he peered around a corner, only to be greeted by the muzzle of one of the tanks. The tank's engine access hatches were open, with parts and tools perched on its tracks. He was content this tank was not going anywhere.

Movement in the tent confirmed the enemy was in there. Without consulting his men, Bassom pulled a stick grenade from his belt, primed it by unscrewing the cap at the end of the hollow wooden handle and then pulled the fuse cord. He then lobbed the top-heavy explosive, sending it cartwheeling into the tent. It thudded onto the ground, the commotion in the tent instantly fell silent, and a large number of enemy personnel dived outside. As the grenade detonated, the enemy soldiers grunted as one as the tent was shredded.

Before the dust had even settled, Bassom's group rushed the British. Most of the survivors were concussed from the grenade attack. Those who tried to reach for pistols were shot dead, whether they had come from the tent or were sitting in the open tanks. Bassom's men made quick work of them, their MP 40s firing short controlled bursts into the chests of their stunned enemies. Any British not attempting to take up weapons were spared, many instinctively putting their hands out as if to protect themselves.

Bassom's group had seized the initiative. Some stood poised, weapons at the shoulder over the dead and shocked British, while the remainder of the paratroopers stormed one building and one tank at a time, yelling for anyone inside to surrender. If there was no reply from within the buildings, grenades were tossed inside. The sheer aggression of the German assault was enough to encourage surviving Tommies to come out. Most bleeding and bruised from the grenade attacks, those still alive came out of the dwellings and tanks with hands behind their heads.

With his men on a high from a well-executed attack,

and with prisoners to show for it, Bassom ordered Stolz to contact other units. 'Friendlies coming in from the south,' called out one of the privates. 'They've picked up our MG 34 team.'

Bassom went to greet the new arrivals, as they jogged in. 'Did you get your containers?' he enquired.

'Yes sir,' called Sergeant Dormann, coming to a halt as his men ran past him to an area where the prisoners were already being assembled. 'Damn radio is broken, mind. We tried to call, but it took one hell of a knock in the drop – chute didn't deploy properly.'

Bassom knew that despite their short sharp victory, his group had pressing matters, beginning with the flak guns. 'Sergeant Werner, stay here with a squad to watch the prisoners. The remainder are to follow me. We have to take care of those flak guns killing our guys on the north side. Let's go.'

'You're gonna need me with a reserve group, then, aren't you?' replied the no-nonsense Nazi.

Not all Germans were Nazis, meaning that not all Germans were members of the Nazi Party. Nevertheless, Bassom kept his non-membership of the party quiet. The problem was that, originating from a harsh dairy farming background in Dornitz just west of Berlin, he and his parents had to work hard over the years to look after his disabled brother, Karl, who was Martin's identical twin. Their father Tomas had a poor opinion of the Nazi Party, an opinion that worsened when local SS began talking about committing the disadvantaged to sanatoriums. So as much as possible the family kept Karl's existence under wraps. The truth was that there were a fair few Nazis in the *Fallschirmjäger* and, outside soldiering, Bassom couldn't stand any of them. Werner was particularly staunch in his Nazi beliefs. Bassom found that on the battlefield Nazis were fearless and unwavering, but in camp they were all barrack-room lawyers, sniffing out any sign of dissent from non-party members. 'No, Sergeant,' Bassom responded. 'You organize things here. I'll call you and a contingent of men forward, should I require it.'

'But Captain, no one including me has risked his arse to babysit fucking crying Tommies.'

Werner had spat out the words, glaring. For a moment Bassom wondered if Werner wanted all the prisoners to be shot, so the entire group could join the attack, but Bassom was not about to have an argument over the desires of career Nazis. He sought to stifle quickly the flame of rebellion. 'Sergeant Werner, I have given you an order, and if I want your opinion about how to attack the enemy, I will ask you for it. Now get on with your job.'

Werner flinched as a Stuka swept overhead, strafing in the direction of the enemy flak guns. 'Yes, sir,' he muttered through clenched teeth, his glare still on Bassom.

3

The sharp thumping of the flak guns rendered most of their crew unaware of Bentley Paine's arrival in the first gun pit, although a few men had their personal weapons at the ready at the shoulder. Some flinched at the sight of sweaty, heaving Paine clambering into their gun pit.

On his way in Paine had observed that only two of the four flak guns were in operation, the two furthest away from his line of approach. Each gun was sited in its own pit, the pits connected by short trenches running between them. Upon inspection of the abandoned flak gun in the first pit, Paine could see little wrong with it, but a huge smouldering crater just forward of the front edge of the pit answered a question that had been forming in his head. The gun crew were huddling in the trench that led to the next pit. The sandbagged trench walls had collapsed due to another huge crater. No one wanted to man the gun and take a chance with another Stuka hit. The Stukas' aim was good, there was no denying it. Paine turned and waved his ad hoc force to follow him in, as he moved with a purpose through the shell-shocked flak gun crew. He didn't have the time to give the crew a pep talk. 'Ensure your weapons are ready to go, men. Prepare to defend this position.'

Paine didn't look back to ensure they had got the message, instead he continued on to the next gun pit. The crew of the second flak gun had not been so fortunate. It appeared they had been peppered with shrapnel. The gunner in the nearest seat was missing his head; it had shattered all over the side of the feed chute. The remainder of the crew were strewn about the pit like partially clothed department-store dummies, each lying in a dark and congealed pool of what could only be their blood. Paine realized that seeing their demise could well have been a factor in the first crew abandoning their gun. He fought hard not to look at their broken bodies, and to focus on the task at hand. His stomach turned as he swallowed continuously in order to keep bile from surging up into his mouth.

Movement caught Paine's attention. To the rear of the gun pit was a soldier, sitting rocking with his knees up to his chest. He was coated in dust, dry clotted puncture wounds all over him. His cheeks were scarred with filthy dried tear streaks. As Paine's force caught up with him, he wasted no time putting them to work. 'Take care of that man,' he said, pointing to the wounded soldier. 'And have that one removed from his station,' he added, indicating the headless gunner.

Paine moved down another trench to the third gun pit. The flak gun was active, its crew feeding the gun as fast as they could, putting shell after shell towards low-flying German aircraft and their ever-descending hordes of human cargo. A big, burly gun commander, a bombardier, caught sight of Paine and broke off to address him. 'Good morning, sir,' he had to bellow in Paine's ear, since there was no let-up in the firing. 'We've hit a few of them. One has definitely crashed.'

Paine nodded, then noticed the narrow footbridge spanning the canal in the near distance. 'Have you seen anything of our company on the far bank?' Their fate was a matter of grave concern, especially if they had withdrawn across the bridge and the flak gun crews had mistakenly shot at them in their enthusiasm.

But the bombardier shook his head. 'No, sir. We've even tried to call them on the radio. No response.'

'Gliders!' came a simultaneous roar from the crew manning the flak gun. Some pointed at slow-moving aircraft, gracefully swooping in to land on the other side of the bridge. The soldiers inside the gliders would pose a real threat if they stormed across the bridge. It had been wired for demolition, but for the life of him Paine had no idea where Captain Green and his sappers were.

'Fire at the bloody gliders,' roared Hallmark. He did not have to repeat himself. The fourth flak gun was still in the game, and the muzzles of the third and fourth guns were quickly lowered, their crews beginning to fire at the wooden aircraft.

Of the four gliders making a final approach along the length of the far canal bank, the flak gun crews could claim at least one kill. The second glider took several hits and broke up as it plunged into the ground. The fuselage cartwheeled, flinging men high in the air, some of whom were thrown over the tall bank and down into the canal far below. The attention of the gun crews then centred on the already smouldering final aircraft. But the three remaining wooden craft all managed to crash-land in huge clouds of dust. As the clouds merged and began to drift across the span of the bridge, the gun crews continued to fire blindly. Mindful of ammunition expenditure, the bombardier ordered both guns to stop firing. The echo of their fire faded out; the skies finally falling silent, even of aircraft deploying paratroopers at much higher altitude.

Hallmark stood on the sandbagged forward lip of the third gun pit in order to get the best view of the area surrounding the bridge. The dust cloud was breaking up and lifting, and he spotted several German paratroopers clambering across the bridge. Enemy engineers. He lurched back and screamed at the third and fourth gun crews, 'On the bridge, shoot at the fucking bridge.' The flak guns erupted into a steady drumbeat. Cannon fire hit Germans and the bridge structure with ruthlessness. As Germans fell between the man-made walls of rock that flanked the sides of the canal, the bridge suddenly disappeared in a huge fireball. The blast from the explosion punched outwards so fiercely that it knocked everyone in the gun emplacement to the ground. Paine felt as if God himself had delivered his best right hook to his entire body. His testicles felt like they had been stamped on, as his lower gut burned. Gasping for breath and writhing in pain, he could do nothing more than let it all slowly pass. The world around him was muffled groaning, ultimately broken by the dull thud of bridge components clattering down over the emplacement. He knew the bridge had been rigged to blow, but it had been a truly massive explosion, and confirmation that Captain Green and his men were still around.

Having their air support circling over the target area made progress difficult for Martin Bassom and his men. It could prove tricky for the Stuka pilots to tell who was who; there was a real chance of taking friendly fire. As Bassom's men advanced, he had to ensure they remained spaced out and not about to walk into an ambush they could have avoided with a little patience. The continuous drumming fire from the British flak guns on the approaching gliders was making everyone really angry. He cursed the planners of the mission. Yes, objectives can be seen better in daylight, and your own forces can regroup and work better, but light also made parachutists easy prey as they drifted under canopy, and made the Junkers aircraft sitting ducks. He would have preferred a night-time assault. Seizing objectives and regrouping would have taken longer, but the British would have had to use searchlights, giving away their positions in the process.

Corporal Muller emerged from the olive groves, stopping then standing still without a care in the world about appearing conspicuous. He could see the bridge but not the enemy flak gun position. Bassom and Sergeant Dormann jogged up to join him, although they kept lower. The rest of Bassom's group soon assembled behind them. Exasperated, Muller pointed at the slow-moving gliders as they came into land. 'Clowns, what on earth do they think—'

His rant was cut short by fire from the unseen British flak guns. The second glider broke up and cartwheeled, his comrades meeting a grim, premature death before they could carry out their duties as parachute engineers. The other gliders got down, but the fourth had caught fire from flak tracer.

Bassom had seen enough. They had to take the flak position. Taking the lead, he waved his men forward at a jog. War was untidy and played by ear. MP 40 gripped in both hands, he was mindful that he would shortly need his one remaining grenade. The flak guns continued to fire but soon stopped, only to recommence, targeting the bridge through clouds of swirling but slowly clearing dust.

An almighty punch to the left side of his body sent Bassom sprawling, his hearing nothing more than a high-pitched whine. A huge explosion had ripped through, flattening his men. Wind was knocked from his lungs, his lower gut burning from the blast. With adrenaline running through him, and despite his pain, he clambered to his feet and looked about for his weapon. He trod on his MP 40 by accident; it was as good as buried in freshly disturbed loose earth. He shook the dirt from the sub-machine gun and roared at his men to get to their feet. They scrambled to maintain their dignity. Ahead of them, he watched debris from the explosion come back to earth. Then he allowed his arms to slump by his sides in disappointment. The main target of their mission had gone. Only the approach ramp of the Corinth Canal bridge remained. The British engineers had demolished it. His group began to move forward towards the flak gun position.

Still recovering from the explosion, Paine slowly clambered to his feet. The first reassuring indication that other men were alive was their mumbling profanities. A lot of dust and debris hung in the air. Hallmark was agitated, but together they checked the other men over. Most were OK; others had suffered cuts and bruises, but nothing worse than they might pick up on a Saturday night in town. Paine clambered to the forward edge of the gun pit, just as the dust from the explosion cleared enough to reveal what was left of the bridge. Those German troops not killed by the flak guns must have been consumed by the explosion, or had gone to the bottom of the canal along with the bridge debris. He worried that although the enemy threat from the north would be reduced for the time being, the destruction of the bridge meant that some of the Kiwis were trapped on the other side.

'Listen up, gents,' began the bombardier 'We have a

job to do. Let's get our weapons and equipment sorted, and then we can take care of our dead. Not ideal, but someone has to do it.'

Bassom had thought his throw was weak and his grenade would fall short, but it bounced on its head and then tumbled into the third British gun pit. As the grenade clattered against the flak gun, he knew his men would have the upper hand in the coming assault.

'Grenade!' roared Hallmark as he dived into the trench leading to the fourth gun pit. But the loud thud of the grenade's detonation caused everyone else to fall, Paine included, their bodies punched by the explosion and punctured by tiny metal splinters.

Hallmark's head was swimming, his hearing temporarily gone, but he got to his feet almost instantly. His Lee-Enfield was jammed in his right shoulder just in time for the first of the enemy paratroopers to come dashing down into the third gun pit, firing a submachine gun from the hip. With no time to aim through his sights, Hallmark kept both eyes open and pointed at the centre of mass of the dusty green enemy charging towards him. Hallmark felt the kick of his rifle as he fired, but the sound of his shot was overwhelmed by the snaps of the incoming rounds that zipped past him, ripping up the sandbagged trench walls. The enemy sprinting towards him burst in a pink mist from the centre of his torso, already dropping like liquid. As he fell, crashing face first, the momentum of his sprint made him almost collide with Hallmark, who side-stepped untidily to his left, already working his rifle bolt to feed the next round. The fall of the German provided a glimpse of a second paratrooper following in his wake. The advancing German grabbed his right bicep, wincing in pain as he went to the ground. The hitting power of the Lee-Enfield's .303 round had once more done its job, two enemy troops taken care of with one shot.

Paine, racked with tiny hornet stings and excruciating pain in his ears, grabbed for his Webley pistol as dust generated by the grenade drifted from the gun pit. By sheer instinct, he pointed the revolver at the fading dust cloud and the German troops within it and continued to pull the trigger until the sidearm was empty. Fearing the enemy would now overwhelm him, he received welcome support from one of the New Zealanders armed with a Sten sub-machine gun, his short chattering bursts giving Paine a chance to clamber behind the flak gun and find another weapon, hopefully the Lee-Enfield he had acquired from the tent.

As his grenade detonated, Bassom knelt down in the first gun pit, abandoned by the enemy, and allowed his small force to go up and over, rushing the stunned defenders in the other pits. He heard his men scream orders at each other in an attempt to dominate the assault. As the dust kicked up by his grenade explosion consumed him, he heard enemy weapons among the sounds of more familiar German ones; the bold snap of an enemy rifle, along with the rapid cracking of what he thought was an enemy pistol. As a third enemy weapon began to clatter, his men suddenly dashed back through the dust, seeking the cover offered by his position. He was somewhat concerned that not all of them were present. The enemy was not going quietly.

A weight of fire bore down on the first gun pit, as some of the New Zealanders gathered their wits, moving forward to fire at the regrouping Germans. Now back in the third gun pit, Hallmark noticed the German shot in the bicep had disappeared. Hallmark took the opportunity to pull those still concussed from the grenade blast to their feet and shove them towards cover. He spotted Paine and hauled him up. 'We can't stay here, sir,' he shouted at Paine's half-deaf ears, and over the din of the Kiwis' fire. 'We need to move back.'

Paine took exception to Hallmark manhandling him and shook him off. He was about to rant at him, but a volley of stick grenades tumbled among the firing Kiwis. Hallmark grabbed Paine by the scruff, pushing him into the trench leading to the fourth gun pit. Paine was enraged; he couldn't have the man continuing to shove him about. But the rippling concussion of multiple grenade explosions knocked the wind and anger out of him.

Bassom's group quickly reorganized themselves. Bassom couldn't account for Corporal Muller and two other men, fearing they had fallen, but rallied his remaining men, some having just thrown grenades towards the incoming fire. As an officer in the *Fallschirmjäger*, Bassom knew he would have to inspire them. He couldn't expect them to do something he wasn't willing to do himself, so he must lead the second assault. Pulling his MP 40 in tight under his right armpit, he stormed down the trench, his men's grenades going off as he approached the second gun pit. Although stunned and shaken by the grenades, he dealt with the nearest enemy troops in quick, brutal fashion; short concentrated bursts to the faces and chests of those who unbeknown to him, had originally manned the flak gun in the first pit. His magazine empty of ammunition, he instinctively dropped to one knee. In a slick, well-drilled manner he had a fresh magazine fitted in a matter of seconds. By the time he was ready to rejoin the assault, the remainder of the first pit flak gun crew had been taken care of, none of them alive enough to be considered prisoners. His men were changing magazines in the second gun pit, checking that their comrades were OK.

As he scrambled to his knees, pulling Paine up against the sandbag fortifications, Hallmark spotted a Bren light machine gun.

'Hallmark, leave me be,' roared Paine in his ear. 'I'm perfectly capable of standing on my own two feet.'

'You two get that Bren covering the trench,' bellowed Hallmark at two flak gunners. As he turned back to

Paine, intent on putting him in his place, a stick grenade thumped into the officer's chest and Paine let out an involuntary yelp. Hallmark grabbed the grenade, lobbing it back the way it had come. Looking across the third gun pit and down the trench leading to the second pit, he observed enemy paratroopers diving for cover, all shouting hysterically. As the grenade detonated in the second pit, he mockingly tipped his helmet at Paine. 'You're welcome, sir.'

Hallmark kept his profile low as he crawled across the third gun pit and in behind the two lads setting up the Bren gun, ready to assist them. But just as they pointed the Bren down the trench leading to the second pit and got the thick, curved magazine inverted on top of the weapon, Hallmark was blinded by a pink mist, his ears ringing once more. As he cuffed sprayed blood from his brow, he was greeted with the horrifying mess of what was left of the two lads on the Bren. Faces and shoulders smashed to pulp, their bodies were slumped over each other. Hallmark's stomach turned as he fought to hold back the burning bile attempting to flood his mouth. Taking a grenade from his pouch, he pulled the pin, sending the explosive bouncing down the trench ahead of him. The grenade came to rest under a dead soldier.

Bassom's men were tending to their wounded in the second gun pit when one of their own grenades came tumbling back at them. As it went off, many yelped and grunted as they caught fragments from the detonation, but despite ringing heads and ears, the tending of the wounded continued. Bassom ordered the medical attention to stop. It was not the time to play nurse. He ordered everyone to collect weapons and ammunition from the wounded. They needed to keep the pressure on the enemy occupying the third pit, and maybe the fourth. They needed to continue the assault and deny the enemy time to gather themselves.

Bassom peered down the trench leading to the third pit, casting a quick glance at the nearby body of Corporal Muller, who was face down, coated in dust, a horrific exit wound just below his left shoulder blade. The other two that had gone down in the first assault were alive; among the wounded, but well and truly out of the fight. Then Bassom spotted two British soldiers setting up a machine gun at the end of the trench. Without hesitation, he scrambled into a crouched firing position and fired short, rapid bursts at them. They collapsed on each other, covering the machine gun. He crawled back into the second gun pit. All of his men seemed to be wounded now, but most were moving about. His heart swelled, for he knew he had a good bunch of lads with him.

The close-quarters thump of a grenade suddenly tossed the corpse of Corporal Muller end-over-end through the air. The body came to rest, draped high over the flak gun in the second pit. Bassom was transfixed by the tortured lifeless face of Muller, who had been one of his best men. From shock came anger, not just from Bassom, but also from his men, some of whom couldn't help shouting hate at the enemy while trying their hardest to disguise their sobs.

Even the British and New Zealanders were horrified at the sight of the German soldier. 'Bloody hell,' Hallmark remarked. He couldn't help but let out a nervous chuckle. Paine found the nerve to peer over the sand-bagged lip of the third gun pit. As well as a better view of the body, he caught the odd glimpse of German helmets bobbing about. He could hear the Germans shouting and screaming but didn't have a clue what they were saying.

'Matey,' called Hallmark to the bombardier, 'go to gun four and have them get ready to fire on gun two. Open fire when you see us moving into the trench. We need to get the hell out of here.' The bombardier set off along the trench leading to the fourth gun pit. Its flak gun was no longer manned, the crew having contrib-uted to the defence of the emplacement, but dusty tin helmets were starting to bob about there.

Hallmark turned his attention to Paine. 'Sir?' But Paine's stare was locked on the bodies of the two dead Bren-gun crew. Paine felt surprisingly calm. Just two dead men. Two more to add to the list. 'Sir?' Hallmark roared. The ripple and snaps of incoming fire began.

'Yes?' replied Paine over his shoulder.

'We need to get out of here. The bombardier has gone to get the fourth flak gun to fire on gun two. We can use that as cover to get out into the olive groves. We can try and make our way south to a port or something. If we stay here, we'll die.'

Paine spun round in the dirt, outraged by Hallmark's suggestion. But then the men in the third gun pit stood as one before Paine and started firing over his head and shoulders. He dived to the ground, fearing they were shooting at him. He wondered what the hell they were playing at. Hallmark joined the other men, feeding round after round into his Lee-Enfield, returning fire at the Germans. Paine was treated to a light shower of hot brass bullet casings clattering on his helmet. He felt an excruciating burning from inside his open collar. Instinctively, he grabbed at the offending item, which he found to be one of Hallmark's spent casings. Paine threw it away angrily.

Hallmark knelt next to him while feeding a fresh clip into his rifle. Red-faced, Paine glared at his irksome corporal. Hallmark looked down at him neutrally. 'Court-martial me later if you want, but we need to get out of here now. Let's go.'

With no grenades left, Bassom's men continued to move up and down the edge of the second gun pit, taking pot shots at the enemy. Bassom knew that charging down the connecting trench would spell suicide. The enemy were fast learners.

Under covering fire, three of Bassom's men clambered over the side of the gun pit in an attempt to rush the enemy. They had not even got five metres when they were cut down by a hail of fire. They were not dead, for they cried out and groaned while rolling about the ground. Bassom feared the enemy would finish them off, but they held their fire, probably choosing to conserve ammunition for opponents still fit to fight. And it made firing at the enemy more dangerous; in order not to hit their own injured, his men were having to stand above the lip of the gun pit. He thought they had to destroy the flak gun position, and fast. Conscious he was losing manpower, he was aware that the enemy could counter-attack at any moment, and he had no idea of their number.

'We have friendlies coming in from the rear, Captain,' Stolz yelled. He was tending to his own dressings, which were seeping blood, as well as trying to position the radio in a safe place.

Looking back at the first gun pit, Bassom caught the bobbing motion of numerous paratrooper helmets coated in dust and scrapes. 'Make room for these guys coming in,' someone called out.

Sergeant Werner emerged into the second gun pit, breathing hard, sweating like a maniac, MP 40 submachine gun in one hand and carrying an MG 34 machine gun by its handle with the other, its bipod legs splayed ready for action. He was also draped in belt ammunition for the MG 34. Behind him followed a dozen paratroopers, all heavily armed and looking fresh. Bassom could have felt a little deflated at the arrival of the Nazi, but Werner brought much-needed men and firepower with him.

Werner moved towards Bassom, but was suddenly

distracted by the body of Corporal Muller, sprawled over the flak gun above them. Bassom realized Werner was actually lost for words, or was perhaps trying to put his words in the right order. As the fresh paratroopers took up fighting positions in the gun pit, Bassom decided on speaking first. 'Excellent timing, Sergeant; we are really feeling the pinch here. We have two more gun pits to assault; we have wounded men caught in the open, and we cannot waste time. We must assault pit three before the enemy regain the initiative. I want six men with grenades.'

Bassom knew Werner was not about to disagree. Werner was a professional soldier, and they were in the midst of an assault. He pointed to half a dozen fresh men. A seventh took the MG 34 from him. Bassom wasted no time briefing the seven men on their mission. 'When I say so, I want one grenade per man thrown into the next pit. As soon as they are thrown, I want the MG 34 up on the lip, firing at gun pit four, and we will rush down the trench and take care of gun pit three. Do you understand?'

'Yes, sir,' the seven-man group replied as one, already priming their stick grenades and checking the magazines on their MP 40s and carbine rifles. In his periphery Bassom could see Werner setting up the machine gun for a quick lift up onto the sandbag wall. Werner gave Bassom a thumbs-up.

'Captain, look!' Hallmark hissed. Paine clambered up next to him to the lip of the gun pit, trying to focus on what Hallmark was pointing at. Paine could make out helmeted troops arriving in the first gun pit. 'We need to get out of here,' Hallmark reiterated. 'We are almost out of ammunition, and I'm guessing they have just been reinforced.'

Paine had to agree that now was not the time to argue about the merits of withdrawing. Hallmark spun round, taking it upon himself to signal for everyone to move towards gun pit four. The men didn't wait around. At a crouch, they made their way into the connecting trench. Following Hallmark, the last two men out, Paine felt the thud of heavy objects hitting the gun pit floor, at least one clattering against the splayed legs of the flak gun. It didn't occur to him that they might be grenades.

Hallmark took off at a sprint into the trench. 'Go, go, fucking go!' he roared. Paine had a lot of failings, but he had learned to listen to his batman and not to look back. Paine screamed and started running.

Realizing the huge risk of hitting their own wounded men in the open with machine-gun rounds, Werner assisted his MG 34 gunner as they lugged the belt-loaded weapon up onto the sandbag wall.

Bassom was at the rear of the assault force as they steamed down the trench, just as the grenades detonated ahead of them in the third gun pit. As the dust from the explosions consumed them, so did the biblical din of the firepower directed at them. Bassom's ears erupted in a high-pitched scream, as displaced air punched his assault force in their faces, forcing them to the bottom of the trench. Bassom's momentum had him stomping all over his men before he finally tumbled into the third gun pit with neither grace nor dignity. The earthquake lasted a few seconds, and then stopped as quickly as it had started.

Dust hung thick in the air, causing Bassom and his men to hack and cough as they fought to organize themselves to continue the attack. Bassom focused on the flak gun in the hot dusty haze, then scanned about for enemy soldiers to engage, but couldn't see any. Behind him, his punch-drunk men were clumsy, some having to lean against the gun pit wall to catch their breath. As the dust lifted and drifted out of the pit, it was evident that the enemy had abandoned it. Mindful of the enemy troops still in pit four, Bassom's group maintained a low profile. 'What on earth was that?' gasped one of the paratroopers.

Bassom pulled his helmet from his sweat-soaked scalp, running his fingers through hair that was slowly getting caked by the dust haze. 'The bastards used the fourth flak gun. Keep low and stay vigilant.'

'All you guys OK in there?' Bassom noticed that there was a hint of concern in Werner's voice.

'Yeah,' one of Bassom's group replied. 'Can you see the fourth gun pit?'

'Yeah, it's empty,' came Werner's response. 'The enemy have run away.'

'What?' Bassom attempted to clarify, his ears still ringing.

'The enemy have run away,' repeated Werner. 'They are gone. Look for yourself.'

Bassom carefully peered over the side of the third gun pit. The Nazi was right, the British had indeed deserted the flak gun emplacement.

4

Captain Bassom's paratroopers cautiously moved in to check gun pit four, unsure whether the British were in the habit of laying booby traps and hesitant as they inspected what equipment had been left behind, for their engineer comrades would normally have been assigned such a task. But the engineers were now dead, blown to pieces when the bridge, the primary objective of the mission, had been blown sky high.

After a time the gun pit was confirmed as safe to occupy. Bassom felt the hot, beautiful Greek afternoon was bittersweet, given what had taken place. Now the dust of battle had settled, enemy opposition in the Corinth area subdued, those who had survived the German attack had either been rounded up or were fleeing for their lives in the Greek countryside. Bassom was confident the routed enemy would soon be taken care of. He and Werner stood at the rear of the flak gun emplacement, observing the grim scene. Their men had fought bravely, but were now playing the horrid role of undertaker. The worst part for Bassom was watching his men sob and try not to vomit as they pulled what was left of Corporal Muller from the flak gun in the second gun pit. Had Muller's body been hit by the brief flak-gun fire from the fourth pit, it would have been shredded too badly to make collecting the remains worthwhile.

Like all good infantry sergeants, Werner had taken care of all his dead and wounded colleagues, ensuring they had been or would be taken away to the cluster of buildings they had initially attacked. Werner had even ensured the enemy dead were treated respectfully, some of his men being tasked with burying them in marked temporary graves in front of the flak gun emplacement. Prior to burial, the enemy dead had been searched for anything of use. Bassom and Werner were surprised to find pay books and other documents which led to the conclusion that New Zealand troops were fighting alongside the British.

'Has Lieutenant Mettlemas begun his sweep south of here?' Bassom asked Werner as they continued to look on. 'We can't allow the British to regroup and counter-attack.'

'Sergeant Dormann is on it, sir. Lieutenant Mettlemas busted his ankle in the drop. Nothing too serious. Several of his men carried him off the drop zone and joined us at the captured British HQ. Consequently, we had extra manpower, so I decided to come here and give you a hand.'

Bassom liked Marcel Mettlemas; they had been room-mates at Stendahl Parachute Training School. A native of

Essen, Mettlemas's father was a steel worker. Both of broad-backed German stock, Bassom and Mettlemas had been offered officer cadet positions in the Luft-waffe, but unlike Bassom, Mettlemas was a Nazi Party member, having grown up in the smothering, yet blink-ered embrace of the Hitler Youth.

'Thank you, Sergeant.'

'What for?' came Werner's deadpan reply.

'For reinforcing us, and helping with the dead and wounded.'

'Hmm,' Werner grunted, walking off without so much as a backward glance.

Bassom didn't have the strength to get angry at the arrogance of the man. After the original assault on the buildings, Bassom knew Werner had probably been right about leading a reserve force to join him in the attack on the flak gun emplacement. But Bassom had not been about to give the Nazi bastard the satisfaction of admitting it. Bassom was tired, his men were tired. He knew well enough that his military masters would judge him later, particularly regarding the failure to secure the bridge. The German paratroopers on the other side of the canal would have to stay put until engineers came south to construct a new bridge; the engineers would eventually arrive with the dull grey mass of the panzers, which were still far to the north.

Bassom observed what was left of the bridge. Its approach ramp was shattered, the buckled steel frame of the bridge span slumped out of sight over the side of the cliff below. He thought once more of the engineers who had been crossing the bridge, all gone now. He could only hope it had been quick for them. Little did he know that the destruction of the bridge would become the subject of historical dispute; was it really demolished by the British, or had a stray round hit demolition charges, naively left on the bridge for later collection?

Racked with thirst, Bentley Paine trudged on. If it wasn't for the cover of the olive groves and the count-less walls of loose rock he had to scramble over, the Germans would have captured or shot him hours ago. It was the dreadful crack and ripple of distant gunfire that spurred him on, for he knew that the German para-troopers, fuelled by their recent victory, were pressing home their advantage and hunting their quarry ruth-lessly. He had no idea where Hallmark was, or the artillerymen that had fought with them back at the flak gun emplacement. In their desperate haste to get clear of the emplacement, confusion had reigned, all sense of direction and military order falling by the way-side. All Paine knew was that between him and a ship there were Germans and an unforgiving range of hills he would have to traverse. It was starting to get dark but no less hot. The Greek climate was punishing for a sol-dier who was injured, exhausted and dehydrated. As he stumbled up a rubble-strewn track that terminated at the foot of another large spiteful thorn hedge, Paine hoped that those he had fought with, in particular his troublesome batman, would make it to a ship.

Paine's bleeding forearms and knees no longer caused him to wince, for his body was now becoming accustomed to the light trauma it was being subjected to. All he had to do was keep going uphill; if he chose to rest, he would be killed by marauding Germans, plain and simple. His delirium due to the heat and lack of water was now getting the better of him, even though he was being lulled into a false sense of security by the oncoming darkness.

After what felt like an age, it was finally dark. Without a care for his fragile frame, Paine slumped against a rickety farmer's gate that was long overdue some maintenance. The close evening air was a little cooler, but Paine cursed himself for not having his water bottle to hand; cups of tea are fine through the night, but during the day, like it or not, a man needs water. What he would give right now for a bottle of foul salty canal water. He was educated enough to know the salt in the water would just magnify the wretched thirst that tortured him, but the fantasy was there nevertheless.

Torch beams and commands shouted in a foreign tongue suddenly told Paine that the Germans were not planning on calling it a day any time soon. He fought to focus and get back on his feet. Just keep going uphill; no compass work, just go up. He knew from his long nights staring at maps in the command tent that he would be able to see the coast from the high ground, a view that would inject some motivation into his numbed brain and limbs, along with a sprinkling of hope. As he began to move, the numbness in his left leg instantly exploded into a sudden attack of muscular cramp. In intense pain, he fought with all his strength not to cry out loud. A bow wave of crushing pain burst through his rock-hard sore muscles. He cursed in a low voice. 'Start moving, damn you, start bloody moving.' For a hundred metres he was about as agile as one of the grand statues that adorned his family home. A rock wall appeared, which he simply couldn't climb, so he was forced to keep to the track leading off to the east. All he had to do was keep moving, there was nothing else for it.

He had thought of home for the first time that day. The battle had purged such comforts from his mind, forcing him to focus on the second-by-second nature of close combat. He began to get emotional, knowing that during the battle he had not performed as he should have done. Hallmark, deliberately or not, had demonstrated how much Paine was out of his depth. Paine acknowledged that there was a lot to be said for cutting your teeth as a platoon commander early in your career. His promotion for secondment to the cavalry in Greece had put him out of his depth. A more seasoned officer probably would have done better. But Paine had been in the wrong place at the wrong time, when the position in Greece had come up. And the arrogant Hallmark was the icing on the cake.

Bentley Paine knew that despite being son and heir to a retail empire, he was now walking for his life on an unforgiving Greek hillside, with German troops hot on his heels. He felt compelled to sit down on a stone wall. How on earth had he got himself into this mess?

He knew the answer to his own question. Spencer Paine, his father, had got him into this mess. The Richmond Furlong Company was the biggest equestrian equipment distributor south of Hadrian's Wall. If you owned horses, or knew anyone who did, you could bet your last penny that all your requirements were fulfilled by the RFC. Like his father and grandfather before him, Spencer Paine had stood strong at the helm of the empire. Outwardly, the Paine household had enjoyed the life that high-society people enjoyed: money, opulence, fine food, high-end booze, fame, a portfolio of properties dotted about Yorkshire and London. During the days before Spencer took the helm, the RFC had sponsored more Grand National and point-to-point winners than any other brand in the United Kingdom and Europe. The royal family had RFC stable hands moved down to London in order to run their stables. The RFC stud farm on the outskirts of Richmond was the bar that all stud farm owners measured themselves against. The RFC always seemed to have the money to throw at any problem, no matter the price.

When Spencer's father died of heart failure, Bentley was just a child. As he grew up, he wanted for nothing.

But as a consequence of their lifestyle, Bentley and his older sister Madison grew up ignorant of the real world. A live-in nanny tended to their every whim, and they were then sent to the finest schools. Nevertheless, as a young teenager, Bentley was already being groomed by his father to take the reins of the RFC, since it had always been known that illness might take Spencer, heart disease being common in the Paine men.

One wet and dreary Wednesday in March, as grey as most days were in North Yorkshire at that time of year, Bentley and Madison were collected from their schools by Connor Firth, the family driver. They were taken home to the huge Paine country manor, which perched on high ground overlooking Richmond village centre. Richmond was picture-postcard beautiful most of the time in spring and summer, and chocolate-box-worthy come autumn and winter. A liberal coating of snow on the hills would give the village a Dickensian feel.

Connor reached the junction that took you to either the manor or the stud farm. Madison insisted that he take them to the stud farm, so she could check on Tango. Tango was a beautiful horse, once a frequent point-to-point winner but of late rather irritable. When Madison had tried to brush him the evening before, he had bucked and kicked like a mustang that had been stung. So her mother had promised to have him brushed and ready to go for when Madison got home from school that afternoon.

The stud farm was well established; a large, thatched

farmhouse with stables running off either side and a huge paddock to the rear. Most of the stud farm staff lived locally; only the estate manager, Alby Shaw, lived onsite in the farmhouse. As Connor drove into the stud farm courtyard, he was perplexed as to why Tango was out, untethered, dashing back and forth. Alby suddenly dashed out of the stables. 'Call an ambulance. Mrs Paine is hurt bad.'

Spencer was in London, finalizing a sponsorship deal, when he received a phone call at his hotel reception desk. Alby informed him that his wife Melanie had been kicked by Tango, resulting in crushed vertebrae and a broken pelvis. Alby and the children were with her at the hospital in Harrogate. Melanie was heavily sedated but stable.

Spencer was on the first train out of King's Cross in less than an hour. The train journey to Harrogate was the longest journey of his life, but he was holding his distraught children by the early hours of the next morning, even managing to get Alby in a bear hug, repeatedly thanking him for taking care of his family. Spencer managed to convince the children that they needed their sleep and should go home. They didn't want to sleep in the manor without their mum or dad there, so stayed with Alby in the farmhouse. Once Alby and the children were gone, Spencer broke down, burying his face in Melanie's breast, cursing himself for not being at the stud farm to help with Tango.

The decline of the Paine family empire became

assured all because of a kick from a beloved family member. Melanie's crushed vertebrae had severed her spinal cord, so she was for ever paralysed from the waist down, her smashed pelvis held together with pins. Her life would be blighted by the need for round-the-clock care.

Spencer had to keep up appearances, so attended business functions alone, since Melanie would not be ready to face the world for quite some time, but then one of the nurses at Harrogate sold her story to the tabloids. Pretty soon photographers and reporters began prowling around Richmond, enquiring about the accident. Alby, an old-school Great War veteran, stood guard at the manor gates with a shotgun, threatening any member of the press with buckshot if they were found in the manor grounds. It was considered ironic she had been crippled by a horse, a symbol of the family empire.

Spencer heard of the press intrusions in London just after he climbed, sweat-soaked, off his conquest. The beautiful young woman had taken a particular liking to him as he sat in his hotel bar, enjoying a few drinks after a long day of tending to potential international clients. He felt he could have his cake and eat it, just so long as the cake remained in London. But the young woman had in fact been an employee of Showcase International Limited, a rival brand based in London, a company who had fought bitterly to the point of spite to tear away a royal contract from Spencer. She wasted no time in selling her story. Before long almost everyone had read it, and he knew it was just a matter of time before Melanie and the children found out.

Bentley and Madison began to learn how much of a bastard their father was. The man had endangered everything most mortals dream of – a loving family, a thriving business – and for what? A bit of fun in a hotel room. Madison and Bentley huddled together at the top of the manor's grand staircase, peering through the banister spindles while downstairs their father pleaded forgiveness from his hysterical wife. The children flinched as expensive ornaments crashed, Melanie bombarding Spencer with anything she could throw at him. The household staff thought better than to remain in the manor, and left mob-handed, seeking refuge at the pub, where the still-lurking press plied them with booze to loosen their tongues.

It was the first of many sleepless nights for Bentley and his big sister, amid screaming, shouting, crashing china and breathless sobs. Spencer was no longer welcome in the same bed as his wife and was kicked out.

Madison began to neglect her studies, since her mother's care demanded more and more of her. She allowed her academic potential to decline, in order to enable Bentley to get through school, which she hoped would make him ready for when their father abdicated his position in Richmond Furlong. Bentley was far too young and inexperienced to even consider a coup. The company was just too big a beast for him to take the helm from his father, at least at the moment. At the weekends, in an attempt to help Madison catch up with her school-work, Bentley began to tend to his mother, with help from a few trusted members of the household staff. But before too long everything proved too much for Madison, and she dropped out of school to help at home.

The finances of the Paine family were not as comfortable as they once were. Before newspaper stories switched to the possibility of war, scandal after scandal saw clients pulling out of contracts with Richmond Furlong, since they did not want to risk their own secrets coming under scrutiny because of an association with the excesses of Spencer Paine – womanizer, drinker and gambler. Vast sums began to vanish from the family's bank account. Melanie became a shell of her former self, despite Madison's diligent care and attention. A letter from Spencer to Melanie explained that almost all of Richmond Furlong's clients had torn up their contracts and walked away. Showcase International had picked up many of the clients. The manor, the stud farm and the household staff were all at risk.

Despite her frailty, Melanie still had a sharp eye for numbers. She demanded that Spencer perform one selfless act for the sake of his children before he fell on his sword, and the bank began liquidating assets. So his final act of lavish spending was to buy the stud farm outright. All the staff except Alby Shaw were dismissed, each with a month's wages and an outstanding reference. Melanie felt that she couldn't send away the man who had saved her life following her accident. The manor was taken by the bank, along with the horses, including Madison's beloved Tango. The majority of the family furniture wouldn't fit into the farmhouse, so was sent to auction. Spencer vowed to change his ways to breathe life back into his company and his family, and with the farmhouse bought and paid for, Bentley, Alby, Melanie and Madison were content to live a very basic life on a stud farm devoid of horses.

Bentley offered to rent out the stables to local horse owners, but nobody wanted to pay the rates Richmond Furlong had previously demanded of its clients. So with a heavy heart he lowered the fees, just to have the stables occupied. There was some interest, and the stud farm had horses once more. But ultimately, even with the farm full, revenue just about covered the household bills. Bentley came to realize how affluent his life had once been. Through the good times his father had spared no expense, but Spencer's public breaking of Melanie's heart had destroyed everything.

With Madison tending to her mother, and Alby not getting any younger, Bentley rolled up his sleeves and helped with the running of the stables. There was no money for paying stable hands. One hot day, while Alby and Bentley were mucking out the stables, Alby made a suggestion. 'Why don't you join the army or something? Do something with your life.'

Bentley hadn't even entertained the idea. The stud farm was the only thing on his mind. 'Going to war is not the kind of life I was hoping for.'

'Pah,' dismissed Alby. 'It's just talk, that's all. No one, not even the blimmin' Jerries, wants another war. Take it from me.'

Bentley felt he was quite clued up on current affairs. 'Hitler has been rather aggressive towards Poland.'

Alby waved a dismissive hand. 'That guy has just got Germany back on its feet, after how many years? Why would he want to ruin all that he's done? He's just making big talk to put the frighteners on his neighbours, that's all.'

Bentley suddenly realized that joining the army would bring in more money for the farm. He could serve a few years, then return a little wiser. 'Would I join as a private soldier, like you did?'

Alby shook his head. 'No, no, no. Not with your schooling credentials; that's officer material. Don't waste all that schooling your father paid for by going in as a blimmin' private. Officer is what you need. If you want, we can find out where we need to go to get more information.'

Bentley was fit, and took the army infantry training in his stride, but no matter how much he put his case to the sponsorship committee at Sandhurst, he couldn't secure a move to the cavalry, because their allocation of officers was full. So he was commissioned into the ranks of the Yorkshire and Lancashire Regiment, mocking himself for agreeing to join the infantry.

After a short spell of leave, with his family complimenting Second Lieutenant Paine on how smart he looked in his service uniform and Sam Browne leather belt, he boarded a train to meet up with a transport ship in Southampton. The ship was bound for Alexandria, on the southern coast of the Mediterranean, almost two hundred kilometres north-west of the Egyptian capital Cairo.

The voyage was long and boring, with brief stops in Gibraltar and Malta and a pick-up of supplies in Souda Bay, Crete. Bentley's vision of Alexandria was what history and literature had fed him. He imagined a panorama of majesty, with the legacies of pharaohs and Caesars engraved in the very fabric of the city. He was bitterly disappointed as they docked. Alexandria was nothing more than a foul-smelling, fly-blown, whore-ridden dump, with everyone trying to sell you something or pick your pocket. By the time a convoy of trucks arrived at the dock to collect his group of new recruits and more seasoned men, Bentley was sweat-soaked and hassled, not to mention downright irritable.

The barracks of 2 Yorks and Lancs was another dump far removed from the disinfected impeccable campus of Sandhurst. As the trucks made their way through the front gate, past the guardroom, Bentley observed how deserted the place looked. The trucks came to a halt outside what turned out to be Battalion Headquarters. Everyone clambered down. The seasoned men, most returning from leave, just slung their kitbags over their shoulders and wandered off, leaving Bentley and the other fresh faces to stand around, waiting for someone to point them in the right direction.

Before long, the new recruits were ushered into the

headquarters building by an old, overweight corporal. Bentley was conscious that he was the only officer in the group. He was ushered upstairs on his own to meet the regimental adjutant. A large powerful-looking sergeant stood stock still on guard at an open door, unshaven, sporting two black eyes, his lips split in several places. In the presence of Bentley, a commissioned officer, he didn't move. Bentley thought to reprimand the sergeant for his lack of acknowledgment, but flinched as a figure appeared through the open threshold that led into an office. In the doorway was a fierce-looking captain. Bentley stood to attention and delivered a very crisp cadet salute. The captain, carrying a handful of papers, remained stony-faced as he looked the young subaltern up and down. His glare then flicked to the much larger sergeant. 'Sergeant Hallmark, you look and smell like shit. I want you back here in half an hour, looking a damn sight fresher than you are now. In the meantime, I intend to try and keep the Egyptian police from nailing you to a bloody cross.'

Bentley watched Hallmark walk away down the steps with a sense of urgency. Bentley quickly returned his focus to the irritable-looking adjutant. 'Second Lieutenant Paine. I've just arrived from England, sir.'

'Great.' The adjutant rolled his eyes and walked back into his office. 'Someone else I've got to find a bloody job for.' The captain turned and waved him into the office. 'Take a seat, Mr Paine. Just give me a minute.' He strode out of the office, still clutching his paperwork.

As he eased himself into one of the rather worn leather chairs, Bentley couldn't help but pick up on what was happening in the next office. A number of typewriters were going like the clappers, and there appeared to be a lot of walking about. The fan on the off-white high ceiling turned lazily, doing nothing to reduce the stifling heat that hung in the building.

The captain reappeared with just one cup and saucer. Bentley got the feeling that the captain was not in the habit of making tea for newly arrived junior officers. The adjutant sat in his chair on the other side of the desk. He slowly took a number of sips, before eventually looking up, putting the cup and saucer down. 'How much news have you received on the way here?'

Bentley was a little confused. 'News, sir?'

The adjutant got to his feet. 'Germany has invaded Poland. It's all gone mad around here very quickly.'

Bentley now understood the frenzy in the adjoining office, but had still to grasp the seriousness of the situation. 'Are we going to war?'

The adjutant shrugged his shoulders. 'I don't know. I really don't. All we know is that we have been warned about a move to Crete. Italy has sided with Germany, and that threatens Greece. We are to move to Crete as a reserve force, for operations on the Greek mainland.' Bentley couldn't help but feel excited about the prospect of action so early in his career. 'All of our platoons have commanders,' the adjutant continued, 'and therefore I have no in-house job for you. I have however been landed a bugger of an external job, but I feel you might be too junior and too inexperienced for that.'

Bentley's stomach leaped higher, his heart thumping harder. 'A special mission?'

The captain glanced sideways at him with a raised eyebrow. 'Not quite.' He got to his feet once more and abruptly left the room.

As the minutes ticked by, Bentley's excited mood subsided. He had got the feeling he was a fifth wheel in the battalion. There would be no platoon command for the time being, and by the look of things he could well be given some other role to play in the pending deployment. To an outsider looking in, the army gives the reassuring feeling that things run like clockwork and happen for a reason. But as an insider now, Bentley was beginning to realize it wasn't always like that.

A scrape and shuffle of boots had Bentley turn and peer into the corridor. The large profile of Sergeant Hallmark was back, looking a little less beaten up. He had shaven, but there wasn't much he could do about the black eyes and split lips. Bentley was suddenly aware the sergeant was giving him a murderous glare. Reassuring himself that the NCO would keep himself in check, Bentley slowly turned away from his unnerving gaze, hoping his first platoon sergeant wouldn't look at him like that. As Bentley swivelled, a brass plaque mounted on the office door briefly caught his eye. He hadn't noticed it as he entered the room. It was rather grubby and faded, not to the polished standard he had grown used to at Sandhurst. It was engraved CAPTAIN LONG REGIMENTAL ADJUTANT.

A few more minutes passed before Captain Long re-entered the office, closing the door behind him without giving the sergeant a second glance. Long took up his position behind the desk, shuffling some fresher-looking paperwork in front of him. 'I said I had a bugger of a job for someone. I've spoken to the commanding officer of the 4th Hussars, and he is content that you can fulfil the vacancy.'

Bentley's eyes lit up. Hussars were cavalry, so this could well be the beginning of something he could exploit, if he played it carefully. He mentally repri-manded himself for allowing his facial expression to imply he was getting carried away with the idea.

'They are due to be deployed to the Greek mainland,' continued Long. 'Their barracks are not too far from here. They have a New Zealand infantry battalion attached to them. God knows why, but that's the military for you. The Hussars require a battle captain – someone to manage their Regimental Headquarters in the absence of their commanders, and to be the infantry link with the New Zealanders.'

Bentley fought to conceal how pleased he was at the sound of the role, his smile reaching from ear to ear.

'It's not an easy job, mind,' Long went on. 'In fact, it might be a royal pain in the arse, if you aren't careful. You'll need a bit of clout, so you will be wearing the rank of captain. Our paymaster is in the process of arranging everything with his opposite number in the

Hussars. They'll pay you a captain's salary, but only for the period of the secondment.'

'How long will I be with them, sir?' Bentley was excited; working with the cavalry and getting a pay rise. He had already arranged to send the lion's share of his salary home to help his family run the stud farm, and the pay increase would be most welcome. He didn't smoke and rarely drank alcohol, so it wasn't as if he needed much money in Egypt or Greece.

The captain shrugged. 'Could be two years, maybe less. They are usually two-year secondments. So, then. How do you feel about it?'

'It's all fine, sir. Thank you for the opportunity to represent my battalion with the cavalry.'

Long eyed him up, unsure whether he was excited or being sarcastic. He dismissed Bentley, telling him to sort out his documents in the paymaster's office before returning in an hour.

As he waited at a counter for the paymaster's clerk to stamp and countersign his documents, Bentley heard an awful commotion – plenty of swearing and shouting, and someone being marched about at a fast pace. Bentley looked about the office. Everyone just got on with their work as if it was an everyday occurrence. 'That will be Sergeant Hallmark in trouble again,' commented a big barrel-chested captain behind the counter. He was built like an ox, with a huge sweaty red face.

Bentley wondered if the captain was the paymaster. 'What did he do wrong, sir?'

'The usual. Drinking, fighting, whoring, fighting some more.' The captain rolled his eyes. 'He's getting demoted to corporal as we speak.'

'How do you know?'

'I'm sorting his reduced wages out right now,' the captain informed him matter-of-factly. 'Hallmark is a good soldier; he just has a habit of finding trouble. Or it finds him.' To Bentley, a good soldier would perhaps steer clear of trouble and be an example for his men to follow, but he wondered if he was being naive.

As the Officers' Mess was a fair trek away, the captain showed Bentley into a kitchen with a kettle, recommending he wasn't late for his follow-up meeting with Long. So just under an hour later Bentley finished his tea and went back upstairs to Long's office. Hallmark was standing further down the corridor, being berated by what appeared to be the regimental sergeant major and an Egyptian policeman. Bentley tried not to eavesdrop, but couldn't help but be drawn to the drama unfolding. Towering over both of his accusers, Hallmark was being threatened with time in a local prison, not to mention a public flogging, the sergeant major allowing the policeman to vent his fury. Bentley felt certain Hallmark would later erupt into a rage, feeling sorry for whoever his platoon commander might be, since it must be one hell of a task keeping Hallmark on a leash.

'Finished staring, Paine?'

Bentley's head snapped forward. Captain Long was

glaring straight at him. Bentley wondered if everyone in 2 Yorks and Lancs was aggressive. 'No, sir. I mean yes, yes, sir.'

'Get in here and shut the door.'

They sat opposite each other in the office, Long explaining the details of Bentley's secondment to the 4th Hussars. There was a light knock at the door. 'Come.' Long's command was stern. Bentley looked straight ahead at Long, thinking that turning might be considered nosey. The door opened, then closed, and in his periphery Bentley could detect someone standing to his left. 'Mr Paine,' said Long, 'you will have Corporal Hallmark with you in Greece, to keep you out of trouble.' Bentley was appalled, for it quickly dawned on him that he would be the poor officer in command of the rogue. Long turned his attention to the large demoted sergeant. 'Corporal Hallmark. You are skating on thin ice. You so much as fart too loud while you are in Greece, and I promise you a long spell in a Cairo jail, do you understand?'

Bentley couldn't quite bring himself to look at Hallmark, at least not yet. 'Yes, sir,' Hallmark replied. 'I'll be good.' Seemingly content, Long nodded and rose. 'I'll make sure this one stays out of trouble too,' added Hallmark as a sting in the tail.

Bentley was suddenly overwhelmed by muscle-crushing cramp. As he woke, he lost his perch on the stone wall and slid to the dry dusty ground. For what felt like a lifetime he was frozen like a fallen statue. He could do nothing more than to wait for his muscles to relax once more.

When his muscles loosened, a wave of euphoria washed through Bentley. He seized the moment and quickly clambered to his feet, but his legs went solid once more. The cramps came more frequently and with increased intensity. Only when agony didn't bring him to the point of nausea did he try and listen for anything that resembled a German search party. He cuffed his red-hot stone-dry brow, for he was beginning to burn up, despite the welcome early-morning chill in the air. He needed water and fast.

Once Bentley managed to compose himself, he turned to see the sun rising, casting a stunning glint on the most beautiful-looking sea. In the middle distance he could make out shipping clustered in a natural bay. It had to be his way off the mainland. Cramp or not, it was where he needed to go. Hoping no Germans were about, he kept to the main tracks. In any event there was no way he could climb over walls or any obstacle, since he was walking like the Tin Man from *The Wizard of Oz*. While on leave before travelling to Alexandria, Bentley remembered accompanying Madison to see the film on its very first day of cinematic release. He wasn't interested in the film, but Alby had offered to see to Melanie, permitting Madison and Bentley to have a little fun for the first time in a long while.

No matter how fast Bentley tried to walk, the bay

never appeared to get any closer. Dread filled him every time he watched a ship sail out of it. He didn't want to be left behind. As he left the high ground, with the sun climbing higher over the eastern horizon, he became aware of other walkers, all heading off the same range of hills. In the far distance off to his right he could see dust kicking up from what turned out to be a convoy of trucks. A brief moment of panic overcame him. Were the Germans at the dock? As he staggered on, he resigned himself to a period of captivity if they were. But the prospect of a German prison camp with running water was paradise compared to his current situation.

The lone walkers began forming into groups of various sizes. One particular group, about three hundred metres to Bentley's right, were heading his way. Quietly confident it wasn't a German patrol, he gave them a casual wave. There was no response, which didn't bode well. His vision swam in and out of focus, and he blinked repeatedly to try and see clearly.

A broken-down stone wall blocked Bentley's route to safety. He stumbled and lost his footing as he desperately climbed over it. Clumsily, he got to his feet but felt very nauseous as he stood up too fast. He needed to rest. So keeping his legs ramrod straight for fear of cramp once more, he leaned against a higher section of the wall. The group that hadn't responded to his wave got ever closer, the lead figure appearing bigger than the others. They all appeared to be armed. Bentley fumbled for his Webley, but even with his clumsy hands he could tell the pistol was not loaded. Why on earth hadn't he reloaded his sidearm? The armed group were now tens of metres away, and there was no way he could get the Webley into action before they opened fire on him.

'Bloody hell, sir,' said a voice. 'Thought the Germans got you in the night. Have you got any water?' For the first time ever Bentley was actually pleased to see Corporal John Hallmark. Hallmark had some lads from the flak gun emplacement in tow, all looking rather the worse for wear. 'Have you got any water, sir?' he repeated.

Bentley blinked rapidly, trying to comprehend the words. 'What?'

'Water, sir,' repeated Hallmark again. 'Have you got any?' Without even thinking about it, Bentley instinctively patted himself down, only to eventually look up at Hallmark with a puzzled expression. Hallmark grinned. 'Never mind. Come on, sir. We need one of them beautiful boats out of here.'

The small harbour was a scene of olive drab and red-speckled misery. Troops from various units, mostly New Zealanders, were having their details taken by equally miserable soldiers armed with clipboards. As Bentley, Hallmark and their group joined the queue, it became clear to Bentley that this was a not-so-glorious withdrawal of Allied forces from Greece; it was in fact an evacuation. Bentley wondered if the Germans were all over the country now. Most of the battered men in the queue stood on their own two feet, quite a few somehow mustering the strength to carry others on stretchers. Any chance of a drink of water was next to non-existent, as the troops crowded towards a low jetty, from where small open-topped craft ferried men to the ships sitting in the bay.

As Bentley's group shuffled up onto the jetty, he observed slightly fresher navy personnel standing there. Water must be at a premium, since the navy guys were promising drinking water on the ships, reminding everyone not to drink seawater. And indeed the white foaming surf tumbling onto the shingle looked delicious to Bentley's eyes. He felt himself moving towards it, but Hallmark grabbed him firmly by the biceps. Bentley looked up at Hallmark, who appeared completely at ease with the whole situation. 'Don't drink it, sir,' warned Hallmark. 'The adjutant will have my head on a pike if you croak it now.'

It was the last thing Bentley heard. He faded out, his legs giving way. Hallmark, to his credit, didn't allow Paine to collapse onto the jetty; he pulled him in tight, then slung him over his shoulder, where he held him for a minute before some medics arrived. As they loaded Bentley onto a stretcher Hallmark joked, 'I promised his mum I'd keep him out of trouble.'

From his position just inside one of the many olive groves that draped the hills, Sergeant Dormann observed the British as they were ferried out to their ships. His radio man had mortar crews on standby, ready to shell the jetty as well as the rest of the embarkation area. Dormann's platoon, tired from their lightning exploits over the last twenty-four hours, were grabbing the opportunity to rest. Dormann once more put his binoculars up to his tired dry eyes. He couldn't determine if there were any British forces conducting a defence of the bay. He was at odds with himself. Attack the enemy when they were most vulnerable and risk a robust British response, or let sleeping dogs lie and preserve the lives of his paratroopers.

Dormann chose the latter. After all, his hounds had killed many a fox during the night.

Battle of Crete,
May–June 1941

5

It was some time before German engineers arrived to commence the building of the bridge across the Corinth Canal. It would take time to construct a new bridge to allow men and panzers to cross, so Captain Martin Bassom allocated his men the usual after-battle tasks, most of which were rather thankless. They gathered up the drop containers that hadn't yet been collected after the jump. They gathered up the parachutes, inspecting them carefully, since *Fallschirmjäger* always packed their own chutes, and there was no reason why a serviceable chute couldn't be used again. They accounted for and dealt with their dead and injured; most injuries had been sustained in parachute landings, although some had broken legs, including Major Olaf Darsch, Bassom's company commander. Major Darsch was a good leader, always at the front, where a parachute officer should be, but his landing had as good as crippled him. He was suffering from at least a broken femur and pelvis, and would be spending some considerable time in hospital. His military career might not suffer too much, but his days in the *Fallschirmjäger* were over. But it was the collection of

German and enemy dead that made Bassom's heart sink. They came in wrapped in shelter sheets and were buried in temporary graves, which were marked accordingly. He was sad for all their families, but was also furious at the waste of expensively trained German talent.

To permit the local German forces to regroup properly, Bassom had his men sweep and clear a nearby airfield. Very soon transport aircraft were arriving safely with additional supplies and taking away German and enemy wounded. He had Sergeant Werner organize a patrol schedule around the airfield and Corinth town. Bassom didn't have the resources to deal with civilian unrest, but the locals kept their distance, so in return he limited town patrols to the outskirts.

The new bridge was completed and the panzers arrived. With Bassom's battalion regrouped, its commander was warned that their next mission would be the airborne invasion of Crete.

Rested and eager to get into the next fight, Bassom's men went about their battle preparations with purpose. It was not in the nature of German paratroopers to think they had fought their war and to languish behind the front line. As far as Bassom was concerned, the *Fallschirmjäger* was the tip of the Führer's spear.

During an inspection of his men's equipment and weapons, both he and Sergeant Werner were summoned to Battalion Headquarters. The summons seemed nothing out of the ordinary, and when they reached Colonel Veck's office, they were waved straight in. Captain Keich, an adjutant, closed the door behind them. Bassom gave the colonel a crisp Luftwaffe salute, whereas Werner clashed his heels together and gave the Nazi salute. Werner's often-performed little charade irritated Bassom, for he felt it was all for show; Werner was a member of the Luftwaffe and yet persisted with his ridiculous dance. The colonel thanked them for their compliments and invited them to sit on the other side of his desk. Removing their caps from their heads, they obliged. They were offered coffee by the adjutant, but both refused, already full of the stuff from earlier in the day.

'Gentlemen,' the colonel began, 'I must say well done to you both. Your men conducted themselves as *Fallschirmjäger* in every sense of the word during the operation. Dashing, daring, courageous, with aggression and honour. Your men are a credit to you both.'

'Thank you, sir,' Werner jumped in enthusiastically.

Werner's interjection irritated Bassom. 'Thank you, sir,' the captain repeated in a more measured tone. 'I will pass on your compliments to the men.'

Veck nodded with gusto. 'Yes, yes. Unfortunate for Major Darsch. He is a fine commander, and I will miss his contribution in the up-and-coming battle. But with grey storm clouds of bad news, there is often a silver lining, yes?'

Bassom was puzzled. 'Sir?'

'Captain Bassom, it has been noted by several members of the unit that you fought with distinction during the operation, and you are therefore to be nominated for the Iron Cross, effective immediately. Congratulations.'

Words gathered on Bassom's tongue, but he couldn't put them in the correct order as he stood to accept Veck's outstretched hand. His thoughts briefly returned to the flak gun emplacement, the smashed frame of Corporal Muller, his men writhing wounded in the dust during the assault. It hardly seemed exceptional or worthy of such a great honour as the Iron Cross. It was almost as if something wasn't quite right. 'Thank you, sir,' said Bassom. He felt the need to sit back down and gather himself, but Captain Keich stepped forward, and Bassom had to accept his handshake. Werner then stood and extended his hand. Bassom forced himself to take it, but his sergeant's sinister grin added to the impression that everything wasn't as it appeared, Werner seemingly knowing in advance that something was awry.

'That'll be all, Sergeant, thank you,' said Veck as Werner and Bassom were about to take their seats. Werner gave Veck a knowing glance, then looked with what seemed to be mock surprise at Keich, who disturbingly closed his eyes and nodded. Werner straightened up and gave yet another heel-clicking Nazi Party salute before leaving the office. Keich closed the door after him, then moved the chair Werner had sat in closer to the desk. He and Bassom sat together, opposite Veck. Bassom began to feel uneasy, the mood in the room not so cordial. He wondered if he had done something wrong.

Veck looked sternly at him. 'You are to take over from Major Darsch. In a few days you will take command of his company for the Crete operation. So again, congratulations, Captain Bassom.' No handshakes were offered this time, making the newly appointed company commander squirm slightly in his chair.

Veck then leaned back in his seat, and Keich reached forward to pick up a light brown document file from the desk. He opened it, then passed the colonel a single sheet of paper. Veck scanned it briefly, giving the impression he had read it previously, before lifting his eyes to Bassom once more. 'I have a communication here from Para HQ back home, Captain Bassom. It would appear that you can be in two places at once.'

Bassom was well and truly lost. 'Sir?'

'A few nights ago an SS police unit arrested a man of your description in the small town of Dornitz. The man was as naked as the day he was born. They came to the conclusion that he was drunk and incapable of coherent speech.' Bassom's stomach turned over. His identical twin Karl's body had grown and matured like his brother's, but his mind had not. Bassom's family had worked hard to conceal Karl's existence, but it sounded as though he had escaped the confines of the family's dairy farm. Bassom couldn't help but lean forward, putting his face in his hands. Veck continued, 'Something you wish to tell us, Captain?'

Bassom took a deep breath and straightened up on the chair. His eyes were bloodshot, for all sorts of scenarios were rushing through his desperate mind. 'I have an identical twin, sir. The naked man you speak of is my brother, Karl.'

'Is dancing drunk and naked in the street the usual habit of your brother?' asked Veck.

'Dancing and naked, yes. Drunk, no. He is disabled and has the maturity of a child.'

Veck seemed stunned. He was in uncharted territory; in all his years he had never encountered a similar situation. Keich was also at a loss for words.

An uncomfortable silence hung in the office, as if all three men were waiting for someone else to break some sort of deadlock. Bassom decided it should be him. 'We live on a farm just outside the village. My brother sometimes wanders off the farm. When I'm on leave I take the blame and pretend it is me. But you're quite right, sir, I cannot be in two places at once.'

'Indeed, Captain, indeed. The communication also reads that a Tomas Bassom was arrested,' continued Veck, 'shortly after your brother was taken into custody.' This news of Bassom's father, a usually silent opponent of the Nazi Party, was a hammer blow, just as Bassom was beginning to rationalize everything in his head. 'It says here,' Veck elaborated, 'that he assaulted the SS men as they marched the naked man away. Who is this Tomas Bassom?' Bassom's entire world was falling backwards into an abyss of darkness and depression. He became embroiled in an image of his father sparring with the SS in a futile defence of Karl. The colonel snapped the image away. 'Captain, who is Tomas Bassom?'

'My father, Herr Colonel.'

Veck unlocked his gaze from Bassom's eyes and went

back to the document. He scanned it again, until his eyes locked on to something. 'Ah. It says here that due to Herr Tomas Bassom's exceptional wartime record, the police commissioner is reluctant to have him sent to a labour camp. It is regretted, however, that Herr Bassom was most vocal when questioned as to why he is not a party member, and was subject to disciplinary measures for speaking out of turn when the subject was broached.' Veck continued speaking, but talk of Tomas and Karl made Bassom's mind drift away to days gone by and his father's tales.

Tomas had been in the trenches when Martin and Karl Bassom were born on 11 November 1918, the last day of the Great War. The armistice hadn't boded well for Germany; the subsequent treaty was a virtual surrender, leaving the country without the resources to wage war again, making Tomas very quickly wonder whether it would be possible to continue his career as a professional soldier.

Tomas's march from France to Germany had been torturous, and on arrival in his homeland there was no fanfare, no family welcome; instead the soldiers were confined to barracks, French troops taking control of all military resources. It was February 1919 before Tomas finally returned to the family farm, to be reunited with his wife Astrid and two new boys. The farm was then run by Tomas's parents, Franco and Magda, who were ultimately forced to reduce the price they charged for their milk because of the deterioration in economic conditions. And things only got worse, as ever-accelerating hyperinflation gripped the nation. Buying basic commodities became increasingly difficult, the currency seemingly worthless, Martin and Karl wondering why the dairy herd was becoming ever smaller, unaware that Tomas was working tirelessly to protect both his boys and his cows from cattle rustlers.

Things became even more difficult when Martin and Karl reached their teéns. They began to behave differently, Karl suddenly unable to tie his shoelaces, his performance at school falling behind Martin's, his reading and writing slower. Tomas initially passed it off as differing character traits, but it soon became clear Karl's disability was getting worse. Tomas removed him from the school system altogether, keeping him at the farm, but Martin's schoolmates noticed Karl's sudden absence and mocked Martin, saying Karl was a halfwit, a blight on society and the Reich. Hitler was by now in power. He was promising the German people many great things including putting Germany back on the map. It was certainly true that the economy soon began to strengthen, the fortunes of the dairy farm fast improving. But Hitler's emphasis on turning the German people into what he called the master race had sinister overtones.

The authorities decided to build a camp on the outskirts of Dornitz. Tomas initially believed it was an army barracks and was hopeful he would be able to provide both the builders and the eventual occupants with milk.

But the construction of an enormous shower block, tall watchtowers and barbed-wire fences made him realize the camp wasn't going to be a barracks, after all. He ordered his family to stay away from the camp because of the dangerous fences, but that wasn't the only reason.

Despite his misgivings about the camp, Tomas eventually secured a contract to supply its kitchens with milk. His family weren't keen on producing milk for the camp, but appreciated the extra revenue. And unfortunately for Tomas the additional work made running the farm a little more difficult, a business equation complicated by his parents becoming frail, Astrid's time taken up with looking after them and Karl. Martin offered to drop out of school to help his father, but Tomas would have none of it. As far as Tomas was concerned, an education would make Martin wise to the world and the arseholes that ran it, enabling him to run with the fox or hunt with the pack. Martin was getting on exceptionally well at school, and was old enough to understand that with the heart of Germany beating stronger, a good education would help him find top employment.

Germany became stronger, but as it did, Tomas couldn't help but notice the camp was getting fuller. Yet the demand for milk from the camp never increased, making him wonder what the new arrivals were drinking. Then one day, while running a few errands in the village, he spotted a convoy of army trucks transporting what appeared to be ordinary men into the camp. He wondered if they were to undertake basic training, but learned while queueing for a newspaper that everyone who was negative about the Nazi Party was being interned as a troublemaker. It was hard to believe that speaking your mind got you locked up, but times had changed.

The camp eventually reached bursting point, but still the demand for milk didn't increase. On hot days in the early summer of 1939 the area smelled foul. Tomas knew the sweet, cheesy, sickly aroma of death all too well. He knew it from the Great War, and had been reminded of it again when earlier in the year his parents passed away in quick succession, mere months apart. Suddenly, trucks full of gaunt-looking men began to leave the camp for God knows where, with the camp almost empty at the beginning of August 1939.

Stories spread about Germany counter-attacking, reacting to Polish aggression. The Bassoms sat around their wireless, listening to news reports. Tomas sat in his chair, staring into space, his eyes glazed. Astrid stood at his shoulder, her hands on the high back of his chair, her eyes full of tears, as Germany tumbled back into a world of madness once more. Tomas reached up for her small hands, feeling crushed that it looked as though war would break out again. Karl sat rocking in his chair, giggling to himself, whistling bird songs. Martin was however transfixed by the radio broadcast. His heart fluttered with excitement as the correspondent spoke over the shrieking of Stuka dive-bombers pounding Polish positions.

Martin spotted a Luftwaffe recruiting stand at the

Berlin apprentice fair he and his father attended as soon as he graduated from school. Tomas tried to steer him away from it, but Martin protested, arguing he just wanted to find out a few facts. The NCO manning the stand was very keen to recruit men into flak gun regiments in Berlin and all over the country. He told Martin that, based on his education, he had the makings of an officer. Martin was very encouraged, thinking it might be possible to sign up but remain close to home. Tomas eyed the NCO suspiciously. In Berlin Tomas was starting to feel like he and Martin were the only people not in the Nazi Party.

His eye caught by another stand, Tomas wandered away, and although he knew his mother and father would disapprove, Martin signed up for the Luftwaffe, his joining date some way away. At least he would grow beyond the farm and wouldn't be fighting in Poland. The train journey back home was almost in silence, Martin feeling his father's disappointment bearing down on him.

Karl became more of a problem. He was still able to get himself to the toilet and back, but would now and again become disorientated and wander naked around the house and farm. Then one night Martin awoke to a commotion – Karl being put back into bed, naked yet smeared in mud and straw, sobbing inconsolably, Tomas and Astrid attempting to soothe him. Martin almost smiled when thinking of the subsequent conversation with his father, almost forgetting he was in Colonel Veck's office.

'In the morning,' began Tomas, 'I need you to go into the village and get bread, OK?'

'Er . . . sure,' Martin replied.

'If anyone says anything about Karl wandering naked and drunk in the village,' continued Tomas, 'pretend it was you, OK?'

The penny dropped instantly for Martin. It was a devious but good plot to keep Karl out of Grabowsee Sanatorium. 'Sure. No problem.'

'Good lad. Now get some sleep.' As Tomas stood, he winked at Martin.

And indeed, the errand to fetch bread proved to be easier said than done. As Martin walked cautiously down the main street of the village, women huddled together, pointing and tittering at him. The reaction of their children made it clear that even they were privy to whatever Karl had done during the night. Some of the children danced around, singing a made-up crude song about drunken naked boys. The menfolk stopped to cast Martin glares of disapproval. He was confident Karl had not harmed anybody but had just made a fool of himself, and potentially the family. Martin queued up behind a line of ladies outside the bakery.

'Young man, come here!' commanded a voice behind Martin. He turned. Two SS policemen stood across the street, glaring at him. Both were six foot tall, if an inch. 'I said come here, now!' the same voice ordered, owned by the less well built of the two officers. He raised his billy club, and Martin felt it best to obey. 'Martin Bassom, correct?' asked the officer.

The gossip mill of the women obviously reached even beyond their families, extending to the SS. Martin realized just how important it was to keep Karl to the confines of the farm. 'Yes, sir.' Relief washed through him as both officers tucked their clubs into their belts.

'Think you're funny, do you?' challenged the other officer.

Martin was at a loss, but decided to chance his arm. 'No, sir. I can only apologize. I have just been accepted into the Luftwaffe, and the family celebrations got out of hand. I'm sorry.'

The two SS men looked Martin up and down, then looked at each other. The bigger officer shrugged his shoulders as if the excuse was acceptable. 'Just as well you aren't joining the SS, then,' the smaller officer concluded, 'because I would have to kick your arse for you, you fucking idiot. Piss off back across the street before I change my mind. Go and mingle with the clucking hens while you wait for your bread, flyboy.'

Martin could feel his blood beginning to boil as he absorbed the insults. But only fools and madmen messed with the SS police. The SS he had heard about were bullying bastards, and if they were all the same, he could only be pleased he had instead joined the Luftwaffe.

Cadet Lieutenant Bassom's basic training in the Luftwaffe was tough and disciplined. There were long marches to and from the firing ranges, long days of shooting various weapons. There were tedious hours of parade drill and numerous room inspections, his instructors always screaming and demanding the impossible. A lot of recruits dropped out because of the harsh regime, but Bassom took it all in his stride. The long hours were not a problem; after all, he was from a farm.

It was during classroom instruction on radios that Bassom noticed a glossy, colourful poster for the *Fallschirmjäger*, the paratroopers. The image of men diving from aircraft, weapons in hand ready to fight, really caught his eye. The message on the poster was simple. The paratroopers were looking for tough, fit, competent volunteers to join their swelling ranks, to lead Germany to decisive victory over its enemies. Bassom was hooked. At first he met resistance from his instructors, who had invested a lot in his training and shortly planned to deploy him to command a flak battery in the western suburbs of Berlin. They even reminded him that Berlin was close to his family farm, so he would be able to go home often, which was unlikely to be the case with the paratroopers. But ultimately Cadet Lieutenant Martin Bassom got his wish. He was transferred to the *Fallschirmjäger*.

In the colonel's office Bassom wondered if Veck had played a little game to see if he would acknowledge that Karl was his brother and Tomas was his father. It sounded as though Tomas had expressed his opinion of the Nazi Party a little too strongly for the Dornitz policemen to tolerate, and had taken a beating. Why couldn't Papa have just kept quiet? The question circled in Bassom's mind. No wonder his mother insisted Tomas keep his views to himself whenever he was out in public. But obviously Karl's arrest had pushed him over the edge. Bassom began to wonder as to the whereabouts of his brother, but a request from Keich registered in his mind: 'Tell us about your father's war record.'

Bassom explained his father just wanted to forget the horrors he had witnessed in the Great War during long nights in the trenches at Verdun. Tomas had been an infantryman and had almost single-handedly destroyed a French trench-raiding party on a frozen December night. The French had seized a radio from a command bunker, killing the occupants with grenades and trench clubs. Tomas chased them into no-man's land in the darkness, killing some of them with nothing more than his trench spade. He returned with the radio, enabling German radio traffic in the area to remain uncompromised. For his actions he received the Kaiser's commendation, and a week later was mentioned by name in the Kaiser's Christmas message to the nation.

At the end of Bassom's monologue Veck and Keich leaned back in their chairs, clearly in awe. The colonel composed himself, national pride beginning to overwhelm him. He had to clear his throat. 'It makes the outcome of that war sting all the more, when Germany's boys were at their best but fighting when times were at their worst.' Silence descended over the office again. But this time it was not uncomfortable, but rather nostalgic. Bassom enquired what had become of his brother. Veck referred to the document, before looking up. 'Your father is currently in custody, and your brother has now been admitted to the sanatorium at Grabowsee—'

'Grabowsee, what the hell?' Bassom forgot himself and the company he was in. He stood up angrily and began pacing around the office, running his hands through his hair. 'It's supposedly for tuberculosis sufferers, but they also experiment on patients there – a horrid place, my father has always said so. They can't keep Karl there, he is not an animal.'

'Captain Bassom!' bellowed the colonel. 'I don't care to hear such claims, for which you have no evidence. May I remind you that you are a captain in the Luftwaffe and should behave as such. Now sit down.'

Bassom stopped, realizing he had gone too far. He adjusted his smock and belt, before taking his seat once more. 'I apologize, sir. This is all coming as a shock to me.'

Veck nodded, before continuing. 'The SS have insisted that you are to accept party membership in lieu of your father and write a formal letter of apology to the SS police commissioner regarding your father's conduct. Only then will the commissioner be satisfied and have your father released. Your father will then be able to take your brother back into your family's care.'

It was blackmail, plain and simple. Bassom was to join the Nazi Party or lose his father and brother. Was the Iron Cross merely a sweetener to make the deal somehow seem more attractive? He was now convinced of Werner's involvement. It made him hate Werner even more. 'Why party membership?' he chanced. 'I swore an oath to the Führer when I enlisted.'

'I'm just the messenger, Captain Bassom,' replied the colonel coolly. 'By all means refuse, but I would seriously think about your options right now. For the sake of your family, I trust a man of your intellect will do the right thing.'

Crestfallen, Bassom found himself looking into his own lap. 'How long have I got, sir?'

'We have mission preparations to be getting on with here, and the time to do them is short. Once operations in Crete are concluded, we will return to Germany, and that will give you the opportunity to do what is right.'

Bassom worried that the return to Germany might be some while away. The *Fallschirmjäger* had enjoyed many lightning victories, but Crete could be a drawn-out campaign. But there was little he could do but focus on Crete, so he nodded to Veck.

'Since Sergeant Major Skorensen never made it out of his aircraft –' Keich twisted the knife '– Sergeant Werner will be acting as your company sergeant major. Let's just say he can help you remain focused on your obligations.'

It was all Bassom needed: that Nazi arsehole Werner would be in his shadow all the time, watching his every move. Denis Skorensen was a good guy, a good leader, taking no nonsense from anyone. 'Is Skorensen dead?' enquired Bassom.

'No,' Keich confirmed, 'but his aircraft took a lot of ground fire just before he jumped. Most of his men were hit, and the aircraft limped back north. They should all be in hospital beds by now.' Bassom was happy to hear Denis and his boys would be OK.

There was little else to say. Bassom stood, giving the colonel a Luftwaffe salute. Keich eyeballed Bassom but didn't comment on his defiance.

Halfway out of the door a sudden realization dawned on Bassom. He spun on his heel and looked back at Veck. 'What would happen if I fell in battle, sir?'

Veck returned his stare. 'All right, Captain Bassom, I will assume you have already accepted the terms proposed by the police commissioner, so I will communicate with him on your behalf. Satisfied?'

It was enough for Bassom. 'Thank you, sir.' He turned and scurried away. Werner was waiting outside, finishing a coffee he had scrounged and looking smug. Bassom had a lot to be getting on with, not to mention a lot on his mind.

6

A British ship chugged slowly into Souda Bay, Crete. Crammed with battered and bloody men, the ship groaned as she finally came to a standstill and was moored to a concrete and timber jetty.

Captain Bentley Paine had been brought back from the brink with some of the most vile yet delicious water that had ever passed his lips. Hallmark had got him onto the deck of the ship with the aid of medics after he collapsed on the loading jetty. Bentley had regained consciousness enough to start taking on water, albeit almost bullied into it by Hallmark. Violent spasms of vomiting, along with increasing stomach and leg cramps, had made it touch and go, but Bentley was slowly able to keep water down, gradually recovering from his extreme dehydration, repeatedly demanding to know where the toilets were. And as he had grown stronger during the voyage his shrapnel wounds from the flak gun emplacement in Greece had been treated in the ship's sick bay.

As the ship docked, Bentley was strong enough to stand at the rail. He and Hallmark witnessed the troops disembark. At the end of the jetty men armed with clipboards took details and directed the troops on their feet to clusters of trucks parked up on a low escarpment. The stretcher-bound were ushered off in a different direction, towards a large cluster of oversized canvas tents that bore the markings of a medical facility. Conscious that Bentley had been through a lot, Hallmark gave him a gentle nudge with his elbow. 'Shall we get you to those tents for a quick check-up?'

'No.' Bentley's answer was cold and to the point. Hallmark eyeballed him out of the corner of his eye while slowly shaking his head. There was just no pleasing some people. Once room on deck allowed them to begin their hot and sweaty disembarkation, they shuffled down the gangway. Bentley did the talking to the clipboard men. Hallmark was stunned at his arrogance towards them. Hallmark was a rough diamond, but Bentley was rude and obnoxious as he barked information to a young sergeant. Bentley came across as so jumped-up, Hallmark wondered how he didn't get a thump on the nose. But the sergeant kept his cool, eventually pointing out a truck to take them to the city of Heraklion, where 14th Infantry Brigade was situated, the parent formation of 2 Yorks and Lancs.

It was a beautiful hot Cretan day. The truck journey was long, dusty and uncomfortable. Those crammed in the back under the heavy canvas sat in silence, which suited Bentley fine, except that Hallmark was crammed in next to him. Bentley was not in the mood to engage in idle chitchat with anyone. He just wanted to see the adjutant at Battalion Headquarters. The whole chaotic debacle on the Greek mainland could not be sorted out until those units that were being shipped onwards to Egypt got reorganized. Bentley's secondment to the 4th Hussars in Greece had been a failure. His ambition to get a transfer to the cavalry and make some headway with regard to regenerating the family business was in tatters. He couldn't even be certain that the 4th Hussars Headquarters had survived the German airborne assault. All he knew was there was no job for him back at 2 Yorks and Lancs, and he would no doubt be farmed out on some other irrelevant assignment, with Hallmark in tow.

His thoughts about Hallmark were becoming toxic. As tough as he might be, as good a soldier as he might be, Hallmark seemed to go out of his way to embarrass him. Bentley thought he had had the battle at the flak gun emplacement under control. No doubt a character like Hallmark thrived in chaos, something that probably put him in a position to push officers and other men around. The sooner Bentley could get rid of the brute, the better. Hallmark's head was hanging on his chest. A seasoned soldier, Hallmark knew how to take every opportunity to sleep.

Suddenly consumed in a cloud of Cretan dust, the truck lurched abruptly to a standstill. Everyone began to dust themselves down. The tailgate was lowered, and just as Bentley jumped from the rear of the truck, Hallmark gave an almighty stretch. The men lined up behind Hallmark had to wait for the theatrics of the yawn to conclude, before he hopped down. He had already decided that Crete was not dissimilar to mainland Greece. He noticed Bentley disappear into one of a cluster of buildings signposted as 14th Infantry Brigade Headquarters. Still somewhat sleep-drunk, Hallmark slowly followed.

As Hallmark entered the dark cavern chosen by Bentley, he took a few moments to adjust to the lower light. Hallmark always felt for the poor buggers who sweated away in the stifling rooms under the heat and glare of lamps illuminating map boards, and amid the constant hum of radio traffic. Instead of trying to track Bentley down in the labyrinth of corridors and rooms, he decided not to get under anyone's feet, so stood looking at a large map of Crete on a wall. To its right was a more detailed map of Heraklion, showing the position of units dispersed to the south of the town and at an airfield to the east. A large paper flag highlighted the position of 2 Yorks and Lancs. Judging by the locations of the various coloured flags on the map of Crete, most if not all of the British garrison was placed along the northern coast. The remainder of the island had smaller flags marking units here and there, but only a few. Crete was a large island, and there were a lot of areas to cover against attack. He couldn't understand why some troops were being shipped on to Egypt; surely they served a better purpose here?

Bentley moved from room to room in the headquarters building, trying to find someone with a link to 2

Yorks and Lancs. He couldn't see the adjutant, but found an unhappy-looking major who wore the insignia of his regiment. The major was talking into a phone handset wedged between his cheek and shoulder while rummaging through a mess of papers submerging what looked like his desk, which had a single chair in front of it. He was too busy to notice Bentley standing before him.

'Well?' demanded the major into the handset. 'Whose idea was it for him to go on bloody leave at a time like this?' Bentley took a subtle step further into the major's periphery. Only then did he get noticed, the major fixing him with a glare. Bentley was suddenly conscious of his appearance after the long journey from Greece; certainly not befitting a commissioned officer. 'So I have to go without a second in command?' the major barked into the handset. 'Is that what you are telling me? It's my company that's in reserve, and you won't even give me what is required to man it?' He paused. 'Hang on.' Pulling the handset from his shoulder, he stared directly at Bentley. 'What?' he bellowed. Bentley wasn't sure if the major was addressing him, so instinctively looked around to find no one, only to turn back and find the major still glaring at him. 'Yes, you. Speak,' instructed the major.

Bentley had learned quickly that young officers can get just as much of a hard time as the ranks. 'Captain Paine, sir. Just returned from the Greek mainland, seconded to the cavalry—'

The major held up a hand, cutting him short. The

handset was wedged back between his shoulder and cheek. 'Gerry, I have Captain Paine here. What's he up to?' Bentley heard muffled chatter from the handset. 'He fucking isn't; I'm bloody looking at him!' Bentley began to feel uncomfortable. Especially now that he was the topic of conversation, dreading what was about to become of him. On his way he had glanced at some map boards. As far as he could see, 2 Yorks and Lancs weren't nearby, so he got the feeling he wouldn't be joining them any time soon. The major put the phone down and busied himself with some paperwork, then, without so much as looking up, finally addressed him. 'Take a seat, Captain. I just need to go and kick someone's arse.'

Hallmark was at the point of giving up on Bentley for the day; the man would find him soon enough. He decided he would hitch a lift or walk back to the Battalion Head-quarters position he had identified on a map, not too far to the south. Then he saw Major Barnett come out of one of the rooms with a pile of papers and a face like thunder. Barnett had once been Hallmark's company sergeant major, and had eventually been commissioned. Barnett did a double-take and headed towards him. Hallmark suddenly developed the demeanour of a wayward teen-ager, caught getting up to no good by a parent. He pulled himself to attention. 'Good morning, sir. How are you?'

'Cut the shit, John. I've known you long enough to know when you are being a sarcastic git. What are you doing here?'

'I'm looking for Captain Paine, sir.'

'Why?'

'I'm his ... er ... batman, sir.'

Major Barnett's eyes went wide. 'What?'

'I'm his batman, sir, for my sins.'

Barnett noticed Hallmark's corporal chevrons. He grabbed the fabric with his fingertips. 'Don't tell me the old man busted you again?'

Hallmark struggled to look him in the eye. 'Yes, sir.'

'For fuck's sake, John,' groaned Barnett. 'I thought we'd put all that shit to bed. I told you to stay off the grog and away from the tarts. What happened this time?'

'Grog, tarts and police, all under one roof. The police were taking a cut from the girls. When my tart handed some money over to them, I demanded they give it back to her. Pimps in coppers' outfits—'

Barnett cut him short with a raised hand, then slowly closed his eyes. 'Come with me. Captain Paine is in my office.'

As they walked back out into the corridor, Hallmark wondered where it had all gone wrong. Barnett was admittedly a fine officer, but why had he been so successful in the military, while Hallmark frequently found trouble, more often demoted than promoted?

Major Barnett strolled back into his office bantering with John Hallmark. Sitting in front of Barnett's desk, Bentley felt most put out. It didn't surprise him that they knew each other, both being experienced soldiers, but the casual nature of their relationship seemed bizarre. Their banter continued, seemingly oblivious to him. Eventually, Barnett turned to address Bentley, who sprang to his feet, sharp to attention. Barnett and Hallmark both flinched. 'Bloody hell, Captain,' Barnett boomed, 'calm yourself. You gave me a fright there.'

'Yes, sir. My apologies.'

Barnett ran his fingers through his silver hair. He still had a full head of it, but the original colour had long gone. 'Battalion in their wisdom feel that you should be my second in command.'

'Thank you, sir.' Bentley beamed, nodding enthusiastically. It somehow made perfect sense to him, and felt like another opportunity to get on.

'B Company has been nominated by the commanding officer to be brigade reserve,' Barnett explained. 'I'm not normally the commander of B Company, but the colonel felt that a relatively new face was less likely to get pushed about, so I swapped with Colonel Austin. Sergeant – I mean Corporal – Hallmark will remain with you, but not as your bloody batman, do you hear me?' Barnett seemed to snarl Hallmark's name, as if sensing that Bentley might not like the idea of Hallmark sticking around. 'We've got the Germans breathing down our necks,' warned Barnett, 'so there's no time for in-barracks bullshit, understand?'

'Of course, sir,' Bentley agreed, keen to defuse the conversation.

Barnett relaxed a little, content Bentley was dancing

to his tune. 'So Corporal Hallmark will act as your deputy, as it were. I have been informed by Captain Long
that you have not long been commissioned, so you will
be in a somewhat unique and potentially overwhelming situation. It might have been better to have a more
seasoned officer perform your role, but Captain Parsons
is attending a wedding back in England, and his wife is
about to give birth. Besides, I can't afford to have you
thrown in as a platoon commander, with a platoon that
have never even met you, never mind trained or fought
with you.'

Bentley knew it made sense for him not to assume a
commanding role with a fresh platoon, given that there
would seem to be so little time to bed in before the
expected arrival of the Germans. Despite his feelings
about Hallmark, he had to admit deep down that he
had carried the day at the flak gun emplacement in
Greece, but Bentley was not about to concede the point
to anyone.

'I don't have time to teach you how to command the
company when I'm absent,' continued Barnett, 'so like
it or not, Captain, you will have Hallmark here to help
you along. Understood?' Bentley snatched a sideways
glance at Hallmark, who wore a look that said he wasn't
all that keen on the job. 'Understood?' Barnett repeated
more forcefully.

Bentley snapped his head back to face Barnett, who
was still looking for reassurance that a partnership
between Hallmark and Bentley could work in Crete.

Bentley realized that Barnett might just have presented him with an opportunity to detach himself from Hallmark once and for all, but he couldn't risk suggesting he work alone with Barnett, since Barnett might then look elsewhere for his second in command. 'Understood, sir,' confirmed Bentley.

'Excellent,' Barnett concluded, bursting into a sinister grin. 'I will give you the tour. The platoon commanders are bringing the men here as we speak. Sergeant Major Pearce is with them.'

Major Barnett led Bentley and Hallmark from the building out into the brilliant Cretan sunshine. They had to shade their eyes until they grew accustomed to the light. Bentley took in the scene about him. Around the headquarters buildings a number of men were digging trenches, reinforcing the dirt rims with copious amounts of rock. Signallers were attending to masts protruding from the dusty ground, held in place with guide ropes and metal pegs. He could make out the cough and splutter of aircraft engines; there was clearly an airfield nearby. To the south was a large imposing range of hills featuring arid patches broken up by olive groves and random clusters of tall, lush green trees. On the upper slopes of the hills sat groups of off-white dwellings with dark roofs. Crete was a beautiful place, but how long it would remain that way was yet to be seen.

'When B Company arrives,' explained Barnett, 'I will have Sergeant Major Pearce site the platoons to dig in while I brief you and the platoon commanders on current developments. The Germans are coming, that's for sure.' Bentley and Hallmark followed him to the northern side of the position. Barnett pointed out a large lush green copse that screened them from the sea, speculating B Company might do well to establish a position in the area. The copse was just one element of cover on the north side of the headquarters building. There would be plenty of space for the company to spread out, and the abundant cover would protect everyone from the crushing Mediterranean sun, particularly in the early afternoon, the hottest part of the day, a consideration even more important than hiding from possible Luftwaffe attacks.

It was mid-afternoon when the lead elements of B Company arrived. They were soaked in sweat. Some of the men wore khaki shirts and shorts, but most were in traditional battledress. They gathered in the shade, drinking from their water bottles. As the rest of the company appeared, Barnett broke away from Bentley and Hallmark to collect Sergeant Major Pearce, taking him north towards the copse. After a brief consultation, a series of nods from Pearce led Bentley to deduce that he had been sold on the idea of siting the company in or near the copse.

Barnett returned alone, leaving Pearce to survey the area. B Company were resting, sprawled out in the shade. Barnett raised his voice to be heard by everyone. 'All right, lads? Glorious day, isn't it? Feels like you're on holiday.' There were chuckles and grins all round. 'Please join

Sergeant Major Pearce at your new home,' Barnett instructed them, jovially gesturing towards Pearce. 'Ditch your gear, just weapons and digging tools. Platoon commanders and Captain Paine, please follow me inside. Corporal Hallmark, assist the sergeant major, please.'

'Yes, sir,' said Hallmark and turned away. Fighting gear was heavy, so the men of B Company left it all behind for now, strewn across the grass, as they headed for the copse, carrying just weapons, picks and shovels. Barnett led Bentley and the platoon commanders towards the buildings. Lee-Enfield rifle and water bottle in hand, Hallmark followed B Company. Many were already swinging shovels and picks beside the copse when he got there. He was happy not to have been invited into Barnett's furnace of an office for a briefing, during which he would have undoubtedly watched Bentley get more and more out of his depth.

Barnett spread out a map of Crete across his desk. The platoon commanders and Bentley crowded round. 'Right, then,' Barnett began, 'let's get the pleasant shit out of the way first. Captain Paine. Sorry, what is your first name?'

'Bentley, sir.'

Barnett was about to speak again when he glanced back at Bentley with a strange look, clearly surprised at such an unusual forename.

Bentley began nodding and shaking hands as Barnett introduced the platoon commanders, all officers in their own right, each holding a pencil and a little map. 'Mr

Arnie Thatcher, 4 Platoon; Mr Barney Taylor, 5 Platoon; and this is Mr Kenneth Hicks, 6 Platoon. Bentley here has been thrown into the mix with limited experience, although he has already fought the Germans on the Greek mainland, so is not as fresh as you might think. However, I will have you men stick with your platoons to employ your own unique fighting styles, so I will be helping Mr Paine learn the ropes at a rapid rate of knots. Everyone happy so far?' There were nods all round. 'Right, then,' Barnett pushed on. 'Intelligence sources have informed Brigade that the enemy are currently preparing for an invasion of Crete. Timescale unknown, and method of getting here not certain. Our higher command is putting their money on an airborne approach, with seaborne follow-up forces. The launch point of the enemy assault should be either the southern end of Italy or the Greek mainland. Intelligence sources have also picked up German plans to seize airfields, which would enable the enemy to push their forces in. You don't have to be an intelligence officer to know that the only airfields on the north side of the island are at Rethymnon and Maleme, as well as the one here at Heraklion.'

The three airfields were spaced out along the coast of Crete facing north across the Mediterranean. Heraklion airfield was just a kilometre or so to the east of the city. Rethymnon was some fifty kilometres to the west, Maleme airfield another fifty kilometres further away, close to the western tip of the island. 'Our job as brigade reserve,' Barnett continued, 'is to move anywhere in the Heraklion sector, wherever the enemy threat is most grave. All understood so far?' Everyone nodded; even Bentley had an idea of what was going on. 'We have various units occupying static positions,' went on Barnett, starting to point a pencil at locations on the map stretched across his desk, 'covering key terrain. That will allow us to move about the defensive area, reinforcing any unit that requires our support. We have the Australians overlooking the main road, off to the east. We have a Scottish infantry battalion at Heraklion airfield. We have our own battalion to the south. Greek forces occupy the barracks just south of the airfield, and there are additional units to the west.'

Bentley noticed that the platoon commanders had been scribbling away with pencils on their own maps. It made him feel a little vulnerable; he didn't have a map yet. As if reading his mind, Barnett pulled one from a desk drawer and pushed it towards him. Bentley took it, then noticed a used ammunition container full of pencils. Picking up a pencil, he began to draw on his map. 'OK, then,' Barnett resumed. 'Our positions. As we speak, the sergeant major and your platoon sergeants are getting the boys dug in close to the copse which lies between here and the sea. The trenches are to be fighting positions only; there is no need for the men to be sleeping in them, as of yet. Once the positions are complete, and you have inspected them, the company will sleep under canvas in the copse. If you don't hear the Germans when they arrive, then you deserve to be shot.'

There were chuckles all round; even Bentley saw the humour.

Arnie Thatcher asked Barnett, 'When does our high command think they will come, sir? The Germans, I mean.'

'In the next few days. The enemy's radio transmissions take a while to decode and translate, but we are looking at the next few days.' Unknown to all but a very few, the British had made considerable progress in breaking the German Enigma code. 'So we are to get our act together now and sit tight,' he concluded, 'while we wait for the show to start. Any other questions?' There were none.

7

Time had passed painfully slowly for Martin Bassom. With all the preparations complete long ago, and orders delivered to all paratroopers, from general all the way down to private, every member of the *Fallschirmjäger* involved with the assault on Crete knew exactly what was required of them. Bassom's company was tasked, along with the rest of his battalion, with parachuting onto Heraklion airfield and seizing the control tower and hangars, in order to secure an entry point for follow-on forces arriving by air. German mountain troops, specially trained to fight in rugged terrain at altitude, would arrive as soon as Bassom's men had secured the airfield. The mountain troops would not allow the British, recently mauled in Greece, a chance to regroup and counter-attack. Crete, as far as Bassom was concerned, was ripe for the taking.

And indeed Bassom's time twiddling his fingers was about to come to an end. Sergeant Werner by his side, he was lined up among a vast number of paratroopers at the airfield on the outskirts of Corinth, all waiting to board an enormous flotilla of aircraft; it was to be a massive assault. The Germans had only just finished constructing the airfield.

'I wish I could share your enthusiasm for this venture, sir,' commented Werner, the negative tone unusual for him.

Bassom felt the need to challenge Werner. 'Unlike you to be half-empty, Sergeant.' He decided to add something friendly but a little sarcastic. 'Are you party members not fearless in the face of the enemy?'

Werner knew all too well that Bassom had little time for Nazi Party members, but there was no question he was a fine officer, so in terms of their professional relationship, that was just fine. That said, Werner had tired long ago of Bassom's constant digs at his membership. These digs seemed to come even when current affairs and the German regime weren't the topic of conversation. Werner had hoped Bassom's meeting with Colonel Veck and Captain Keich would change his attitude, but perhaps it was not to be. Werner shuddered at the likely content of the full and comprehensive report on Bassom's conduct he had undertaken to write for Keich, worried about the possible consequences for the captain and perhaps even his family. Werner had been told that Bassom was under instructions to accept party membership as soon as the men returned to Germany. Veck and Keich had also told Werner that Bassom was under considerable pressure to comply. As well as compiling the report, Werner had been charged with keeping Bassom focused, whatever that meant. Werner was at a loss as to why Bassom warranted such attention, given he was to join the party. But if the party wanted a detailed report, far be it for Werner to question his masters. Werner often wondered why he and Bassom had such different attitudes, thinking the answer lay in his upbringing.

Born in late 1911, the Great War largely passed young Julius Werner by. However, he remembered masses of soldiers marching through the streets of his home city of Detmold, some sixty kilometres south-west of Hanover. Perhaps talking about that struggle could ease the tension between the two of them.

'What did your father do in the last war, Captain?'

'What?'

'Your father, sir. I take it he served in the last war?'

Bassom relaxed a little, surprised however at the question. 'He was an infantryman. He fought at Verdun, among other places.'

'Officer?'

Bassom shook his head. 'No, no. He was a private soldier. Just a young dairy farmer.'

'Interesting.' Werner rubbed his chin.

Bassom was instantly irritated, thinking only that Werner was fishing for material to put in his report once the Crete operation was concluded. Bassom was not going to allow the sergeant to conclude their brief exchange. 'And yours?'

Werner was surprised at the sudden return.

'Oh, um. My father was a baker.'

Eyebrow raised, not convinced in the slightest, Bassom scoffed: 'A baker?' The young officer assumed the upstart was the offspring of some Town Hall Nazi official.

Werner, relaxed as he was, frowned at the challenge. 'He was indeed a baker, sir.'

Bassom was disappointed that Werner did not rise to his latest jibe. He could see that the sergeant was offended when he had scoffed at his father's occupation, and the tension remained between them for some time.

It was the warm Greek sun that eventually wore them down to small talk once again. Werner shook his head, puffing out his cheeks. 'I don't pretend to be a great tactician,' he confessed, 'but I think we played our ace when we dropped into here. I don't think the British will perform so poorly when confronted with a second airborne assault. And to make things worse, we will be part of the second wave to fly into the drop zones, so there will be no element of surprise whatsoever. My misgivings could be wrong, I suppose.'

Bassom couldn't help but agree. Werner's observations were not without merit. The British were a lot of things, but they were not foolish.

Bassom looked around the airfield. Some men dozed, some read books, played cards or smoked. A fair number just sat in their packed parachute harnesses, lost in their thoughts. Bassom's own thoughts were worries. His father was in an SS police cell, his brother Karl in the Grabowsee Sanatorium. Bassom's mother would be at home, no doubt worried out of her mind while trying to keep the farm going. It was a lovely bright, warm, clear day. It would be a shame to go back into battle on such a fine day, but Bassom just wanted to get on with the mission, so he could get home to his family. Time was a cruel mistress when you wanted it to move quickly.

'Company commanders, inspect your men!' shouted Colonel Veck, who was in his own parachute harness, ready to go. 'Once complete, board your aircraft. Good luck. See you on the airfield in Crete!'

The men erupted in roars. Many paratroopers clambered to their feet, but all remained in their lines, along with the drop containers full of weapons, medical supplies, radios and ammunition. Bassom inspected each of his men carefully. All stood to attention. Each individual inspection was the same. First he ensured the soldier's parachute was fitted and packed correctly, then he gave his harness straps a good pull just to be sure it was fitted properly. He then ensured his helmet was secure, for the last thing you wanted was for it to get ripped off in the slipstream as you left the aircraft. Then he inspected the paratrooper's smock, ensuring it was done up correctly, and equipment stowed in the pockets was secure. Some of the men wore knee pads out of personal choice, but most did not. Bassom didn't wear them. He found them uncomfortable, and they reduced his mobility. As each individual inspection was concluded, the paratrooper inspected would put his static line clip between his teeth and head off to his aircraft. Holding the clip with your teeth ensured it would not get caught on something, prematurely opening the parachute as you climbed into the aircraft.

The airfield at Corinth was a hive of activity. Sand and dust was blown through the ranks of paratroopers by the exhaust of aircraft as they spluttered into life.

Only Bassom and Werner awaited inspection. They began to check each other's equipment and chute. Regardless of rank, everyone was checked: once on the ground, and once in the aircraft, just prior to the jump. While checking Werner's chute Bassom had a sudden devilish impulse to tamper with it, to prevent him jumping from the aircraft. He didn't want to sabotage the chute so it didn't open properly, not wanting the Nazi to come to any harm. It would just be better if the bastard didn't come along on the mission, to ensure Bassom remained 'focused', as Adjutant Keich had put it. But he wasn't sure how to do it, at least not quickly and without suspicion.

Bassom and Werner strode over to their aircraft, the jump master ready to assist them on board, since chutes and equipment made clambering into any aircraft a sweaty challenge. Once inside Werner made his way up to the front, taking a seat behind the pilots. He would be the last to jump. Bassom would be the first, after the containers went out of the door.

On Bassom's aircraft everyone was seated and ready to go. Suddenly, the din of the engines and propellers drowned out any chance of conversation. Once airborne, you could communicate, but it generally involved shouting or hand signals. The tempo and pitch of the engines increased as the aircraft began to taxi, ground crews waving the paratroopers off.

Bassom found himself mulling over Werner's words. Being part of the second wave of parachutists would indeed increase the danger, but Bassom quietly hoped the British were not up for a fight, or would be in no shape to resist properly, or would not be there. Getting home to his family was at the forefront of his mind. As he looked towards the front of the aircraft, he could tell by the looks on his paratroopers' faces that they were thinking similar thoughts. Even Werner wasn't displaying his usual arrogance. A sudden increase in engine pitch signalled the acceleration of the aircraft down the airstrip. The noise coming from the tyres became horrendous, but as the aircraft lifted, the din instantly subsided. They were airborne, on their way to Crete. Bassom quietly wished his men well and spared a thought for those paratroopers in the first wave, who would already be fighting for Maleme airfield in Crete.

The Greek morning was beautiful. Yet Bassom had no idea that most of his men would never see another one.

'Sir? Sir?'

Bentley Paine opened his eyes and allowed the dark looming mass above him to swim into focus. He was yet to decide whether the siting of B Company Headquarters on the top floor of 14th Infantry Brigade HQ was a gift or a curse. Yes, a comfortable canvas cot bed under a roof was nice, but the copse would be much cooler, and the building was constantly full of the crackle-buzz of radios, along with the incessant chatter of typewriters. He wondered if the brigade clerks were ever allowed to sleep. His vision cleared. The image of John Hallmark became clear, not looking his usual cocksure self.

'Major Barnett wants you now, sir. We've got Germans landing at Maleme.'

Bentley sat bolt upright. He gave a big stretch and ran his fingers through his stiff matted hair. 'What time is it, please?'

'Just after eight, sir.'

Bentley clambered off his bed and hurriedly pulled his boots on. Without even doing the laces up, he followed Hallmark downstairs to Major Barnett's office, where a group stood before large maps of the island and Heraklion pinned to a wall. A colonel stood poised with a long wooden pointer, waiting for everyone to gather. There was a sudden commotion. The group turned as one to witness Barnett's platoon commanders stomping in, dressing as they went.

Once everyone had assembled, the colonel tapped sharply on the Maleme area of the map of Crete. 'Gentlemen. A short time ago a German parachute force began landing on Maleme airfield. Friendly forces dug in around the airfield inflicted heavy losses on the enemy, hitting both their planes and the parachutists under canopy. But our men are now being overwhelmed by not only the mass of parachutists landing, but enemy glider-borne forces too. The enemy have quickly gained a foothold on the airfield, and are really putting the pressure on the remaining defenders. We are to be ready for an enemy force to land here. Please have runners posted, so we can feed information to you as we receive it. Thank you.'

The room emptied with a sense of urgency. Bentley went back upstairs to tie his laces and gather what fighting gear he had, which was nothing more than his webbing, a Lee-Enfield rifle, a helmet and a Webley pistol. He had what he felt was enough ammunition, and made sure he had a full water bottle. Realizing Hallmark was elsewhere for once, he left the building, tagging onto Major Barnett on his way to the copse. B Company had clearly been resting in their tents, but the platoon commanders were rousing them. Many were already heading for the freshly dug trenches beside the copse, some carrying Vickers machine-gun kits. It suddenly dawned on Bentley that he wouldn't have a trench to fight from. He felt rather foolish wandering around, pretending to know what he was looking for. By accident, he found himself looking at Barnett, who was in a trench with his radio man and Sergeant Major Pearce. Barnett was busy, a radio handset wedged in his ear. His radio man scrambled out of the trench to reposition the ground-mounted radio antennae, in an attempt to improve signal strength.

'Looking for your trench, sir?' Pearce asked Bentley, grinning.

'Er . . . yes, Sergeant Major, yes, I am.' There was no point lying.

Pearce chuckled as he clambered from the trench, rifle in hand. 'Follow me, sir.' He led Bentley to where 5 Platoon were dug in. Bentley could make out Barney Taylor and his radio man, trying to sort their set out. Just behind their trench was a second freshly dug, vacant trench. 'Here you are, sir,' said Pearce, gesturing to the vacant trench. 'No harm done.'

Bentley felt relief wash over him, glad he didn't have to dig a trench himself. 'Thank you, Sergeant Major. Who dug this for me?'

'Johnny Hallmark, sir. You have a good man with you there. You can't go wrong with that lad.'

Bentley climbed into the trench and got himself comfortable. He silently thanked the wayward Hallmark for his efforts. 'Have you known Corporal Hallmark long, Sergeant Major?'

Pearce knelt down. 'My entire career, sir. Went through basic training with him. He's a wild card and a rough diamond but a man to have at your side in a tight spot. He's a good 'un for someone from Lancashire.'

Bentley appreciated the humour in Pearce's comment and let out a stifled chuckle. 'Where the devil is the man?' Paine demanded as he looked about the position.

'He's acting as a runner. I took the liberty of nominating him, sir.'

Pearce took his leave and left Bentley to his own devices. He peered about his trench and beyond, and could just make out the crude earthworks of the other 5 Platoon trenches. Most were dug into a rough hedge line, overgrown with what appeared to be reeds. He became aware of how much of the company position he couldn't see. He didn't think the foliage would fool any parachutists drifting directly above them, but at ground level it did the job. With plenty of trenches forward of his, and a Vickers team dug in forward right, the company was orientated with their backs to the sea. Bentley couldn't understand the reason for this straight away, but once he realized the position was skewed towards Heraklion airfield to the east, it all made sense. He was slowly figuring things out for himself, and as far as he was concerned, Hallmark would soon be surplus to requirements.

Noon came and went, and the Mediterranean sun was punishing. Some trenches enjoyed the shade of foliage around them, but many didn't. Bentley watched Hallmark as he dashed back and forth, delivering information to Major Barnett.

It was well into the blistering early afternoon when the distant drone of aircraft snapped Bentley from his heat-induced doze. It was coming from out to sea, behind the company and slowly growing. Everyone turned, shading their eyes as they tried to spot the planes. Some climbed out of their trenches, pointing excitedly at numerous black dots flying in formation on the horizon.

'Vickers and Bren guns only, guys, Vickers and Brens only,' Hallmark shouted, dashing from trench to trench.

The Bren light machine-gun and Vickers medium machine-gun teams began getting their weapons elevated.

Bentley spotted Major Barnett, running between the trenches. 'Wait for my command, men, wait for my command. Remember what you've been taught, boys. A solid stream of fire, six aircraft lengths in front. Go for the aircraft. Those with rifles and Stens can deal with the parachutists as they land, OK? Aircraft are the priority.'

Bentley was starting to feel strangely excited about the prospect of firing on those who had almost chased him down like a fox on mainland Greece. As he readied his rifle, Hallmark slid in beside him. 'Remember, sir,' reminded Hallmark, 'let the gun teams take care of the aircraft. Don't try and get the bastards until they hit the deck. You will only waste ammo—'

'Thank you, Corporal. I did manage to hear the major.'

Hallmark's mood instantly soured. He gave Bentley a sideways glance.

A vast armada of German transport aircraft took shape, coming into focus over the sea. An air-raid siren began to wail from Heraklion airfield. Bentley could see troops dashing about the Brigade HQ building, some taking up fighting positions on the rooftops. The aircraft looked as though they would bypass the company, instead heading for the airfield. Some of the Vickers and Bren boys were cursing, fidgeting behind their weapons; the order to open fire delayed and delayed. Just as the lead aircraft approached the coastline, small black dots began trailing from their tails. Parachutes blossomed, and the flak guns surrounding the airfield began to thunder away in a steady bass beat.

It was enough for Major Barnett. 'Fire!'

The red light by the door illuminated. 'Action stations!' roared Bassom's jump master. As one, everybody clambered to their feet. Once standing and stable, they each took the static line from their teeth, securing it to the fixed line that ran the length of the aircraft. With the aid of the jump master, Bassom inverted the drop containers, so they too could be clipped to the fixed line. With one of the containers leaning heavily on his thighs, the jump master called out, 'Equipment check.'

It was easier said than done, as the aircraft slewed slightly in turbulence. Corporal Stolz checked Bassom's chute. Bassom shuffled to his right so he could look out of the open doorway. He could see coal-black puffs of smoke bursting above and below the aircraft flying alongside. He remembered Werner's words at Corinth airfield. What were the planners thinking? The British had plenty of warning. And the Maleme drop must have given away the German intention to attack airfields.

The red light blinked out, replaced by a green one. The jump master flipped a drop container out of the door. As it was ripped away by the slipstream, there was an almighty thud and flash. Bassom's vision swam back into focus on what he thought was a prematurely deployed red and green canopy. Deaf with the exception of a high-pitched whine in his ears, he struggled to catch his breath.

It was as if a huge force had stamped on his lungs. He fought with every gasp to draw in air. His lower gut burned intensely as he clambered onto his hands and knees.

His vision became acute. The red and green canopy was in fact the smashed cadaver of the jump master splattered all over the inside of the aircraft, everything coated in clothing shreds and clumps of muscle and bone. Bassom attempted to stand, pushing himself up on a warped and buckled drop container, then he felt the force of rushing air roaring through the torn-open side of the aircraft. The full extent of the horror became apparent. Most of his men were piled on top of each other, droplets of blood flicking from them. Almost buried, Stolz managed to pull himself free from the combined weight of his dead comrades. At the back of the green and grey blood-flecked pile of men, Werner was hacking away at their static lines, the pile of corpses blocking his exit from the shattered aircraft.

Black smoke from the port engine billowed in over the dead and barely alive. The smoke rendered Bassom blind, and he could feel hot engine oil and fuel spraying over him. His still-impaired hearing only allowed him to perceive a low hum, but as a pair of rough hands gripped him by his smock, the deafening soundtrack of chaos suddenly returned, like a steam locomotive screeching through a tunnel. He fought for breath, but did nothing more than inhale smoke, fuel and oil. With one rough shove, he was out of the aircraft door, coughing and spluttering as he went.

The parachute harness that ran either side of Bassom's crotch snapped sharply up, reminding him that his canopy had fully deployed. He still gasped, fighting for clean air. His eyesight unrestricted, he had a grandstand view of the brutal demise of many of his comrades. Aircraft fell in droves, flames licking from them, human torches continuing to jump, hopelessly too close to the ground for their parachutes to deploy in time. Drop containers smouldered as hails of tracer bullets pulverized them and any men drifting close by. He could see the open expanse of Heraklion airfield, well off to the east. His attention snapped back up towards a swift series of explosions. One of his men under canopy screamed. Tracer bullets had set the paratrooper's grenades off, but Bassom was amazed and horrified that the man was still alive. Tracer bullets snapped and whizzed close to Bassom. He had no idea where on the ground the hail of fire was coming from. It looked as though the British were well hidden, a lesson they had undoubtedly learned from mainland Greece.

Bassom's brutal descent ended when he crashed hard into an olive tree, one branch thumping him under the chin. With his head ringing once more, and pain shooting through his lower jaw, he came to rest in a tangled heap. Overwhelmed by fatigue and shock, he struggled to decide what to do first, his training temporarily evaporated.

Bassom could hear men shouting in a foreign tongue and German shouts for assistance. On more than one occasion high-pitched screams were replaced by deep belly laughter and cheers. Bassom's mind became clear in an instant, for he quickly realized his men were being killed while attempting to rally. Scrambling for his knife while trying to free himself from his harness, he was suddenly confronted by what appeared to be civilian men with dark skin and rough unshaven faces. They wore off-white blood-speckled shirts and dark waistcoats, their broad-brimmed hats pushed back on greasy unkempt hair.

The largest man raised a blood-dripping axe to finish Bassom off, but the man's chest suddenly exploded in a pink and black mist, causing him to drop like an empty sack. The remainder of the civilians were then felled by a hail of bullets. Bassom fought to get out from under the axe-wielding man. Once up, he looked around at the civilians; all down, some groaning from their injuries. Then sudden movement and noise caused him to panic. He scrabbled for his pistol.

'Relax, sir. They won't give you any more trouble.' The bloodied Werner grinned at him, a battered but angry-looking Stolz in tow. Bassom knew his life had been saved by Werner and his radio man and couldn't help but be grateful.

Stolz helped Bassom to his feet. 'Take it easy, sir. Let me help you out of this damn harness.'

As Stolz set about removing Bassom's harness, Werner prowled among the dead and wounded Cretan men, kicking each one in turn. Those who groaned were shot in the head, their scalps shattering, brain matter and blood pooling instantly underneath. As Werner finished off the last Cretan, he noticed Bassom scowling at him. Werner was unfazed, quoting one of the German Parachutist's Commandments: 'Fight chivalrously against an honest foe; armed irregulars deserve no quarter.'

Bassom believed it was wrong to kill civilians, but the entire drop had been a crucible of death: the flak guns blasting the aircraft, the hail of lead whizzing through the paratroopers under canopy, and now the locals butchering them on landing. It was this last element that made the situation on the ground very different from anything they had encountered in Corinth, where the locals had hidden. He looked around the olive grove. German paratroopers were lying stricken on the ground. Others had been hacked to death while suspended in the trees, unable to defend themselves. Realizing it wasn't the time to debate the killing of civilians with Werner, Bassom nodded gravely, knowing the battle for Crete was going to be savage and unforgiving.

8

Major Barnett's Vickers machine-gun and Bren-gun teams couldn't help but crucify the low slow-flying German transport aircraft. With each long greedy burst, fragments of planes were smashed from the formation. British troops all around the position cheered as engines caught fire, and aircraft began to plummet towards the sea. Some enemy paratroopers escaped their beleaguered planes, only to find watery graves more quickly.

While Barnett's gun teams displayed excellent marksmanship, the focus on the aircraft soon evaporated, the number of German parachutists drifting under canopy being far too great to ignore. Most of the parachutists were easy pickings, as pistols, Sten guns and Lee-Enfield rifles joined the fusillade of fire upwards. Screams from the air confirmed British accuracy, some parachutists hit multiple times as they thudded into the dusty, stony earth surrounding Brigade Headquarters. Some survived the descent, but most who landed were enthusiastically mown down while rushing towards the drop containers, many of which were riddled with bullets. A few parachutists made it to the green copse and the excellent cover it provided in the form of trees and the B Company tents.

Eventually, the parachutists stopped dropping from the sky. Barnett had attempted to control the mass slaughter from the company headquarters trench, while Sergeant Major Pearce tracked the surviving parachutists. 'Enemy are sheltering in the copse, sir,' Pearce confirmed. 'A dozen, I'd say, plus one of their containers. We have to get a platoon in there, sir. There are many more of us than them, and we can't have them threaten Brigade HQ.'

'Agreed,' said Barnett. 'Get Mr Thatcher over here.' Barnett's radio operator contacted the commander of 4 Platoon.

Bentley Paine was reloading his rifle after firing umpteen shots at the descending parachutists. He observed Arnie Thatcher join Barnett, then clambered from his trench, concerned he might be missing out on something. 'Wait here,' Bentley called back to John Hallmark, who watched as he sprinted away, unconcerned as to the motives of the pompous fool. The flak guns at Heraklion airfield were still pounding, but British fire had otherwise withered away, so Hallmark was more concerned with shooting at Germans attempting to recover their drop containers in the open.

Bentley slid into the company headquarters trench. 'We have enemy troops in the copse,' Barnett informed Thatcher. 'The sergeant major counted at least twelve, and they have one of their containers. It's probably full of weapons and ammunition.

'Arnie, I want you to take your platoon and form a screen on the forward edge of the copse. When you are in position, I want an aggressive push through the copse. You cannot allow those German bastards to get their act together. Drive them into the sea, Lieutenant.'

'Yes, sir.' Lieutenant Thatcher dashed away back towards his trench.

'Anything I can assist with, sir?' Bentley asked Barnett.

'First, Captain, don't ever share a trench with me again,' Barnett rebuked him in a matter-of-fact tone. 'You are my second in command. One well-placed shell could wipe us both out, and we can't have that. At least one of us has to stay alive to run things, even if everyone in the company headquarters trench is killed.' Bentley was shocked at the reprimand, particularly given the circumstances, but he knew that he understood little about the tactical necessities of company leadership, so he nodded meekly. Barnett slapped a heavy hand on Bentley's shoulder. 'Steep learning curve, Captain. I don't mind cock-ups. Just don't repeat them, and we will get along fine. Mr Thatcher has been tasked with taking care of the copse, so I would like you to return to your trench and shoot at anything that looks German, understand?'

'Yes, sir.' Bentley clambered from the trench and jogged back over to his own. Hallmark was taking greedy swigs from a water bottle as Bentley slid in beside him. 'Everything OK, sir?' Hallmark enquired. 'What's happened?'

Bentley was not in the mood for talking to him, but knew it was wise to share information. 'Four Platoon are to clear the copse. About a dozen enemy paratroopers were seen in there. We have orders to sit tight until further notice. Engage anything German.'

'Fair enough.' Hallmark cuffed his mouth with his dusty sleeve, put away his water bottle and took his Lee-Enfield rifle in his huge paws. Germans in the immediate vicinity were keeping low. Dead enemy lay all around, with groupings around several of the visible drop containers. It looked as though the Germans were not willing to make further attempts to retrieve them. Not that most of the containers would be worth retrieving, British fire having pulverized the majority beyond use. Having noticed that few heavy weapons had been carried by the descending parachutists, Hallmark wondered what weapons and ammunition the Germans in the copse might have. 'Why would you not jump with your weapons, ready to fight?' he thought out loud. Bentley had had the very same thought while observing the enemy paratroopers coming down, knowing he had killed a few before they had a genuine chance to fight back.

Bentley observed 4 Platoon move into position along the edge of the copse. There was enough cover in the copse to make its interior dark. He was growing impatient with what seemed to be Thatcher's lack of urgency. Barnett had ordered Thatcher to drive the Germans into the sea. 'What the hell is Thatcher waiting for?' groaned Bentley. 'A bombing raid? He should get his men in there and take care of it.'

'Sir, it's not that straightforward,' Hallmark replied. 'Even if the Germans in the copse are a small force, they have the advantage of excellent cover. All they have to do is sit there and play the waiting game. They have water, shade, and I bet a month's wages they have a couple of machine guns. I could swear I saw a drop container fall in there.'

Bentley was incensed by Hallmark's attitude to the delay. 'So we are all just supposed to sit here?'

'Four Platoon have been tasked to clear the copse, so all everyone else can do is sit and wait. The Germans know that if they break cover, we will kill them, so why would they come out? They must have seen what happened to their comrades in the open.'

This wasn't enough to appease Bentley's anger. 'It pains me to see a man doing himself a disservice. Your off-duty antics are stifling your flair and apparent aptitude for command and soldiering.'

Hallmark's face dropped, even though he hadn't a clue what Bentley was driving at. He sat back against the wall of the trench, not entirely sure if Bentley was being serious. Having had the last word, Bentley enjoyed what he considered to be a small victory, even though his remark had contained an implied compliment.

Time passed slowly into the late afternoon, the Germans in the copse penned in. There had been no action around Brigade Headquarters, although distant sounds of battle echoed around Heraklion, varying from raging conflict to minor exchanges of fire.

Bentley and Hallmark were both becoming droopy-eyed, succumbing to the lethargy-inducing heat. They watched Barnett and Pearce climb from their trench and make their way towards the headquarters building, where a small group of what appeared to be local men had assembled, heavily armed with guns and farming tools. Barnett talked with the group, but Bentley noticed he wouldn't accept their handshakes. Then Barnett pointed them in the general direction of Bentley's trench. The group waved enthusiastically towards Bentley. He was puzzled by it all, but gave a limp wave back, not even sure he was the focus of attention. The group approached the trench. 'Bloody hell,' blurted Hallmark, looking rather anxious. 'Tell them to go away, sir. We don't need to be mixed up with those guys.'

Bentley frowned. 'What are you talking about? They are on our side.' He decided to twist the knife a little. 'Corporal Hallmark, have you been sleeping with their wives or something?'

'What?'

'You appear uncomfortable.'

'Look at them. Look at their fucking weapons.'

Bentley observed the scruffy group approaching him. They were all armed with what appeared to be German weapons. They also had pitchforks, axes and shovels, all of which glinted a pinkish red in the sun, clotted blood fresh on the blades and forks. Their once-white shirts were smeared with blood. Bentley's stomach turned. Then he noticed they were wearing gold rings, some men even sporting rows of watches up their forearms. But before he had the chance to start asking questions, the Cretan men were upon them, standing over them, their shadows providing relief from the sun.

'Hello. Hello, sir,' a short unshaven man offered. He had a German MP 40 sub-machine gun in each hand. Even the braces that held up his oversized trousers were soiled with faded red. He put down one of the MP 40s and extended a blood-smeared hand. By sheer instinct, Bentley accepted the handshake, before realizing why Barnett hadn't earlier. The man had an iron grip, and his hand was sticky. Bentley also noticed he had a gold ring on every chubby finger.

The man offered his hand to Hallmark, who reluctantly accepted it. Bentley felt relieved; at least they hadn't offended the Cretans. 'How can we help you, gentlemen?' Bentley asked.

The man picked up the MP 40, one in both hands once more. He took a deep breath, as if trying to find the right words. 'We kill Germans. Many Germans. Germans in trees, we kill them. Kill many Germans.'

As he spoke, the others in the group repeated over and over, 'Many Germans.'

'OK,' responded Bentley, not sure what to say next.

Hallmark saw that Bentley was struggling to keep

the initiative. 'Where are the Germans?' Hallmark asked. 'Are they close?'

The group looked at each other, muttering in Greek. It was as if Hallmark's words or his Lancashire accent were a new experience for them. The short, chubby-fingered Cretan smiled, giving Hallmark a broad grin of rotten, tobacco-stained teeth. 'Yes, many Germans, we kill.' Bentley realized the locals' English wasn't up to much. He decided that he should at least thank them for their efforts, but then the short Cretan pointed to the copse. 'You have Germans? Germans in trees?'

Bentley breathed with relief. 'Yes, Germans in trees.'

The entire group raised their weapons towards the copse. Those who had cigarettes spat them from their lips. They began strolling away from Bentley's trench, heading for 4 Platoon's position at the edge of the copse. 'Tell the OC not to have 4 Platoon go in there with them,' warned Hallmark.

'What?'

Hallmark rolled his eyes. Bentley didn't like his attitude. 'If the locals want to go into the copse on their own,' Hallmark rephrased, 'tell Major Barnett to let them. Don't let 4 Platoon go in there with them.'

Bentley became agitated. 'Are you stark raving mad?'

Hallmark was beside himself, deciding not to explain it again. He jumped from the trench and sprinted away. 'Where the hell are you going, Hallmark?' bellowed Bentley. 'Get back here.'

Hallmark found only Barnett's radio operator in the

company headquarters trench. It was good enough. 'Call 4 Platoon,' Hallmark instructed. 'Tell them to hold their position. But allow the Cretans to proceed if they wish.'

The radio man looked at Hallmark as if he had three heads but took a handset from a canvas rucksack. After adjusting his radio, he passed the handset to Hallmark, nodding. 'Hello Four Zero Alpha,' said Hallmark into the handset. 'This is Bravo Zero Bravo, over.' Barnett's radio man raised his eyebrows. Hallmark had used Barnett's call sign, his radio identity. Thatcher's radio operator would believe that he was talking to Barnett unless the reception was perfect.

The handset crackled. 'Four Zero Alpha. Send. Over.'

Hallmark composed himself. He already knew he would be in deep trouble for taking matters into his own hands, but had to back his own horse. 'Bravo Zero Bravo. Hold your position. Allow the civilians to proceed if they wish. Do not move into the copse with them. Over.'

There was a long pause. Hallmark peered out of the trench like a meerkat, watching the Cretan group move into the copse without 4 Platoon. The handset crackled again. 'Four Zero Alpha. Roger that. Out.' With a wave of relief washing through him, Hallmark dropped the handset back into the canvas rucksack.

'So what the hell was all that about?' the radio operator asked.

Hallmark was about to respond, when Barnett's voice cut him off. 'That's what I would like to know.'

Hallmark looked up to find Barnett, Pearce and Bentley looking down at him. Bentley's glare bored deep into Hallmark's eyes. Bentley felt Hallmark was always on a mission to humiliate him. But Hallmark had now presented him with an opportunity for revenge, perhaps even an opportunity to permanently disengage himself from the corporal. Hallmark looked at the stern expression on Barnett's face, wondering if he had pushed his familiarity with the major too far. Hallmark had known him for a long time, back when Barnett was an NCO fresh out of basic training. But now was not the time to test their camaraderie. Hallmark could only make his explanation plain and simple.

'Apologies, sir, but I feel it would be unwise for Mr Thatcher to follow the locals into the copse at this time.'

Barnett knelt above him, his stare not so much as flinching. 'Why is that, Corporal Hallmark?'

'The locals, sir. They are covered in fresh blood which isn't theirs, and they are wearing Nazi gold and weapons. One of them has half a dozen watches up one forearm, sir.'

'It's like finders keepers, right?' asked Bentley. No sooner had the flippant question left his lips than he regretted it. Hallmark, Pearce and Barnett shot him disapproving glares.

Hallmark swallowed hard before answering Bentley's question, albeit directing the answer at Barnett. 'My brother was at Dunkirk, sir. He saw what happened to captured French troops and civilians who looted the

German dead. It didn't end well, sir. And if the enemy discover their dead have been looted, they get nasty.' He shook his head. 'A collection of enemy gold and watches could be worth a king's ransom, but looting, you just don't do it.'

'Er . . . absolutely,' Bentley half-stammered.

Barnett glanced at his radio operator. 'Did 4 Platoon get the message to stay put?'

'Yes, sir.'

'OK, then,' sighed Barnett. 'Good call, John. Just run it past me next time. OK, matey?'

Relief washed through Hallmark, even though no admission was forthcoming from Barnett that there hadn't been time for consultation before sending 4 Platoon the message. Hallmark usually didn't care much for an officer's approval on anything, but Barnett wasn't your average officer. 'Yes, sir.'

'Right, then,' concluded Barnett. 'Get your arse out of my trench and piss off back to your own.'

As Hallmark climbed out of the trench, all hell broke loose inside the copse. Tracer snapped and screamed in all directions. Bentley, Barnett, Pearce and Hallmark all hit the deck, swivelling to face the copse, weapons in hand. Near the copse members of 4 Platoon kept as close as possible to the ground, crawling like men possessed to the sanctuary of the nearest trench. Barnett slid into his trench beside his radio man. Before long, Barnett was trying to talk on the radio, but looked as though he was being drowned out by the firefight. The thud of a grenade resulted in some screaming from the copse. Bentley had no idea who was doing the screaming, but the snaps of what could be pistol shots cut it off immediately. Silence descended. 'If the Germans discovered those men wearing their comrades' jewellery and watches,' Hallmark remarked, 'there will be no mercy.' Bentley realized the sense of Hallmark's earlier comments on looting.

'Roger that,' said Barnett into the radio handset. 'Keep your eyes peeled, Four Zero Alpha. Some might get back out to you. Out.'

Hallmark and Bentley got to their feet and began to make their way back to their own trench. It occurred to Bentley that noble as it was for the local population to want to resist the German invader, there were disadvantages to their involvement, and a certain amount of diplomacy should be used to keep them out of the fight. He ran the firefight in the copse back through his mind. There had been short controlled bursts of disciplined fire from heavier weapons, which had certainly not been the work of over-enthusiastic amateurs. The bursts had been followed by pistol shots, more than likely shots of execution. Bentley knew in his heart that the Cretan men were dead.

Martin Bassom was still taking time to tune into the environment he had been so violently thrown into. The olive grove offered him some priceless shade. His heavy clothing and equipment were not ideal for summer operations, never mind the middle of the Mediterranean. Standing unsteadily, he leaned against a tree, removing his helmet to give his sweat-soaked scalp a chance to breathe. Sprawled out before him were the bodies of the Cretans who would have hacked him to pieces, if it hadn't been for Corporal Stolz and Werner.

Sergeant Werner was dragging the Cretan bodies into a neat line, heavy-handedly stripping them of anything that was the property of the Reich, including his comrades' personal possessions. 'Fucking thieving bastards,' Werner raved, 'all of them. What use are fucking family photographs to them?' As well as photographs, he was assembling many items in two neat piles on the ground: gold rings, watches, weapons, ammunition, food rations, pay books.

Knowing he was ultimately responsible for it all, Bassom began looking through the pay books. With each name he read, he felt his stomach tighten, anger and sorrow competing to overwhelm him. He could understand the venom in Werner's voice. Some of the names in the pay books cut deeper than others. Some belonged to veterans of the magnificent victories of 1940. Others were of men who had joined the ranks of the *Fallschirmjäger* in 1941, in time for the Corinth Canal mission in Greece. Such fine soldiers. Decent men who were trained to peak physical condition, only to be murdered by farmers armed with axes and pitchforks. As Bassom dwelled on the murdered, he could feel the rage within him begin to rise at an alarming rate. He shook his head as he fought to keep control of himself.

Stolz was cleaning clotted blood from ammunition. You had to conserve ammunition, since paratroopers could fight only with what they could carry, plus whatever could be recovered from the drop containers or scrounged. He looked up at Bassom, then stepped over to place a gentle hand on his shoulder. 'Are you OK, sir? Are you wounded?'

Bassom blinked hard. He couldn't show weakness when Werner was around. He was still searching the dead, as if it was his daily routine. 'I'm fine, Stolz,' answered Bassom. 'Thank you for your concern. I'm fine. Please assist Sergeant Werner. We need to check on our men who got caught in their harnesses.'

Two more survivors of the drop suddenly appeared. The paratroopers were injured, but not by enemy action, rather by the occupational hazards of parachuting. They limped in, sweating heavily yet bristling with weapons appropriated from dead comrades. The two parachutists were not known to Bassom or Werner; they were from another company. The fact that there were only two of them led Bassom to believe they had fared no better than his men.

The two new men helped Bassom, Werner and Stolz to scour the olive grove to locate comrades, dead or alive. Bassom's small ad hoc group found dead men up in the trees, murdered before they had hit the ground, some looking like hacked meat in a butcher's shop.

Bassom had them cut down, formally identified, then wrapped in their parachutes for burial. Their ammunition taken by Bassom and his men, the dead men's empty weapons were inverted into the dirt, with their parachutist helmets placed on top as crude grave markers. Bassom couldn't help but wonder if Crete was to be the graveyard of the *Fallschirmjäger*.

A commotion from above alerted Bassom's group. A parachutist was still alive. They hadn't spotted him at first. He was badly tangled in his own rigging. Werner climbed up to free him from his harness. It was evident the man had been crying, his eyes fixed on a dead comrade hanging nearby, who had been sliced to ribbons by the Cretans. Werner put an arm around the shoulders of the shocked and distraught young parachutist in what Bassom thought was a rare display of compassion. 'If you had tried to assist your friend,' Werner said gently, glancing across at the dead man, 'you would be dead too. Don't beat yourself up about it.'

As the young paratrooper was cut down, he fell to the ground and looked up at the captain standing over him. 'I'm sorry, sir. I couldn't move. My rigging wouldn't—'

'Calm yourself, young man,' Bassom soothed. 'If you had moved, they would have spotted you and killed you too. I must ask a question. Was it enemy soldiers or farmers that killed the men around you?'

'Farmers, I think they were farmers. Laughing, they were. Fucking savages.' This convinced Bassom that no quarter should be given to those who weren't fighting in uniform. The young parachutist shook himself out of his self-pity and stood up, cuffing his half-dry tears with his smock sleeve. 'I am ready to serve the Führer and the fatherland, sir. I will not show weakness to these savages or the enemy, so help me.'

Bassom placed a hand on his shoulder. 'I know you won't, my friend. But for now we must try and recover the living from this olive grove.'

For another heartbreaking hour, Bassom's group encountered many German dead, mostly dispatched by axes and clubs. But those discovered alive swelled the ranks now under his command. Most were not from his company, leading him to further dread what had become of his men, but he felt that he already knew. If they had landed in the open, the British would have killed them. If they landed in the cover of the many groves that dotted the area, the locals would have butchered them. The choices for the descending Germans had not been great. And in addition Bassom had little idea where he was in relation to his objective of Heraklion airfield, which didn't bode well for his newly formed group.

9

Martin Bassom had little idea where he was on his map because he had failed to notice any meaningful reference points. During his descent he had been conscious of drifting ever further from Heraklion airfield and had not learned anything geographically useful since landing.

Sergeant Werner took on the role of lead scout and led Bassom's ad hoc force gradually downhill. Through a sudden break in the grove he observed something other than olives. He signalled the group to halt and take cover. Silence descended, bar the distant sounds of battle and the constant clicking of insects. Getting onto his belly, Werner crawled forward for a better look at what lay ahead then called to the man behind him in a rasping whisper, 'Buildings up front. I need Captain Bassom.'

Whispered down the line, the message finally reached Bassom, who wasted no time in crawling up next to Werner, who was already looking at the scene ahead with binoculars. Bassom fished his own from his smock. Beyond a small clearing in front of the olive grove was a small farm. A network of rough low stone walls divided livestock pens from an open courtyard. A dairy farm boy, Bassom found it bizarre that no animals were visible, but then he panned his binoculars across the farm, registering movement beyond it, just inside the forward edge of yet another olive grove. Cattle. They kept their cattle under the trees, very wisely using the shade. 'Any sign of people?' he whispered to Werner.

'Not yet. I'm going to need three men plus myself to check the buildings. What are we looking at here? Three, maybe four buildings, if you include that small barn at the back.'

'You need three men?' Bassom clarified.

'Yes, sir. Three. Preferably ones who are not limping. We have a few men now, but I know resources are slim.' Bassom nodded his approval of Werner's proposed patrol. Werner crawled back away from him to a point where he felt he could risk standing up. As Werner picked his team for the patrol, Bassom scanned the buildings with his binoculars once more. There was still no sign of human life. Then it flashed through Bassom's mind that the bastards were probably out, hacking Germans to bits. Or perhaps they had already been gunned down by Werner and Corporal Stolz.

Bassom heard Werner crawl up behind him. 'We are ready, sir. We will move around from the right, clearing each building in turn.'

Bassom nodded. 'The remainder of us will line up here. We'll give covering fire, should you need it. After all, we have no idea if there are British patrols in the area.'

Werner got slowly to his feet, waving his team to join

him. Each man was armed with an MP 40 or carbine. Bassom watched as Werner led them towards the farm, his pace slow and deliberate. Bassom whispered back for Stolz and the rest of the men to form a firing line. They crawled slowly into position on either side of him. As Stolz took up his fighting position, Bassom noticed that he looked rather small without a radio strapped to his back. This reminded Bassom he was in dire need of a radio. He had to find out what had become of his company, and the remainder of the battalion for that matter.

In the clearing Werner was all too aware of how exposed his patrol had become. The farm complex was bathed in brilliant sunshine save for the main building. It had a low red-tiled roof and was afforded some shade by a small cluster of tall trees. As Werner led his men further right, he cast a quick glance back, just about able to make out Bassom's fire support position.

As Werner came level with the courtyard, the chickens there became excited and clucked loudly. He went slowly down on one knee, pulling the butt of his MP 40 into his right shoulder, waiting for one of two things to happen. Either an inquisitive farmer would peer out to investigate the commotion made by the chickens, or British troops might pile out, fighting as they came. Werner had no issue with shooting British or Cretan civilians, given what he had seen in the olive groves, but nothing currently gave him an indication of human presence at the farm, as the chickens skipped away, settling back to their business. He cast a glance at his team.

Like him, they had weapons at the ready, their faces like stone. And like him, he didn't think they cared about the difference between Cretans and the British.

The first outbuilding checked by the patrol was clearly decades old. The wooden structure was held together by wrought-iron brackets and copious amounts of twine. The rickety double doors were slightly ajar, and as Werner took a careful step across the threshold, the aroma of rotting straw and animal waste caught the back of his throat. He wished Bassom had led the patrol; Werner was a city boy, unlike the farmer Bassom, who would have been more used to the scents and atmospherics. Despite the foul odour, Werner pushed further inside the outbuilding. It didn't take long to check it was empty, so he made his way back outside. He suddenly realized there were actually six buildings in total, the view from Bassom's position restricted.

The next building smelled worse than the first. It had a complete roof and sides, but the gable ends were open to the elements. Werner could make out off-grey metal barriers running through the centre of the open-plan structure. The vile smell was overpowering but also familiar, although he couldn't be sure what it reminded him of. As he backed out of the building he asked his team what it was. 'Sergeant, I think it's the milking shed,' offered one of the young parachutists. 'That's the smell I'm getting, anyway.'

As if on cue, the cattle in the olive grove groaned and began shuffling about. Something had spooked them.

Werner and his men tensed. Werner could hear his heart beating in his ears, his knuckles white on his MP 40. Then beyond the cows he detected movement. 'Make yourself known to us,' he barked. 'With your hands up, or we will open fire.'

There was no reply, but the movement from beyond the cows continued. Werner was not taking any chances. He spun to alert his men to the movement, and they fanned out to his right. As one, the group advanced slowly through the milking shed. It didn't offer the best of cover, but Werner felt more secure inside. As he and his men took up fighting positions around the shed interior, the cows suddenly moved together, trotting away from the area. 'Prepare grenades,' he hissed to his men. 'Throw them on my command.' Each of his three men rested his gun across his knees and pulled a stick grenade from his webbing.

'*Fallschirmjäger*,' called a desperate voice from the grove. 'Don't shoot, don't shoot. We have wounded.'

Werner looked at his men, who in turn looked back at him, shrugging their shoulders. He had to make a judgement call. Could it be British troops trying to trick him? Or wounded comrades trying to find fellow parachutists? 'Come forward slowly,' Werner called back, 'and make sure we can see your hands.'

The movement in the grove became more heavy-footed, as if men were pleased they no longer had to move quietly. A filthy and exhausted-looking paratrooper emerged, hands held high, weapon slung behind his back. Werner recognized Sergeant Dormann. 'Dormann? What the hell are you doing, sneaking about like that? We were about to throw grenades, you buffoon.'

Dormann couldn't help but let out a wide grin. 'Take the piss all you want. Just help me with these men.' As Werner followed Dormann into the grove, he saw that he had managed to round up a dozen or so men, some of whom were wounded. Dormann's men had managed to recover a drop container, which they had dragged along by its chute. The container was caked in grime and filth, but Werner was still able to recognize the chute as white, which indicated the container held weapons and equipment. A medical container would have been better, but he wasn't about to criticize Dormann for his efforts.

Werner used some of the extra manpower offered by Dormann to finish the search of the farm, before signalling Bassom's group to join them. Bassom was very pleased to see the familiar face of Dormann. All along, Bassom would have preferred Dormann's presence to Werner's, but given the circumstances, he was just pleased to have more fighting power at the farm. As the parachutists began to get established, making the wounded as comfortable as possible, Bassom asked Werner and Dormann to join him in the farmhouse kitchen. The delicious aroma of freshly cooked bread seduced them all immediately, especially Werner.

'You never get tired of that beautiful smell.' Werner spoke yet his eyes remained closed as he enjoyed the moment. Bassom reminded himself that Werner's father was a baker. With sentries posted, they relaxed a little at the kitchen table, pulling out their sweat-soaked maps and notebooks. Stolz joined them, working to set up a radio that had been found in the drop container. Bassom unfolded his map and stroked it flat on the table. 'Dormann, what landscapes did you cross to get here? Have you had any opportunity to get your bearings?'

Dormann pulled his helmet off, allowing his scalp to breathe. He puffed out his cheeks as he ran his fingers through his dirty salt-and-pepper hair. 'I landed on open ground. God knows how I wasn't hit by enemy fire. Two of the boys that went for the drop container were hit, right in front of me. I dragged it into some reeds that lined a stream and hid for a while. The enemy were dug in on some high ground overlooking my position. I couldn't move from the reeds, and all around me the men in my plane were shot like pheasants as they drifted down. And the enemy fire just increased, once our guys landed. I don't think a single man landing anywhere close to me survived. Eventually, when the enemy began shooting at a wave of parachutists landing elsewhere, I took my chance to move into the olives. In the groves I managed to pick up most of the guys who arrived here with me, but it looked as though a lot of our boys landing among the olives were picked off by the locals. The whole drop was awful.'

Silence draped itself over them. Bassom came to realize that his whole battalion might have been virtually wiped out. Not the best start to a mass airborne operation. He fought to keep his mind on the task in hand. 'Did you notice any landmarks, key features, anything?' he pushed Dormann. 'I have a distinct feeling we are well to the east of our objective.'

Dormann got to his feet. His filthy trigger finger began pointing to features on the map. 'This water feature. I think I landed close to it. This is the high ground which has enemy troops dug in all over it. I encountered a few of the guys I brought here as I dragged the container from the reeds and towards the olive groves.'

Bassom studied the map. He thought they were way off the target area of Heraklion airfield. Any attempt to get there, especially in daylight, would be suicide. To even get a look at the airfield, they would somehow have to get past some high ground occupied by the enemy. He didn't have the manpower for an assault, but perhaps his force could try to infiltrate their way through in the darkness.

'Sir,' suggested Werner, having also worked out their rough position, 'if we were to establish a base here for now, then perhaps we might get more men coming in. If Dormann's efforts are anything to go by, more of our boys will be forming into groups, trying to link up. Our force here might grow in size, enough to enable us to break out towards our objective. We'll have to be on our game here while it is dark, otherwise we might end up shooting at our own.'

Bassom considered Werner's idea. It was sound enough, but time was against them. The element of surprise had been lost even before they flew over the drop zone. Bassom was concerned that an enemy force might take the initiative and sweep through the olive groves. If his force stayed at the farm, they could end up surrounded. And to make matters worse, they were low on equipment and supplies. Going without food was one thing, but his men, fit and wounded alike, were going to need an ample supply of water, sooner rather than later.

Bentley Paine was summoned to the Brigade Headquarters building along with the platoon commanders. The company were still in their defensive positions around the buildings. Major Barnett had his commanders gathered round and was standing in his office once more, his map spread over his desk. Pencil in hand, he pointed to features on the map. 'We've been tasked with a clearance patrol in front of the Australians dug in on the high ground to the east. They've spotted a number of enemy troops in and around the olive groves to the east of this bridge.' Everyone leaned in to see the bridge better. 'Arnie,' Barnett continued, 'your platoon is to remain in place here, as we can't afford to expose this building to the bastards holed up in the copse. The remainder of the company, 5 and 6 Platoons, will accompany me on the patrol.'

'But what if the enemy in the copse attack?' Not for the first time, Bentley's mouth engaged before his brain, but this time he didn't receive a sharp glare from anyone.

Barnett nodded. 'I've been thinking about that. They won't come out, not after the landing they had. Right now they know they are safe, and I'm sure they know they are severely outnumbered. If our patrol sneaks out, the Germans in the copse probably won't notice we are temporarily fewer in number.' He noticed that Lieutenant Arnie Thatcher didn't appear too happy. 'Don't worry, Arnie; you'll be fine. You have a good defensive position, and the enemy won't try anything stupid here. If the patrol is not back by nightfall, be sure to double up on your sentries through the night, OK?'

Thatcher swallowed heavily. 'Yes, sir.'

'Right, then,' concluded Barnett. 'We all have jobs to do. Brief your men, and I want the patrol heading out in ten minutes. We are already starting to lose daylight. I would rather have the patrol done before dark, or it might just get stuck away from here until the morning.'

Barnett gave 4 Platoon one of the Vickers machine-gun teams in return for a couple of Thatcher's more lightly armed men. The patrol was on the move within fifteen minutes. John Hallmark was at the very rear of the long column, Bentley just in front of him. Bentley still despised Hallmark but had to admit he felt a little more secure, knowing the corporal had his back. The patrol moved slowly east, skirting south around Heraklion airfield and the Greek-occupied barracks nearby.

They came upon two land features that looked like a pair of breasts pointing skyward. 'Now that is a set of knockers,' Hallmark remarked. 'Wouldn't you agree, sir?'

Bentley sighed as he rolled his eyes. Hallmark was not only crass but predictable. As the column skirted the north side of the pert twin features, Bentley could only reflect on the lack of females in his life. Besides his mother and his sister Madison, his only real contact with the fair sex had been the household staff at the family manor. None of the girls in the employ of the Richmond Furlong Company were ever about long enough for him to get to know. His thoughts suddenly turned to his father. Bentley wondered how many housemaids his father had screwed in his study while everyone else was out of the house. Bentley had no evidence to support his theory but certainly wouldn't have put it past him.

The route to the eastern perimeter of the twin peaks began to gain height, and there was a long frontage of rocky high ground. At the top troops were moving about. Bentley recalled Barnett talking about an Australian unit on the high ground. Barnett led the patrol up the reverse slope, before halting them just short of the skyline. As the mass of sweaty, heavy-breathing men took the opportunity to sit down and rest, Bentley was required at the front of the column.

'We are wanted up front. Let's go,' confirmed Hallmark. Bentley got up and took off without acknowledging him. Hallmark had experienced his fair share of officers, but Bentley was definitely one he would remember, for all the wrong reasons. Hallmark clambered to his feet and set off after Bentley.

They arrived at a cluster of rocks which had been

arranged to form a crude defensive perimeter. They could see Barnett under a canvas bivouac sheet that served as a crude headquarters, talking to a man who appeared to be his Australian counterpart.

Off to his left, Bentley was stunned by what he saw. He counted at least twenty bodies wrapped in green mottled parachute canopies. The boots worn by the bodies were hobnailed under the sole, similar to those he wore. It suddenly dawned on him that the Australians had gathered up enemy dead. 'Do you think there are any enemy left in the area?' he asked Hallmark. 'A lot of them have been killed already, it appears.'

Hallmark shrugged. Barnett's Australian friend looked over at Bentley. 'That's just those on this side of the hill,' he confirmed. 'The forward slope is covered in them. But I'm not risking my guys gathering them up till after dark.'

Barnett waved Bentley and Hallmark over to join him. Bentley clambered into the crude headquarters, realizing it offered protection from the slowly cooling sun. Hallmark was left to perch on some rocks in the open, but at least he could see the map spread out on the ground under the canvas. The Australian officer used a sorry-looking pencil to point out features on the map. 'On the east side, at the base of this position, is a stream. It's not that deep. The water is drinkable. Lining both banks are long reeds. We hit a lot of the bastards before they could take cover in the reeds, but we didn't get all of them. We ended up turning round and fighting those who landed behind us. So some enemy may still be in the reeds. But my guess is they've scarpered into the groves just beyond. Hence I need your guys, Simon, to conduct a clearance, sweeping across our frontage.'

'No problem, mate.' Barnett grinned. 'We can do that for you.' Bentley was unfamiliar with the Australian officer class. From the little he had heard, they seemed to talk as roughly as their men. Barnett, however, spoke almost as plainly. Bentley supposed that not all officers were cut from the same cloth but shuddered at the thought of Hallmark ever becoming one.

'Don't force it, though,' the Australian continued. 'It'll start getting dark soon. See what you can do, and if needs be come back up here. Then have another go in the morning.'

'Thanks for the offer,' replied Barnett, 'but I've left just one platoon to keep some nearby enemy from over-running my Brigade Headquarters, so I want to return there as quickly as possible.'

'Fair enough,' the Australian responded, shaking his hand. 'Then we shouldn't waste time talking.'

Barnett decided that to start the clearance they would come off the slope, skirting the north side of the hill. There was a road bridge over the stream, so his plan was to cross it cautiously, then push south towards the olive groves. 'Remember, gents,' he concluded to his commanders, 'the enemy could still be hiding in the reeds. So make sure your guys aren't walking with their thumbs up their arses.'

But by the time Bentley and Hallmark crossed the unremarkable bridge it was apparent there were no Germans hiding nearby, so the patrol moved slowly up to the forward edge of the first olive grove. Still at the very back of the column, Hallmark didn't think he was the only one to notice the shredded remains of a white parachute hanging off the side of the bridge, so as the rest of the company advanced, he sneaked away. Wading a few feet into the stream, he craned his head under the low bridge. Convinced he was about to discover a dead parachutist, he was surprised to see a large silver and green container, clearly supplies for the German assault. He wondered if there might be something useful inside, but now was not the time to find out. Scrambling out of the stream, he sprinted to regain his position behind Bentley, who had somehow been oblivious to his escapade.

Barney Taylor's 5 Platoon picked up blood trails that led into the groves, so the Australian officer had probably been right to suggest the enemy taking cover in the reeds had later headed there. Barnett ordered the patrol into a T-shape to sweep through the groves, with 5 Platoon advancing in extended line abreast. Barnett and his radio operator would follow a little behind, along with Kenneth Hicks, 6 Platoon Commander. Bentley, Hallmark and Sergeant Major Pearce would follow Barnett's group, leading 6 Platoon in single file.

The patrol began the sweep. It wasn't long before a series of cracks echoed through the olive trees, snapping and thumping above their heads. They instantly fell onto their bellies, men shouting at each other in an attempt to deduce the direction of the incoming shots. Some looked as though they were about to return fire, but the thumps and snaps stopped as suddenly as they had started.

'What the hell is that over there?' Pearce asked Hallmark, looking off to the left, having to bellow over the shouting. Pearce had a short fuse at the best of times. Before Hallmark even had a chance to reply, 'Stop!' roared Pearce. 'Stop, stop! Shut the hell up, everyone!' The commotion reduced significantly. Hallmark was already transfixed by what Pearce had spotted.

Having panicked during the short period of incoming fire, Bentley had composed himself, once again forced to acknowledge that better men than him would carry the day. He knelt up next to Pearce and Hallmark, then straightened his battledress. 'What on earth are you looking at?'

Hallmark and Pearce gave no answer, but instead got to their feet, weapons in their hands, and made their way towards what they had seen. Bentley decided to follow. Some way away was what appeared to be a pile of dead bodies. The pile was centred round a green and red mass dangling from a tree. It soon became clear that the red and green mass was in fact a badly wounded German paratrooper. The three bodies around him were Cretan civilians, their bloodied knives and meat cleavers lying on the ground. There was a pistol in the paratrooper's bloodied hand, some of its working parts off to the rear of him, indicating the magazine was empty and no longer a threat. The paratrooper, his harness still caught on some branches, had managed to kill the Cretans before they could finish him off, but it was clear he was mortally wounded, his breathing rasping and rattling. Both of his legs were distorted. His left collarbone was shattered, cut deep by what could only have been one of the cleavers. He spluttered and coughed up a large amount of dark clotted blood, only then looking up at Bentley, Pearce and Hallmark.

The paratrooper's bloodshot eyes locked onto Hallmark's, who wasn't thinking about dispatching him, but rather wondering where the nearest medical facility might be, intent on saving him. But then the paratrooper suddenly expired; no fanfare, no last words, he just faded away.

'So what now?' Bentley asked, his voice devoid of emotion. As far as he was concerned, it was just one less German to fight.

Pearce pulled at the parachute canopy. 'We wrap him in his parachute, take him with us.'

Bentley didn't like it. Pearce seemed oblivious to the implications of giving preferential treatment to enemy casualties over supposed friendly ones. 'And the civilians?' wondered Bentley.

'They can come and collect their own,' Pearce stated coldly. 'But we will take this man and put him with his comrades at the Australian position.'

Major Barnett joined the group and surveyed the

scene around them. Bentley took his chance. 'Sergeant Major,' he protested, 'it is unwise to treat German dead well, but leave the citizens of this island where they fall.'

Hallmark and Pearce focused their glares on Bentley. 'With all due respect,' Pearce argued to Bentley, but for Barnett's benefit, 'civilians, as much as they love their homeland, should not be getting embroiled in a fight that should be left to armies. The locals are already proving to be more of a hindrance than a help, and in future when they offer their services, I would prefer it if you and Major Barnett told them to go away. For now, we should take this German soldier back and place him with his dead comrades.'

Bentley was about to open his mouth again, but Barnett cut him off. 'Sergeant Major, maybe Paine has a point. It is bad form to leave the Cretan dead where they fall. After all, we are here to help Crete resist its attackers, and like it or not, this soldier is an attacker.'

Hallmark watched a smug grin form on Bentley's face. He knew Pearce had seen it too, but also knew Pearce was too professional to react. Having known both Barnett and Pearce for a long time, Hallmark reminded himself of the days when neither would have thought twice about wiping the smirk from Bentley's overpriced cheeks. 'Sadly,' concluded Barnett, 'we don't have the resources to transport Cretan or German dead. So wrap this German soldier in his chute. Mark his position, but no more.'

Pearce nodded. But Hallmark wasn't satisfied, either

with Barnett's conclusion or Bentley's attitude. 'What if locals loot or mutilate the body?' he pushed. 'The Germans will retaliate.'

Barnett looked him in the eye. 'That is one thing we cannot control. We just have to do our job. If the locals take trophies from bodies, I won't lose sleep over it, and neither should you, unless of course the Cretans start looting our dead.'

Pearce helped Hallmark wrap up the valiant dead paratrooper, putting his helmet on top of a long stick rammed into the soil.

They returned to the patrol and Barnett called a meeting of his commanders. It was getting dark quickly under the trees. He led them out onto open ground, knowing the clearance patrol had barely started. He spread out his map on the ground, and they all got onto their bellies, surrounding it. He gestured to a group of buildings on the map. 'We have what appears to be some buildings not too far away. Could be a farm. If I was a betting man, any enemy troops that made it in here could well have gathered there.' Bentley stretched his neck, squinting to see the buildings on the map. 'We won't push in there tonight,' said Barnett. 'It would be dark by the time we got close, so we'll sit with the Aussies tonight and sweep through the buildings at first light. Does anyone have any objections to that?'

Taylor and Hicks shook their heads.

Bentley thought they looked happy not to have to patrol through the maze of trees in the dark. The darkness would make it easy, even for wounded enemy, to spring an ambush. It was however disappointing that the patrol wouldn't return to Brigade Headquarters before nightfall.

The patrol made its way back up the hill to rejoin the Australians. As they were holding the fort and standing guard, the patrol could at least concentrate on getting a good night's sleep, but in a crude, rocky trench Hallmark struggled to rest in the warm, uncomfortable darkness. Bentley's squirming form next to him didn't help. Hallmark closed his eyes, cursing himself for forgetting about the German parachute container at the bridge. Images of dead locals and looted German bodies troubled him. The fact that the Cretans had taken it upon themselves to get embroiled in the fight was commendable, but it was also foolhardy. In uniform you stood half a chance of being granted quarter if captured by the enemy, but civilians taking up arms were much more likely to be shot out of hand.

Hallmark opened his eyes, then sat up. Having briefly fallen asleep, he allowed his vision to adjust to the low light. Bentley was no longer there. It wasn't quite pitch black, but it took Hallmark a while to identify the glow of cigarettes, as the Australian troops went about their night routine. Not far below him, he eventually made out the wrapped-up enemy bodies. An individual walked among them, stooping over each dead German in turn, gently interfering with the parachute canopies. Hallmark wondered why an Australian might tend to the dead at so late an hour. The man walked up towards him. Hallmark eventually recognized his profile, just before Bentley climbed into the trench next to him, beginning to make himself comfortable. 'All right, sir?' Hallmark enquired. 'Did you go for a stroll because you couldn't sleep?'

'You're right, I couldn't. So I went down the slope to look out over the olive groves below, not that you can see too much in this light, and I noticed something glint beside one of the enemy bodies down there. It was a broken piece of thin silver necklace. I thought it was part of a dog tag, so I searched for the rest of the necklace, but came up with nothing.'

'Did you see any grub or coffee on the dead Germans?'

'No,' Bentley answered. He yawned and turned away from Hallmark, leaving him a view of the back of his head.

Despite his exhaustion, Martin Bassom struggled to rest. He had spent some hours alone, sitting at the kitchen table in the farmhouse. Stolz had got the radio going but failed to make contact with anyone. So being competent enough with a radio set to adjust the antenna and frequencies, Bassom had tried to radio others himself, but no one answered his calls. While fiddling with the radio he had fought to keep his cool, silently reassuring himself there were friendly units out there.

A perimeter had been set up around the farm

complex, and during the course of the night more battered and bloodied parachutists had arrived, Werner
and Dormann working tirelessly to integrate them into
their ever-growing force, having their wounds tended
to as much as possible. Bassom wondered again where
the owners of the farm were. Perhaps they had fled the
area for fear of being caught up in the fighting. Or perhaps they had joined the British, sharpening their
knives and axes for the coming battles.

Bassom again cursed the doctrine that insisted containers must be used in a parachute drop, knowing
many brave parachutists had died on the ground trying
to retrieve them. To keep himself awake more than anything, he made annotated sketches in his notebook of
what he referred to as a 'leg bag', designed to be securely
attached to the parachutist and containing the weaponry and ammunition he required to fight effectively
as soon as he hit the ground. Bassom acknowledged
that larger quantities of ammunition and medical supplies could still be delivered by drop container, but
assuming good teamwork between parachutists, leg
bags would provide the fighting resources needed to
get to the containers without sustaining heavy losses.

It occurred to him that the leg bag might increase the
risk of serious injury on landing, perhaps resulting in a
shattered pelvis or broken femur, but thought the risk
could be negated by supplying the parachutist with some
form of mechanism to release the bag just before landing,
which would also reduce the risk of drowning, should the

parachutist be unfortunate enough to land in water. Maybe a rope could even attach the parachutist to the leg bag, following activation of the release mechanism. The rope would make it possible to pull the leg bag in after landing on the ground, without the parachutist having to crawl to retrieve it; any movement over the ground always increased exposure to enemy fire. And the rope could be detachable, thereby stopping the bag pulling the parachutist under in the event of a water landing.

Werner entered the kitchen. Bassom gave him the briefest of acknowledgments before continuing with his sketches. Werner made his way over to the stove and poured two tin cups of coffee from a pot. He sat with Bassom, handing him a cup, looking down at the contents. 'Not what you are used to, sir, I'm afraid. We just have the usual sweat that the quartermaster feels is acceptable coffee.'

Bassom put down his pencil. 'Thank you, Sergeant. The night is long, and I am tired, so any coffee is welcome.'

'It has been one of those days. But you will be pleased to know that although many of the newcomers are injured or wounded, we have almost a full platoon fit to fight.'

'That's good to know. Any of the newcomers bring machine guns?'

'No. We only have the two MG 34s Dormann brought with him. Also, that radio on the table is our only one.'

Bassom cupped his coffee with both hands, peering into the cup as if looking for inspiration or salvation. 'Not exactly going to plan, is it, Werner?'

Werner put his cup down. Not liking this negativity, he leaned in, his friendly demeanour gone. 'Listen here, Herr Captain,' he hissed. 'The men will follow you to hell and back, if that's what you demand of them. I will not have you speaking like that. It's not good for morale. So stop feeling sorry for yourself and drink your damned coffee.'

Bassom leaned back in his chair, his tiredness instantly evaporating. His coffee forgotten, he fixed his gaze on Werner. Bassom could feel his blood boiling. Who did Werner think he was? Did he think being a Nazi Party member gave him better social and professional standing than a commissioned *Fallschirmjäger* officer? Bassom knew Werner's comments had nothing to do with the morale of the men; no one else was in the room. They were instead to do with the fact that Bassom had shown weakness, somehow risking the prestige of the bloody Nazi Party. Bassom knew his failure to join the party was the ace up Werner's sleeve, and Colonel Veck and Captain Keich had given Werner the chance to exploit it by asking Werner to keep an eye on him. Keich was himself an ardent Nazi, and Veck could be described as sympathetic to the party and its aims. So this jumped-up arsehole of a sergeant consequently thought he could speak out of turn at any time, knowing Bassom would have to watch his tone and words. Bassom vowed that should Werner fall in the coming days, dead or wounded, he would not go too far out of his way to recover him, nor would he allow his men to risk their lives to do so. In the meantime he would have to play along because of the need to release his father from SS police custody and have his brother Karl discharged from Grabowsee Sanatorium.

The lingering aroma of bread prompted Bassom to retake the initiative.

'Tell me about your father, Werner. A baker, you say?'

The sergeant glared at the officer, suspicious at the sudden turn in conversation. Bassom held up his hands in faint submission. 'The time will pass quicker with polite conversation.'

Werner relaxed, taking another sip of his foul coffee. 'My father was not required to serve in the army, since being a baker was a reserved occupation. But he decided to serve nevertheless, on the Eastern Front.'

'As a baker?'

Werner nodded. 'As a baker. Wounded twice during the course of the war, a burst eardrum retired him to home service. Before long he was discharged and went back to baking in our home town.'

'Where is that?' Bassom was now more interested.

'Detmold.'

'I have heard of it, but never ventured too far west as a boy,' the captain confessed.

Werner gave a slight smile, still cupping the tepid coffee with both hands. 'After the war, much like your family no doubt, we really felt hardship. Hyperinflation had Father struggling to earn enough to purchase the flour needed to keep up with the town's demand for bread. The Jewish owners of the flour mill on the out-skirts of the city were ruthless, knowing that local bakers like my father couldn't afford to venture further afield in the hope of finding more reasonable rates.'

Bassom was about to cut the sergeant short when he started blaming the Jews for everything going bad after the war, but thought better of it. The last thing he needed was for the Nazi to add that conversation into this precious report. He allowed Werner to ramble on.

'Father found that passing the price increases on to his customers just wasn't realistic. One by one, the local bakeries folded, including ours. The only bakers left in Detmold and the surrounding villages were run by Jews, who got a far more reasonable rate from the flour mill. How on earth is a baker supposed to do his work when he can't even afford the materials? Tell me that, Cap-tain.' The sergeant flung his tin cup across the room.

Bassom allowed the sergeant to calm down, getting up to fetch the thrown cup and refilling it in an attempt to defuse the situation. Werner accepted the replen-ished cup from the captain, nodding his thanks.

A few minutes later Bassom noticed that Werner had craned his head to one side, taking an interest in the sketches in Bassom's notebook. 'What's that you got going on there, then? Anything I can help you with?'

Bassom fought the desire not to flip the table and grab Werner by the throat. He composed himself, before briefly explaining the concept of the leg bag.

'May I see?' pushed Werner. Bassom blinked slowly as

he slid the notebook across the table. Werner spun the notebook to study it. As Bassom finished the remains of his terrible coffee, the interested look on Werner's face was replaced by an increasing look of disappointment. Bassom guessed that Werner knew the leg bag concept was a good one, certainly worthy of high-level discussion, and was jealous he hadn't thought of it himself.

Werner seemed to lose interest in the sketches, sliding the notebook back to Bassom. 'I'll go and see if we have any more men coming in.'

'Good idea. Why don't you do that?'

As Werner left the kitchen, Bassom slumped back in his seat. Left to his own devices once more, Bassom's head filled with memories of days when decisions had not been half as difficult. He stared at the silent radio. Either no friendly units were listening, or they no longer possessed the means to communicate. For all he knew, the rest of the German forces on the island could well be dead or dying.

10

On top of the hill with the Australians, John Hallmark sat cross-legged among the rocks, reflecting on his lot in life, not to mention how he had got lumbered with the likes of Captain Bentley Paine, the third earl of sod all.

Born to a prostitute, John Hallmark had grown up with lots of so-called uncles, bankers, miners and policemen alike coming and going from his family's dingy, damp Victorian terrace in the rough streets of Carlisle, Cumbria. Their landlord was an uncle too, charging John's mother reduced rent. Her reputation even extended to the circus when it was in town.

John's school life was satisfactory at best. He wasn't dim by any stretch; both he and his brother Michael could read and write. When the weather was bad they would sit in the school library until the caretaker locked up for the evening. One day in the playground two teachers pulled him off a fifteen-year-old boy, who suffered a broken jaw and smashed cheekbone. John was taken to the headmaster. Barney Jacobs was tough but fair, but was also a rough old bastard. Jacobs had fought at the

Somme during the Great War. He had a terrible gravelly voice, thanks to inhaling mustard gas and coal dust from his subsequent work as a miner. 'What am I to do with you, Hallmark?' he growled. Jacobs secretly liked John and knew that caning him would be futile; it wouldn't make any difference to his behaviour.

John shrugged. 'Kick me out of school?'

'Pah,' cackled Jacobs, waving a dismissive hand. 'What good would that do? I know life at home is not great, Hallmark, so that wouldn't help you at all.'

John didn't like the reference to his home life but knew Jacobs had a point. 'No, sir. It would not. I could leave school and go down the pit.'

'The pit?' Jacobs roared. 'What bloody good would that do? You have an education. No, no, no, I won't have that.'

'What then, sir?'

Jacobs leaned back in his captain's chair, which creaked. Interlocking his fingers, he glared at John, who met his stare unerringly. Then Jacobs raised both eyebrows simultaneously as if he had experienced a eureka moment. 'You, Hallmark, could join the army.'

'The army?' John had considered it before but was surprised Jacobs now mentioned it.

'Why not?' croaked Jacobs. 'You're fit, tough. You can read and write. You know what's right and wrong with this world. After all, boy, you live with examples under your own bloody roof.'

John's eyes narrowed to a glare. 'Meaning?'

'I mean you have a lot to offer the world, young man. So why don't you go and see some of it for free.'

'Join the army?'

'Join the army,' repeated Jacobs. 'But there is one condition.'

John was puzzled that joining the army came with conditions. 'What?'

'You finish school.'

When John got home, a pair of circus tickets was lying on the kitchen table. His mother told him to find Michael and take him to the circus. Picking up the tickets and looking at the fancy red lettering, John couldn't remember whether he'd been to the circus before, but the thought of the tickets being used as payment to his mother made his blood boil. He was about to screw them up and throw them in the sink when there was a loud continuous banging at the front door. 'John,' his mother said, 'there's some money in the biscuit tin. Get yourself some supper.'

John caught up with Michael at the pie shop. Like John, Michael couldn't remember ever going to the circus, so with hot pies and tea in their hands, they slowly made their way there.

Hundreds of locals were descending on a huge gold and red marquee, searchlights advertising the circus illuminating the low clouds. Michael and John couldn't help but feel ten years old again, engrossed in the splendour and magic of the show. Outside, between the rigging lines of the marquee and a circle of colourful caravans and carriages, John noticed a large group of men gathering around what appeared to be a crudely built boxing ring. A bookie stood in the ring, taking money from an enthusiastic mob of spectators in return for small slips of paper. There were already boxers in opposite corners, getting ready. They looked far from professional as they took off their caps, slid their jackets over their gloves, slipped their braces off their shoulders and removed their off-white shirts.

'Two bob a fight, two bob a fight,' called out the bookie to the mob. 'Win tonight's dinner. Two bob a fight.' John wandered over to the ring. The fight was untidy and sluggish. Both fighters were unfit. But then the shorter, tubbier man threw a cracking right hook to his opponent's head. The slighter fighter stumbled against the coarse ropes of the ring, then slid to his knees, before vomiting. The referee, who also happened to be the bookie, waved enthusiastically to conclude the fight. The tubby fighter raised his gloves as his opponent was pulled roughly from the ring.

'Who's up for fighting the champ?' challenged the bookie-cum-referee. 'Two bob in yer pocket, if you take the champ down. Come on, two bob.' The champ became a little bothered by the glare of John Hallmark and he recognized the boy from somewhere. Clearly confident he could give the teenager the hiding he probably deserved anyway, the champ pointed a gloved hand at him. John pushed his way through the crowd, but it wasn't long before they began parting for him like the sea parting for Moses. Shouts filled the air as he clambered into the ring, taking the corner opposite the champ's. 'Fight, fight, fight, fight . . .' the crowd chanted.

The bookie approached John. 'How old are you, son?'

'Fifteen.'

'Bloody hell. You're big for fifteen, lad. Sure you want to fight?'

'Yeah.'

'Good. I won't tell 'em yer age. What's your name, son?'

'John Hallmark.' But his voice was drowned out by the noise of the crowd.

The bookie stepped in closer. 'What?'

'John Hallmark.'

'Ever boxed before?'

'No. I don't box, I fight.'

'Yeah. Well, you're gonna need to put these on.' The bookie handed John a pair of sorry-looking, filthy boxing gloves.

John took the gloves but then tossed them to one side. 'I don't box, I fight. You want a show? I'll give you one.'

'Well, that's what I'm talking about.' The bookie giggled as he spun round to address the tubby champ. 'No gloves. Get 'em off. No gloves.' The champ gave John a menacing leer as he slipped off his gloves. The bookie resumed his role as referee, his arms rising to call for order. 'Ladies and gentlemen,' he shouted. He paused for effect, the crowd quietening. 'Our challenger's name is John Hallmark.' The crowd roared, then silence descended. 'Our challenger has insisted the fight be without gloves.' The crowd roared again, but this time subsided to a low buzz. The bookie was happy; a fight without gloves was a novelty, sure to attract more money in bets. And so it proved as he reached through the ropes time after time to take bets.

The champ walked over to John, raising his voice. 'When I've finished knocking the shit out of you, boy, I want a free spin on yer mother. I know she likes a winner.' He couldn't have said anything more infuriating but, not taking the bait for now, John merely sneered at him.

The champ returned to his corner. The referee stood at the centre of the ring, his pockets jammed with money. 'One round,' he announced to the crowd. 'Three minutes. You win or lose; there are no draws. Begin on my say-so.' He backed away into a neutral corner. The crowd grew deathly silent. 'Fight!' he roared.

John jogged out of his corner, dancing quickly around the ring, denying the champ room to move. The champ tried a jab to get the range, but was suddenly overwhelmed by John's sheer firepower. The champ's efforts to cover his head were in vain, each punch having John's full force of fifteen stone behind it. The champ struggled back into a corner, desperately trying to block the blows and keep himself upright on the ropes.

John had barely got into his rhythm when the bookie and others pulled him from the bludgeoned champ, who was unconscious, only the ropes holding him up. John was shoved roughly back into his corner. The bookie placed both hands on his chest. 'What the hell was that, boy?'

'A show. Isn't that what you wanted?' John massaged his knuckles, thinking he would have to fight his way out of the ring, then somehow get through the crowd, the majority of whom had probably lost money. The champ was taken away on a stretcher. The crowd began chanting John's name. Anonymous hands clapped him on the back and shoulders.

The crowd began to disperse, as police visits to circus boxing spectacles weren't unknown, especially if word got around about a severe beating. Before long only John and the bookie remained in the ring. The bookie shook John's hand. 'Well, you're the new champ.' He grinned. 'Got any plans with your life I should know about?'

'Sorry?'

'Ever thought of making this a profession?'

John remembered the conversation with his headmaster and the absurd idea of joining the army. The bookie's proposal was very different to that. 'I am interested,' admitted John, 'but if I am to perform like a monkey, I have a condition.'

The bookie eyed him suspiciously. 'Go on.'

'Sixty–forty in my favour.'

'Fucking behave. Think yourself lucky I let you in this ring, you cheeky bastard.'

'Fine. Find another fat old man to be your champ. And when you do, I'll come back and beat him, just to spite you.' He climbed through the ropes and jumped to the ground, intent on heading for the Feathers. He didn't think the bookie would risk following him.

'Hang on a minute, will yer?'

John turned to see the bookie standing above him, both hands on the top rope. 'What?' rasped John, no longer in the mood to listen to nonsense.

'Forty-five–fifty-five,' the bookie offered.

'In my favour,' pushed John.

'You've got some balls on you,' grunted the bookie. 'All right, in your favour.'

'Plus my two bob for beating your champ.' The bookie smiled and fished two shillings from a bulging pocket.

Night after night, week after week, John fought and won. No gloves, no rules. Both he and the bookie made money, and lots of it. When John left school, word began to get around about his prize-fighting exploits. And with no more school, the bookie started arranging fights all over Cumbria. Town after town, village after village, the challengers came and fell.

Things changed in the Hallmark household. Michael signed up for the army, feeling life in Carlisle no longer had anything going for it. John had accumulated some money from his fighting, and managed to convince his mother to move to a nice little terrace in Preston. His mother got a job, pulling pints in their new local. By 1936 John's mother was settled in Lancashire. It beat Carlisle, but John knew he needed some direction and purpose in his life. He couldn't just sit in the pub, as his money wouldn't last for ever. So John followed Michael into the army. Unlike Michael, who felt he could do well in the Royal Engineers, John settled on joining his local county infantry regiment.

The sun was coming up, but sleep had been impossible for Corporal John Hallmark. He leaned back, listening to the sporadic sound of automatic fire and grenade detonations coming from the direction of Heraklion. It had continued most of the night, sounding as though neither side was giving an inch.

Columns of thick black smoke rose skywards from behind the town. One of the columns slowly became a lighter ash-grey as its source came into view; in the harbour a ship that must have been struck by Stukas was fighting for its life. Hallmark guessed that other boats had not been so fortunate as to stay afloat, but knew it would only be an hour or so before German bombers returned to finish off the stricken ship. In the early-morning light he also observed the orange flicker and glow of burning houses somewhere in the town.

There was a stifled cough from underneath a dusty blanket, and Hallmark looked at the curled-up form of Bentley Paine. His thoughts returned to the captain's night-time stroll down the hill.

Hallmark turned, his eyes summoned by the glow of dawn flooding over the summit behind him. Looking back at Bentley, he considered being a little mischievous, but a scrape of boots sounded and Sergeant Major Pearce stood over them. Hallmark nodded in acknowledgement. 'Hey, Jim.' He grinned. 'How was your night?'

'Crap.' Jim Pearce's reply was deadpan. 'Aussies talking all bloody night.' Strangely, Hallmark hadn't been disturbed by them. 'Give the captain a nudge,' said Pearce. 'The boss wants to speak to him.' He walked away, picking his way through the rocks.

Bentley was awakened with a rough shove. His eyes flashed open to see the unshaven face of Hallmark grinning down at him. Bentley would have settled for someone rather more pleasing to the eye. 'Major Barnett wants you, sir. I think he'll want us to get the olive grove cleared quickly for the Aussies.' Bentley sat upright. He felt absolutely terrible. He hadn't been able to sleep until perhaps an hour before first light. The uncomfortable position he occupied hadn't helped, not to mention Hallmark's fidgeting. Hallmark clambered to his feet with a huge yawn. 'I could murder a cup of tea. In fact, I'd settle for German ration coffee, if anyone has got any. That's why I asked you if you had found some.'

'What's that supposed to mean?' asked Bentley.

Hallmark leaned back, surprised by Bentley's reaction. 'Calm down, sir. I was just being hopeful.'

Suddenly uncomfortable, Bentley rubbed his rough hands over his battledress jacket. 'I saw no tea, no coffee and no food. Not that I was looking for anything but a missing part of dog-tag chain, thinking a tag might still be attached to it. I suppose the Aussies must have taken everything when they searched the bodies.'

'Captain Paine!' Major Simon Barnett yelled from somewhere. 'I want everyone ready to go within the hour before it starts getting hot around here.' The slowly building heat wasn't the only reason Barnett wanted the patrol concluded quickly. He was keen to get back to Brigade Headquarters.

The patrol was fed, watered and ready to move within the hour. They came down off the hill and across the bridge over the stream once more, Hallmark again noticing the un-salvaged German drop container. A commotion suddenly sounded. 'Ah shit, not again,' said Hallmark. 'Why can't they just sling their hook?' A large group of Cretan men was approaching.

The Cretan group didn't stop, instead filing past, all smiles and hellos. Bentley tried to return their goodwill gestures, but Hallmark just glared at them. The Cretans' hands were covered in dried blood and adorned with gold rings. They were proudly carrying wrist watches and German weapons. Bentley continued his attempts to exchange pleasantries. Hallmark glanced at him but decided to say nothing, thinking Bentley would just ignore him.

Hallmark spotted movement in reeds further along the stream. Some Cretans had found more dead German paratroopers. They had lined them up and were looting them. 'Hey, you lot,' Hallmark bellowed. They looked over at him. 'Fuck off,' he warned. 'Leave them alone. Go on, piss off.'

'Hallmark,' stated Bentley, 'you aren't exactly

diplomatic, are you? It may come as a surprise, Corporal, but those chaps are on our side.'

Hallmark ignored Bentley. The looters looked at each other, then shrugged their shoulders, as if they didn't understand Hallmark. But the message must have got through. Leaving the bodies, the looters moved away, heading for the rest of their group, who had clustered around Pearce, Barnett and his radio operator. Bentley deduced that the Cretans would be assisting them in some way.

Hallmark headed towards the reeds. 'Fucking thieving bastards,' he shouted at the looters. He reached the dead paratroopers, carefully wrapping them back in their parachutes, but not before noticing their personal effects were gone. 'They're fucking dead,' he roared at the looters. 'Leave them alone.'

Bentley drew a breath to shout at Hallmark, but just then Barnett called for him, so he picked up his rifle, stuck his helmet on his head and made his way over to the large and enthusiastic Cretan group laughing and smoking around Barnett's small gathering.

An air raid siren began to wail from Heraklion airfield. Above the echo of the klaxon, the drone of aircraft grew louder and louder. Bentley stopped, looking out to sea. High up he could make out the dark profiles of planes in a V-formation. One at a time, they broke formation and went into a steep dive. Haunting screams confirmed they were Stukas, their dives growing to a crescendo, before each dropped its bombs and pulled out of its dive, rising flak following them. Rising smoke columns confirmed hits on the airfield and perhaps on ships in the harbour.

'Captain Paine,' shouted Barnett, 'are you joining us, or do you want an ice cream while you watch the air show? They are not interested in us, at least not right now, anyway. Now get your arse over here.' Bentley spun on his heel and jogged towards Barnett, whose small British group now seemed overwhelmed by Cretans. Hallmark stormed up to the group, still cursing under his breath. He was clearly upset, so Barnett signalled to Pearce to calm him. Barnett had known Hallmark for most of his army career. Hallmark was a drunk and a womanizing fool, but he was an honourable man when it came to fighting; after all, it was all he knew.

Some fresh cow's milk didn't do much to improve Captain Martin Bassom's morning coffee. Nothing could disguise the foul coffee that German soldiers were issued in their rations. Sitting at the kitchen table in the farmhouse, Bassom forced it down all the same. Bad coffee was certainly better than none. During the night there had been another unexpected boost to their manpower. Parachutists, some wounded, others unscathed, had been attracted to the buildings, stumbling across Bassom's force by chance. It had been thanks to the alertness of the sentries around the walls that none of the new arrivals were shot at. A medical drop container had also been hauled in. It was badly damaged, and although it held no radio, the additional medical supplies were helpful in treating the wounded. The increase in man-power had enabled Bassom and Werner to order patrols into the olive groves, starting at first light.

Bassom went out to the courtyard. The sun was up. As he sipped his vile coffee, he decided his force would have to try to take Heraklion airfield, their primary objective, with whatever strength and fighting gear they could muster. After the Stuka attacks of the day before, he had heard distant battle sounds during the night. Given the slaughter during the drop, he doubted the *Fallschirmjäger* had managed to take the airfield.

Bassom could hear Stukas dive-bombing what must be the airfield. It was confirmation that their objective remained in Allied hands. The planes roused some of the paratroopers who had been dozing around the farm buildings.

As Bassom finished his coffee, he noticed the first patrol returning. They were in a hurry. The first man to jog into the courtyard was Sergeant Dormann. Werner was not far behind. The remainder of the patrol clustered in the yard, gulping greedily from their water bottles. Some lit cigarettes and passed them around.

'Need to show you something, sir,' Dormann gasped. He and Werner made their way to the farmhouse. By the time Bassom joined them at the kitchen table, a map of the area was already spread out. Dormann used a kitchen knife to point at features on the map. 'There's British infantry in this area. There's a bridge over a stream on the other side of the grove, and they crossed the bridge as we were doing our sweep. They have partisans with them, sir. We watched the Cretan bastards loot our men in the reeds. The British just watched for a while, until one of them shooed the locals away.'

Discovering the enemy were so close meant Bassom couldn't worry too much about yet more looting. He leaned on the table, looking at the knife, the point of which was spearing the position of the bridge on the map. 'How many infantry?'

'Sixty, give or take,' confirmed Dormann. 'And that's without the partisans.'

Excluding the Cretans, that sounded like two large British platoons. Bassom's force had increased in size considerably, but he only had about half that number ready to fight. 'What weapons do the British have?'

'Just rifles and sub-machine guns,' Dormann reported. 'We couldn't see anything bigger than that.'

'Sergeant Werner,' enquired Bassom, 'how many men do we have now?'

'As of the last count, thirty, sir. Six of those are still unfit to fight because of their wounds.'

It was a little worse than Bassom had expected. The British in the area outnumbered them more than two to one, never mind the Cretans. 'What's our weapons status? Any more containers brought in?'

'No, sir,' Werner confirmed. 'We just have the two MG 34s. Plus carbines, pistols and MP 40s. And a fair few grenades among us.'

Bassom stood up straight, running his fingers through

his stiff matted hair. Despite his desire to move on Heraklion airfield, he needed to protect what he already had. He pulled a pencil from his smock and leaned over the map again. 'We have to be ready to take the enemy on.' He began to mark the map. 'I want you, Sergeant Dormann, to take one MG 34 and half the men, and set up on the outer stone wall facing the grove. Have the 34 on our exposed left side, just in case the British attempt to flank us. Werner, I want you to set up opposite, your 34 on our right flank. I will be at the centre, and on my command you are to open fire, should the enemy approach us. Do you both understand?'

Werner and Dormann nodded.

'The British have no machine guns,' continued Bassom, 'so when they start to fall back, I want your group, Dormann, to go over the wall to follow up. As always, we need to hit them hard, before they have a chance to regroup and counter-attack.' Dormann nodded, a wicked grin emerging on his tired, dirty face. 'Remember this. Don't chase them out as far as the open ground, since my guess is they still have additional forces on the high ground beyond the stream. I know I would have forces up there, if it was me. Werner, ensure your guys divert their fire, to help Dormann's group press home the advantage. If in doubt regarding the position of any of Dormann's men, just stop firing altogether. Clear?'

'Yes, sir,' Werner acknowledged.

'Let's move, then,' concluded Bassom.

*

Barnett was huddled close to the reeds by the bridge leading over the stream. The dawn sun was low in the sky, but
it was nevertheless becoming uncomfortably hot. His
radio operator was with him, along with Pearce and Hallmark. They had managed to extricate themselves from
the large Cretan group, who stood boldly together in the
open, further down the stream.

Bentley approached Barnett's group, swallowing
hard, knowing his message might not go down well
with his boss. 'The Cretans want to take the lead, sir.
They feel that it's their homeland, so they should be
first to kill the enemy.'

Cheers suddenly erupted from behind. The Cretans
had dragged a couple of dead German parachutists
from some reeds and were stripping them of their possessions. One large brute stamped on the face of one of
the dead Germans, then inspected the paratrooper's
mouth to discover if gold teeth had been dislodged.
They dragged a third dead man from the riverbank,
who was still entangled in his parachute rigging
lines. They took out knives, cutting the lines away, then
began stripping items from his body in a methodical
manner, anything not of value being tossed into the
stream.

'Fucking savages,' Hallmark cursed, turning his back,
unable to watch. He wondered why the Cretans showed
no interest in the drop container under the bridge.

One of the Cretans wandered towards Barnett's
group, proudly holding up a newly acquired watch and

pay book. 'What do you think he is going to do with those things?' asked Bentley rhetorically.

'If that fucker so much as talks to me,' Hallmark hissed, 'I'm gonna shove it all up his arse.'

But the Cretan turned away towards the olive grove, waving to his countrymen to follow him. Barnett shook his head. 'Bunch of amateurs, the lot of them. Clowns.' Bentley had to agree. As the Cretans sauntered towards the olive grove, they adopted no formation. It was as though they were hunting birds. 'They know of a farm complex,' advised Barnett, 'a short distance beyond the olive grove. Looks as though it's the cluster of buildings I spotted on the map last night. It's a dairy farm, apparently. They are confident the Germans won't have found the place, so they want to ensure the family that owns the farm are safe before helping us to clear the remainder of the grove. I suppose we should follow the Cretans into the farm, just to make sure they don't do anything too bloody stupid. Bentley, you can stick with me for this one. They seem to like you, so if I want them to do something remotely soldierly, you can tell them, understand?'

'Sure, sir.' Given the language barrier, Bentley wondered how Barnett had got this information out of the Cretans. Bentley also wondered how he could tell them to do anything. But he smiled like the cat that got the cream, empowered by the request. It would be his opportunity to prove to the major that he was an asset to the company and not a burden. Hallmark rolled his eyes.

'I want 5 and 6 Platoons to follow us into the grove,'

Barnett continued, 'with Sergeant Major Pearce bringing up the rear. But I don't want us anywhere near the Cretans, in case they decide to start shooting at stuff.' There were nervous chuckles as the group dispersed.

Bentley followed Barnett and his radio operator across open ground as the last of the Cretans entered the olive grove. 'I've got a bad feeling about this,' said Hallmark through gritted teeth. He was far from comfortable with the idea of following the noisy Cretans into the olive grove. He felt both they and the locals were walking into the unknown, if not an ambush.

Werner spotted the partisans in the olive grove, but had heard them first, cheering and laughing. 'The partisans are leading, sir,' he said to Bassom. 'The British may still be out in the open.'

'Monitor the Cretans' movements. I want to hit them before the British can commit.'

'The Cretans keep stopping to loot our dead, sir,' said Werner. 'The British will catch up with them soon.'

'Looting? OK, keep me posted.'

Werner rejoined his men. Dormann appeared next to the captain. 'What on earth is the cheering in the grove about?'

'That's the partisans looting our dead.'

'Bastards.'

'Indeed.'

'Shall we attack them, sir?'

'No. We will wait for them to come to us.'

'And the British?'

'Werner thinks they might not have entered the grove yet. We'll just have to deal with that card when it is thrown.'

Dormann went back to his position. The cheers and laughter faded away. The Cretans were trying to approach the farm quietly, but from behind his wall Bassom could see and hear them begin to emerge into the clearing between the olive grove and the farm.

'Can't they be quiet?' Hallmark hissed. Barnett wore an angry look on his face as he agreed with the NCO. The British patrol had encountered dead paratroopers in all sorts of grotesque conditions. The olive drab smocks of the paratroopers had been pulled open, what remained of their personal effects strewn about the ground. Hallmark had noticed one dead man in particular. The young parachutist was propped up against an olive tree, his rigging lines tightly wound around his neck. He looked as though he had been garrotted. At his feet was a picture of him smart in his uniform. His sweetheart was beside him, hugging him. Hallmark knew he shouldn't, but he got out his knife, making short work of the rigging lines. Some in the patrol looked at him, amazed he had stopped in a potential battle situation. After a few heaves, he managed to pull the parachute canopy free of the branches overhead. He covered the paratrooper with it, tucking the photo inside. It was all he could do for the man.

*

The Cretan partisans sauntered across the clearing between the farm and the olive grove. Bassom fought hard to contain the urge to order his men to open fire, but not all of the locals had yet emerged from the olive grove. Even at this range, he knew they hadn't noticed his men because of the rough and untidy profile of the tops of the stone walls, a profile that blended in with the usually conspicuous shape of parachutist helmets. He wished he knew where the British were, but you couldn't have everything.

The last of the Cretans stumbled into the clearing. 'Fire!' roared the captain.

Hallmark rejoined Bentley just as the farm buildings came into view across a clearing beyond the edge of the olive grove. The Cretans were approaching the farm. Suddenly, from positions on the left and right sides of the farm complex, the whole world erupted in a stuttering ripple of gunfire as MG 34 machine guns were raised onto the walls,. The partisans didn't stand a chance, many falling in the opening salvoes, pink mist registering a series of simultaneous hits that shattered heads and torsos in the blink of an eye.

It was a massacre. Some tried to run back into the grove, but most were cut down. A few made it to cover, though, a few others playing dead. The machine-gun bursts carried through into the grove, splintering trees, shredding branches. Barnett and his radio operator crumpled. Bentley and Hallmark both dived to the ground for cover. As Bentley tried to get his Lee-Enfield rifle into a position where he could return fire, Hallmark urged him not to risk raising his head. 'Fan out, fan out, don't bunch!' someone shouted. Bentley didn't recognize the voice, having no idea who seemed to be commanding them in what was a one-sided firefight. He crawled over to Barnett and his radio man. Barnett was still alive, crumpled against a tree, groaning, but the body of his radio operator was a pink and dusty pulp. Suddenly, Barnett was hit over and over again, convulsing.

'Stay where you are, sir, stay where you are!' Bentley heard Hallmark roar behind him. But as smashed bits of trees rained down upon him, he instinctively wriggled to his left. 'Get back here!' shouted Hallmark. Bentley nodded then turned, beginning to slide towards Hallmark. With every stretch and drag, Bentley could feel the German bullets snapping just above him, striking timber or meat and bone. Some British troops began to return fire.

Bassom looked on as the enemy running back to the olive grove were cut down by the sharpshooting of Dormann and Werner's men, the MG 34 machine-gun teams and those who had subsequently begun using MP 40s, carbines and pistols to open up in support. Bassom had noticed the movement of the British in the grove and knew some of them had been hit.

He knew it was time to take the initiative and ran over to Dormann's group. Dormann's MG 34 crew were still blazing away from their now exposed position, but the others were firing and moving from behind the stone wall in a fashion that would lead the enemy to believe they were fighting a much larger force. The technique was to fire, duck down, scramble a few metres, then come back up to fire again. 'Assault now, assault now!' commanded Bassom.

Dormann looked round and nodded. 'Grenades!' he roared. As Dormann's MG 34 crew continued strafing the trees at the front of the grove, his other men prepared their stick grenades.

The grenades were lobbed at the treeline. Some made it that far, clattering off branches. Some fell short, among the Cretan partisans lying in the open.

Grenade detonations shattered the forward edge of the olive grove. 'Go!' screamed Hallmark. 'Break clean, break clean.' With caution out of the window, he stood, dragging Bentley away by his webbing straps. Bentley stumbled to his feet, only just hanging on to his rifle. He began staggering along behind Hallmark, who roared at everyone he passed to fall back to the stream. Most followed Hallmark, the pace increasing to a sprint as Pearce began shouting orders to retreat.

Dormann leaped over the stone wall first. His MG 34 team stopped firing. The remainder of his group followed him, vaulting with the dexterity of athletes. Copying him, they then dived onto their bellies to fire at the moving figures beyond the treeline, a few of whom fell. Fire from Werner's group faded. Dormann got to his feet. 'To the treeline!' His men followed him across the clearing without hesitation. Although two of Werner's group fell to shots from the retreating British, they also climbed over the wall, following Dormann's men across the open ground.

Bassom was the last to advance towards the grove. As he reached it, he was stunned to see so many British troops fleeing, knowing if they realized how small his force was, they might have pushed harder to reach the farm. He watched Dormann coolly feed another round into the chamber of his carbine. Dormann pulled it firmly into his shoulder, aiming at an enemy soldier standing on his own, waving the fleeing British through the grove. Dormann fired, and the enemy soldier collapsed to the ground, encouraging those close to him to sprint harder.

Knowing they were just taking pot shots at a retreating enemy, Bassom ordered his men to cease fire. The last echoes of the battle travelled through the grove.

Bassom looked at the men closest to him. They all had sweat running down their temples, their chests heaving. He patted a few of them on the back, making sure he raised his voice, so everyone would hear. 'Excellent effort, men. Well done.' It had indeed been a well-executed ambush.

11

The survivors of the British patrol sat in the reeds by the stream. The Australian unit watching over them from the high ground brought little comfort. The patrol had been hit hard. 'There must be at least a company of them in that farm,' John Hallmark gasped, 'maybe more. Don't you think?' A company would typically consist of between eighty and one hundred and fifty men. No one disagreed with him. Maybe it was because everyone was so shocked by the debacle in the olive grove.

Hallmark looked over at Bentley Paine. Bentley was a wreck, shocked and shaken, overwhelmed by the sheer violence of the ambush. He tried to control his hands by clenching his fists, but it just made the shaking worse. Bentley was unable to forget the sudden way that Simon Barnett and his radio operator had been killed. Hallmark didn't like Bentley much but he had to look after him, come what may. Hallmark leaned towards him, grabbing both trembling hands in one huge paw. Bentley looked up. Hallmark looked serious. 'It's OK, sir. It's over. Take a little time while I try and find out who managed to get out of there, OK?' He knew the job of accounting for the men would normally fall to a sergeant major, but he hadn't seen Pearce for a long time.

Bentley couldn't get the words out to tell Hallmark that Barnett and his radio man hadn't made it, although Hallmark suspected as much, since he hadn't seen Barnett in a while, and was used to him being at the front of everything, wherever they went. Hallmark slowly released his grip on Bentley's hands and pulled himself to his feet, thinking the captain had finally realized he was out of his depth. Hallmark still hoped to find the platoon commanders Taylor and Hicks alive and in one piece. With Bentley incapable, they might have to take over the patrol. Hallmark prayed he wasn't the only surviving NCO.

Martin Bassom stood in the courtyard as his men dragged, kicked and punched the half-dozen unwounded partisans they had captured. After all he had witnessed, it was too late to feel sorry for the Cretans. Some British survivors were also brought in, including a sergeant major by the name of Pearce, whose shoulder had been shattered by Sergeant Dormann's bullet. Dormann ordered the British to be held in one of the outbuildings, their wounded to be treated with whatever medical supplies could be spared. In terrible English he told the British to assist with treatment, but already an unscathed British private was helping a German paratrooper fit a sling to Pearce's shoulder.

In front of a wall, the unwounded Cretans were made to kneel before the captain, their hands on their heads, their faces swollen and bruised. They looked up at him with sheer contempt. Three surviving Cretan wounded were dumped down next to them. Lying on the ground, the wounded didn't have much of a rebellious streak left in them, looking fearful.

Sergeant Werner stormed into the courtyard. He held out his cupped hands, full of the possessions of German parachutists. Watches, rings, pay books, money, letters and photos from home, and to top it all off, numerous gold teeth. 'Found this stuff on the Cretan dead in the olive grove,' he spat.

Bassom could feel rage building in his chest. 'Search them.' His men descended on the Cretans like locusts on a fresh harvest. The search revealed the same types of items that Werner had discovered on the dead. They were piled on a wall, each pile indicating the culprit on which they were found. The injured began to sob. The largest of the uninjured cursed the Germans, before spitting at them. Werner stared straight at Bassom. Staring back at him, Bassom knew he just needed to say the word. He wasn't a fan of the Nazi , but his patience with the Cretans had expired some while ago, and Werner was just the man for the job. Bassom nodded.

Without hesitation Werner pulled a Luger pistol from a holster. The other Germans backed away. Werner put the pistol in the left eye of the still-cursing partisan and fired. The round smashing through the partisan's skull flicked him back like a rag doll. His twisted frame remained half-propped against the wall.

He let out a gurgling groan. His life expired, his bowels failing.

Werner moved to the next man, who had his eyes shut tightly, trying not to flinch. Werner shot him in the face.

As a third uninjured man was executed, the three kneeling to his right pleaded to Bassom for mercy, sensing only he could stop the carnage. He merely looked them up and down with contempt in his eyes. Werner moved over to his next victim. He put the pistol to the Cretan's left eye and pulled the trigger, but nothing happened. The surviving three unwounded Cretans were wincing and sobbing so hard they had no idea of the pistol malfunction. Werner wasted no time with the weapon, dropping it to the ground. With hand outstretched, he spun round and eyed one of his men. The chosen parachutist responded by handing his rifle to Werner, who quickly worked the bolt to feed in a new round. Werner shoved the muzzle into the cheekbone of his fourth victim and fired. The crack of the shot rippled through the farm complex, much louder than the pistol. The partisan's head shattered.

As Werner worked the bolt again, the shoulders of the next Cretan were bouncing as he sobbed, his hands over his face. Werner pointed the rifle down and fired. The fifth partisan's hands and head shattered as one. As Werner shot the last uninjured prisoner, Bassom was forcing himself not to intervene. Werner clearly revelled in the power he had over life and death. Bassom knew Werner wasn't done yet, but just wanted it all to be over as quickly as possible. Knowing all of his men wanted justice for the looting of their dead comrades, Bassom couldn't afford to show weakness.

Werner turned his attention to the three injured Cretans and the piles of looted material in front of them. The Cretans were sobbing uncontrollably. Working the bolt of the rifle feverishly, he shot each of them in turn. Werner reloaded the rifle and handed it back to its owner. 'I don't think our British prisoners will give us any trouble now. Don't you agree, Herr Bassom?'

'No, Sergeant Werner, I don't think they will.' He set the men to work, gathering up any British weaponry in the olive grove, before making his way into the farmhouse with Werner and Dormann. As Bassom seated himself at the kitchen table, pulling his helmet off, he felt sure he heard a baby crying. Werner was in the process of pouring water from his bottle into the kettle, when Bassom spoke. 'Listen. Can you hear that?'

Werner stopped pouring. He and Dormann stood completely still, as they tried to focus on the noise. 'I think ...' said Dormann hesitantly, 'I think it's a baby, sir.'

Bassom slowly pulled himself up from the chair. He looked up towards the ceiling, then, shaking his head, he glanced at Werner, who said, 'But we checked upstairs. The place is empty.'

The three men stood quietly once more, trying to fathom where the noise was coming from. Werner slowly knelt, and then bent down further, putting his ear to the rough tiled floor. It made the sound of crying more acute. He lifted himself up on both knees. 'It's under this floor,' he mouthed in barely a whisper.

Bassom scanned the kitchen floor in the hope of finding a cellar hatch of some description and noticed that in the far corner the pattern of tiles didn't correspond with the remainder of the floor. He carefully paced over and knelt down. He slowly ran his fingertips along the edges of a trapdoor. He looked back over his shoulder, beckoning Dormann and Werner over. 'No shooting,' Bassom mouthed, copying Werner's lowest whisper, looking at him rather than Dormann. 'Just get them out, OK?' They heard someone hushing the baby. Werner glared at Bassom but nodded all the same.

Bassom bounced on his haunches as he heaved the tiles upward. They were hinged on one side, and beneath them was a rough wooden ladder, leading down to a well lit cellar. 'Out, out, now, get the fuck out,' roared Werner. Women and children cried, as did the baby, but there was no movement. 'Out, out, now,' Werner repeated.

'OK, OK,' sobbed a woman. She climbed the ladder, holding on with one hand, carrying a toddler with the other. More girls and women, their ages ranging from perhaps ten to their mid-forties, came out of the cellar. Werner pulled the last woman out by her throat. 'Any more?' he barked at her. 'Any more down there?'

Bassom could tell the shocked and shaken woman had no idea what Werner was asking her. 'Werner, let go of her. She can't understand you.' Bassom heard young male voices coming from the cellar. Two teenage boys clambered up the ladder.

Werner shoved the woman towards Dormann, dragged the boys from the opening, punching them, then kicking them up the backside. Bassom told Dormann to lead the Cretans into the courtyard, reflecting that at least some of them must belong to the farm family, but wondering where the older men might be.

When the women saw the executed Cretan men at the stone wall, they became hysterical. They dropped to their knees and hugged their children, shielding the children's eyes from the horror. Even the steadfast Dormann dreaded what Bassom and Werner might have in store for them. The captain had permitted the executions, after all.

Bassom followed Werner into the courtyard. Two *Fallschirmjäger* were already in the process of frisking the teenage boys. The other men weren't entirely sure what to do with the women and girls. Bassom ordered them to be searched. He was conscious of the panic that the sight of the executed was causing. 'Move the women into the paddock once you have searched them,' he boomed above the wailing and crying. His men were struggling to frisk the women, who were unwilling to let go of their children.

Eventually, all of the Cretans stood in the paddock. Bassom's men had scoured the farm for shovels and now he beckoned the two teenage boys forward. Fearful the boys were about to be executed, the women shielded them, but Bassom pointed to the shovels then the ground. The Cretan boys began digging. Bassom received a few surprised looks from his men, not to mention a look of sheer disappointment from Werner. But before Werner could protest, Bassom gave him an order. 'Have the British come and help with the digging. The women won't leave their children unattended.' Werner eyed him. Bassom kept his expression deadpan, uninterested in Werner's opinion.

Werner reluctantly walked off to where the British were being held. As he entered the outbuilding, he began shouting orders.

Bentley was still numb from the ambush. What remained of the patrol had rejoined the Australians among the rocks on the reverse slope of the hill. Hallmark was moving from position to position, checking on shell-shocked survivors. Bentley fought hard against his still-trembling hands as he attempted to drink from his almost empty water bottle. Spilling most of it down himself, he gave up. He cursed himself for not coming up to par once more. Due to his hesitation, the brute Hallmark had taken the lead again. As Bentley watched columns of smoke drift skyward from Heraklion town and from freshly stricken ships out on the water, he considered matters. Although Hallmark was a pain in the arse, there was a lot to be said about the man in battle. Aggressive, forthright, and at least he was morally straight. Bentley reminded himself that Hallmark had been a sergeant, which explained why he was better and quicker at reading battle situations. Bentley took stock of his own shortcomings. He had yet to command a platoon, never mind being second in command of a multi-platoon patrol that had been originally close to company size. He happened to be the wrong man in the wrong place at the wrong time. The adjutant had had to find him a job. How the hell was he to know it would develop into something like this? Bentley hoped he wasn't the only officer left.

Hallmark clambered back into their position among the rocks and got out a notebook. Bentley didn't like the way he puffed out his cheeks, thinking it was a prelude to bad news. 'Right then, sir,' began Hallmark. 'Out of an original fighting strength of sixty-six men, we have thirty-eight that are fit to fight.'

'Oh, my God,' Bentley gasped. 'We lost about fifty per cent of our fighting strength,' confirmed Hallmark, 'not to mention the local volunteers.' He had waved dismissively when mentioning the Cretans. As far as he was concerned, they had been more of a hindrance than a help. 'If my maths is correct, we have thirteen wounded. They are currently being treated by the Australian medics. Both platoon commanders, Misters Taylor and Hicks, were badly bashed up by grenades. Hicks is full of grenade splinters, and Taylor is temporarily deaf from a nearby detonation.'

'Bloody hell,' Bentley managed. He let out a vomit-fumed belch. 'What of their sergeants?'

Hallmark shook his head. 'Both got hit as we withdrew. They are alive but won't be bossing anyone around for some time. There are nine other lads with various wounds. Three of them are stretcher cases. The remainder can fight, but I wouldn't send them on any patrols right now.' He then shook his head slowly. 'Major Barnett and Sergeant Major Pearce are unaccounted for, along with thirteen other men.'

Bentley was almost sick, remembering the horrific demise of Barnett and his radio operator. 'Barnett and his radio man didn't make it. They were cut down by the opening salvos of machine-gun fire.' Hallmark gave him a grave look, then nodded. Hallmark and Barnett had been close. Barnett had been one of the very few officers he truly respected. Bentley realized the patrol had been decimated in the ambush, and it now dawned on him that he was the only unscathed officer. Hallmark was certainly his deputy, in the absence of the sergeant major and the other NCOs. So, like it or not, Bentley would now have to depend on the volatile Hallmark all the more.

There was a scrape of boots on rock. Bentley turned and looked up at an unfamiliar Australian NCO. 'Excuse me, Mr Paine, sir. I've been told to grab you. Colonel Austin would like to speak with you.'

Bentley was at a loss for words. The sheer idea of being in command appeared absurd. He looked round to find Hallmark studying him. Hallmark could read his face and looked up at the NCO. 'We'll be right with you. Give us a minute?' The Australian nodded and moved away. Bentley put his helmet on and gathered up his Lee-Enfield rifle. He ensured his map and notebook were to hand, then pulled himself to his feet. Hallmark could tell all was not well with him, so put a gentle hand on his shoulder. Expecting his hand to be brushed away, and Bentley's arrogance to kick in, Hallmark was surprised to receive a pleading look, as if Bentley was a child who needed guidance. 'Are you OK, sir?' enquired Hallmark. 'Seriously, I'm not taking the mickey here.'

Bentley nodded. 'I'm OK. Just bear with me if I'm not filling the major's boots as quickly as I should.'

'OK. Let's go see what the colonel wants.'

Bentley followed Hallmark towards the canvas sheet that marked the Australian headquarters position. Hallmark had been in the army long enough to know that, ambush or not, the remnants of the British patrol would soon be in the line of fire again.

12

'We need water, sir, lots of it,' reported Sergeant Dormann. Sergeant Werner stood beside him at the kitchen table in the farmhouse.

Martin Bassom nodded as he sat studying the map on the table. It wasn't just his own men's thirst that needed to be quenched. He had kept his word, allowing the Cretans to leave, providing they headed into Heraklion, but the British prisoners needed water in the crushing Cretan heat. Outside the sun was setting, but the heat was reluctant to fade with it. 'I will lead a patrol tonight,' Bassom decided. 'It will fetch us all some water. Sergeant Dormann, you and your men will accompany me.'

Dormann nodded, but Werner piped up, 'And what am I to do, sir? Babysit the prisoners and the wounded?'

Bassom eyed Werner. 'That is exactly what you will do. Earlier you demonstrated to our British prisoners that you are not a man to be messed with, so with you at the farm they will behave themselves. Don't you think?'

Werner nodded.

'Sir, why are you taking the patrol?' asked Dormann. 'It's sergeant's work, not a captain's.'

Bassom waved a dismissive hand. 'Dormann, I understand where you are coming from, but I think the enemy still occupy the high ground. If I'm right, I need to try and understand what they are doing up there. We have Heraklion airfield to capture, and therefore need to find a way over the hill, one way or another. My main concern right now is where on the stream we should set up tonight.'

Dormann leaned in, his trigger finger pointing to a location on the map. 'The bridge. Here, sir.'

'Why?' Bassom was surprised. 'The enemy are bound to have that approach covered.'

Dormann nodded. 'I agree, but when I was in the reeds after the drop a white-chuted container landed close to the bridge, different from the one I dragged in the other night. The enemy were shooting from the high ground, so I couldn't even begin to look for the second container. There's every chance it's still out there. We could really do with it.'

Bassom nodded.

'What if the partisans or the British have already opened it?' Werner interjected.

Bassom shrugged. 'That would be bad luck on our part. Dormann has a point. We could use another weapons container. How much ammunition did we get through during the ambush?'

'Too much, sir,' Werner said. 'Especially on the MG 34s.'

Bassom sat up, forming a steeple with his fingers. They didn't just need water; they needed ammunition.

His eyes turned to map locations, flicking across the olive grove, the farm, the bridge and the high ground on the other side of the stream.

'Sir,' said Dormann, 'we can complete three tasks in one patrol. We fetch water, potentially recover the container, and get a decent look at the high ground while the enemy are probably sleeping.'

Bassom was sold on the trio of objectives. He considered his patrol route to the bridge, knowing it would be best to remain in the olive grove for as long as possible. There could be hundreds of enemy troops on the high ground, waiting for him and his men to come out into the open.

'Colonel Austin,' Bentley Paine asked, John Hallmark sitting next to him, 'you want my patrol to put in an ambush tonight?'

'Yes, Captain, that is correct.'

'Fine. Where?'

'Here.' In the fading light under the canvas sheet marking the Australian headquarters position, Colonel Austin used a short stubby pencil to point at the stream on his map. From the position on the stream he was pointing at, the forward edge of the olive grove looked to be some two hundred metres away. 'The enemy know we are up here, and after yesterday I think they might come out tonight. The reeds should give you good cover, and if the enemy do appear, we will put up flares to light them up for you.'

Hallmark pointed at the map with his own pencil. 'I spotted one of their drop containers caught under the bridge here. If the enemy do come out tonight, they may well be inclined to try and retrieve it, so perhaps we should set up around the bridge. But the enemy look to be company strength, so they might be difficult to stop.'

On any previous occasion Bentley would have been irritated by Hallmark's comments. Why hadn't he mentioned the existence of the container before? Why was he being so negative about the patrol's ability to defend and retrieve it? But after the ambush Bentley had to admit that despite his attitude he was a strong leader and a competent soldier. So Bentley welcomed his observations. 'Yes, Corporal Hallmark is right. The bridge makes an ideal choke point. And with the enemy likely to attempt to retrieve the container, it's an ideal place for an ambush.'

But Colonel Austin wasn't having any of it. 'Captain, I've got men and firepower covering that bridge. I can pulverize it back to the Stone Age with my mortars. I don't need you to set up there. What I need is for you and your men to set up further along the banks of the stream, and encourage the Germans to come out. If the enemy are stupid enough to come straight out of the grove, you get to kill them. And if they somehow get to the bridge by another route, they will get shelled. Understand?'

Bentley and Hallmark looked at each other. The colonel's plan might work in theory, but even Bentley knew that a surprise mortar attack would only be effective if the bridge had been fired on before, and the lack of damage to the bridge strongly indicated it hadn't. It wasn't good enough to take targeting information from a map. After you first fired mortar rounds, you always had to adjust your aim for fall of shot. The enemy probably wouldn't hang around at the bridge, so by the time the Australians were ready to fire their mortars again, they would have scarpered, perhaps even finding the time to scavenge the weapons container.

But orders were orders, and Bentley wasn't ready to punch above his weight.

The noise of distant, sporadic battle carried far into the night. It remained warm and uncomfortable, but on the edge of the olive grove all Bassom could hear was the trickling stream and the constant rattle of insects. Standing just inside the grove, he could make out a rough dirt road that led west to the bridge. He could see the long reeds that marked the banks running along the stream and the dark hill beyond it. He adjusted the radio rucksack on his back, which was full of empty water bottles. The radio remained in the farmhouse kitchen.

With the full moon stuck behind a long thick bank of cloud, Bassom waved his men to their feet and began to lead them out onto the exposed open ground, heading in the direction of the bridge. On the way through the grove he had entertained the idea of staying away from the bridge, abandoning the idea of searching for the weapons container Dormann had seen in favour of quietly filling the water bottles. All of Bassom's men were racked with thirst, as were the British prisoners. But running out of ammunition was equally dangerous, so Bassom knew he needed to try for the container. Better to be thirsty a little longer than dead.

The moon broke out from behind the clouds. Bassom slowly slumped down onto his belly, his men following suit. Peering out from under his helmet, he couldn't help but acknowledge how intimidating the hill was, and how crucial it was not to be seen from there. The moon swept its searchlight glare over his men, sprawled on the open ground. He felt as if there were countless British soldiers up on the hill, every one looking at him, the area about to erupt with flares and tracer bullets, forcing his men to sprint back to the olive grove. He thought of Dormann's earlier comment. Maybe it was sergeant's work.

Thankfully the cloud screened the moon once more. As his men got to their feet again, Bassom realized the bridge was closer than he had thought. He entered the reeds, forced to a painfully slow pace as his boots squelched in soft mud. To his immediate right, the bridge stood a little taller than him. He was delighted to spot what was probably the very container Dormann had talked about, jammed underneath. To his left, his men infiltrated the reeds like ghosts, an MG 34 team on their far flank providing cover while his other men filled their water bottles, in between taking greedy gulps. Dormann and Bassom followed suit, drinking most of the fresh contents of their own water bottles before refilling them. Bassom carefully scanned the area for any signs of enemy activity. Dormann slipped the rucksack from Bassom's back, and they began filling the water bottles it contained. Once all of them were filled, Dormann took the lead in salvaging the weapons container.

The British patrol sat uncomfortably in the reeds. To compensate for their losses, two Australian Bren-gun teams had been allocated to them, positioned on either flank. Bentley and Hallmark settled down for a long, warm, damp night, the local insects trying their hardest to eat them. The Allied patrol had occupied its ambush position not long after dark, entering silent mode: no sleeping, no talking, no smoking, no eating or drinking. Even movement was frowned upon, since the mere parting of the reeds could give them away to an eagle-eyed enemy in the olive grove. Ambushes were long, tiring, uncomfortable tasks.

Only the trickling stream, the insects and the distant battle noise kept Hallmark from being seduced by sleep, of which he feet deprived. He still thought the ambush would have been better sited at the bridge, feeling certain the container would attract scavenging German paratroopers, and was convinced the chances of catching the enemy out on open ground were next to zero. He fixed his gaze on the dark, sinister edge of the olive grove, wondering what had become of the men missing from the German ambush. Were they dead, wounded or captured? Bentley had told him that Major Barnett and his radio operator wouldn't be coming back. It was such a shame. Hallmark looked at Bentley to his left.

The young officer's head was heavy with fatigue. It would slowly droop, before lurching back up. Hallmark knew Bentley was exhausted. If Bentley fell asleep, Hallmark wouldn't make a scene, at least not at the ambush site. A subtle conversation during the day might do it. Hallmark couldn't check the other lads were awake; moving might attract enemy attention. The constant trickling of water was working on him like a sedative, and resisting sleep became even more of a struggle.

Bentley wasn't quite asleep; not yet, anyway. Tiredness fogged his mind and body. He was thinking about his life up to that point – soaked and exhausted on the bank of a stream in Crete, waiting for an enemy that would have to be either stupid or desperate to come their way. Despite earning a captain's salary to help those back at home, he found himself overwhelmed with guilt about his sister Madison, stuck tending to their mother's every need. It was no life for a young woman with her whole life ahead of her. He even spared a thought for his father, who would most probably be partying in London with his chums. Bentley doubted that the almost complete ruin of the family business would take the shine off Spencer's playboy attitude to life and made a silent promise to himself that he would climb the rank structure as quickly as possible, networking as he went. That would improve his salary further, and he was confident he could get the Richmond Furlong Company back on the map.

The sporadic chatter of distant gunfire continued to echo through the reeds. Bentley was no longer sure which direction it was coming from, but in the dark silence his senses had become much more aware of his immediate surroundings. No one spoke. Some shuffled around, one or two stifling coughs, but there was nothing else. And he was fine with that.

Bassom scanned the high ground, fighting the urge to close his eyes in the warm, dark, insect-filled air. Dormann and two other men were slowly and deliberately cutting away at the container's rigging lines with their knives. They each concentrated on one line at a time, for silence was of the utmost importance.

When the weapons container was separated from its parachute, Dormann crawled slowly under the bridge, getting soaked in the process. The other two men were standing almost chest-deep in the flowing stream. They kept their grunts of effort as quiet as they could as they fought the current as well as the waterlogged container full of supplies. Dormann became visible again, helping the other two men manhandle the long container away from the bridge. The moon broke through the clouds once more, and the man nearest Dormann slipped, cursing under his breath, but between them the three men managed to pull the container into the reeds next to Bassom. In the light of the moon, he could tell it had taken enemy fire in the drop, punctured numerous times. Opening the container in the reeds would make too much noise. It would have to wait until they returned to the farm, where Werner would supervise the task. Bassom shook the hands of Dormann and his two helpers as the German patrol prepared to move.

Numerous boots crunched above them on the bridge. A bolt of fear shot through Bassom like an electric shock. He slowly craned his head up, but he couldn't make out anyone, just the rough, ridged side of the bridge span. Surely it wasn't a German patrol. Bassom looked slowly to his left. Amid the reeds he could make out the helmets of his men. He wondered if any of them could see who was on the bridge, but couldn't risk moving down the line to ask, for fear of detection.

Above the sounds of the insects and the flowing water, Bassom heard a cough and what he thought was a match striking. The aroma of tobacco smoke filled his nostrils, so strong he could barely contain his desire to cough and sneeze. Another hacking cough tore the air above him. Someone on the bridge spat into the water. Bassom didn't think it was a British patrol; they wouldn't conduct themselves in such a noisy manner. As the moon drifted behind cloud again, he looked at the darkened profile of Dormann, who shrugged to indicate he didn't know who it was.

Again, boot leather sounded, scraping on gravel. Bassom looked up, this time to see a dark figure urinating into the stream. Bassom scrutinized the silhouette. The person didn't appear to be wearing a helmet of any kind. The torso was too slim for him to be wearing webbing or military equipment, but he had a long-barrelled weapon inverted over his shoulder. Bassom's stomach tightened. Partisans. But he had to be certain. The figure above looked down, focusing across the stream on the bank opposite the captain and his men. He began chatting excitedly in what had to be Greek. Two others joined him, looked down, and then all three vanished from view. Bassom wondered if any of them were the older men who hadn't been found in the farm cellar.

Six figures appeared at the end of the bridge on the far bank. Two clambered down into the reeds, their comrades watching from the top. What had they seen? Another container, perhaps? Almost waist-deep in the reeds, the two wading Cretans began chattering loudly.

Bassom caught sight of rigging lines wrapped around their forearms. It was then that his heart sank. He could see the parachute canopy was dark. It was either a parachutist or medical supplies. The Cretans were clearly happy with their discovery. As they dragged the soaked parachute and its load up onto the bank, all of Bassom's men must have been able to see it was a parachutist. He was twitching, still alive, still in his harness. Sadness swept through Bassom, but as angry as he was, he was professional enough not to give his men away by opening fire. There was nothing he could do for the parachutist. Bassom just hoped he was killed quickly. The partisans used knives to cut the equipment and clothing from the parachutist, mutilating him. He stopped moving. Two of the Cretans stamped on his head, their comrades laughing out loud, and then they took turns to beat the almost naked body with boots, fists, weapons, rocks. Bassom's blood boiled. He and Dormann gripped their MP 40s tight, Bassom's heart beating like a drum in his chest.

Another scraping of multiple boots sounded up on the bridge. More Cretans had arrived. Bassom glanced left, hoping all his men had heard them. The partisans on the bank called out to those on the bridge, whooping and chanting. Bassom toyed with the idea of opening fire. The Cretans were all armed, but he fancied the chances of his men.

A light thud accompanied a long streaking sound high up in the sky. Everyone looked up. There was a small pop. The area was drowned in brilliant white light, as if a huge torch had been switched on, now tumbling in slow motion back to earth.

Bassom regained his focus. As one, the concentrated rifle and machine-gun fire of his men rippled out of the reeds. His ears screamed at the noise. The partisans on the bank were obliterated in under a second. Their bodies flinched and burst as the bullets smashed through them. Some of Bassom's men quickly turned their fire to the bridge, whizzing tracer decimating most of the Cretans on it. Some were quick enough to dive on their bellies to crawl off the bridge. Bassom felt his anger and tension lift, the sudden violence of battle a release.

Dormann tapped him on the shoulder. 'Stay here, sir.' He spun round, pointing at two of his men, who were busy reloading their rifles with fresh clips of ammunition. 'You, follow me.' He led them up the bank onto the bridge span to finish off the survivors. His men's shadows danced sideways and grew longer as the flare got closer to the ground. Just as its light began to fade, another flare burst high in the sky. Bassom watched Dormann and his men go out of sight as the first mortar bomb fell with a loud crump. He knew the round had come from the high ground, confirmation the enemy were up there. He also knew that with someone up on the hill observing in order to correct the mortar impacts away from the bridge, his men were about to be hit hard.

Hallmark snapped out of his near-sleep stupor when he heard the gunfire to his left. He could see a flare drifting high in the sky under its parachute. The firefight seemed centred around the bridge. He jumped to his feet in one swift motion.

Bentley woke from his drooling slumber to see Hallmark standing over him, illuminated by flare light.

'They are at the bridge,' barked Hallmark. 'I fucking said they would be there. Let's go.' No British soldiers followed him as he stomped off down the bank of the stream. Like him and Bentley, they had all been half-asleep or worse. But a more alert Australian Bren-gun team latched on behind Hallmark.

Bentley got awkwardly to his feet. Gathering the

remainder of the patrol, he headed along the bank. Well ahead, Hallmark kept his eyes fixed on a gentle bend in the stream, knowing the bridge wasn't far beyond it. Through sense of feel only, he ensured his Lee-Enfield rifle was ready to go. He was sure they would encounter Germans around the bridge. As he reached the bend, he slowed to a walk, waving the rest of the patrol behind him down into the cover of the reeds, knowing that to advance any closer would put them in sight of the bridge.

As the patrol settled in the reeds, Hallmark picked out Bentley, who was stumbling his way through those men who had overtaken him. Hallmark didn't wait for Bentley to decide what to do. 'Crawl forward until you can see the bridge,' he ordered the Bren-gun team. 'Stay in the reeds. If you see the enemy, open fire. We will be coming past you, OK?'

'Sure thing, mate,' replied the Australian NCO commanding the Bren team. 'Just don't be too long moving up, that's all.' He grinned.

As the Bren team scampered forward through the reeds, keeping low so they wouldn't be seen, Bentley slumped down next to Hallmark. As Bentley caught his breath, he heard the first mortar round hit, accompanied by a fresh, bright flare. He couldn't help smiling at Hallmark. 'You gave me a fright when you got up and ran off. I thought you were having a nightmare or something.'

Hallmark looked at Bentley. 'Nightmares only happen if you fall asleep, sir.'

Bentley could tell Hallmark wasn't happy with him, but decided not to challenge his remark.

Bassom's force stopped firing as he clambered up onto the approach ramp of the bridge. He saw Dormann and his two men on the bridge span, checking the fallen Cretans were no longer a threat. As the light from the second flare began to fade, a second mortar round thudded onto the open ground between the bridge and the olive grove. The second round was closer to the bridge than the first, the aim of those on the high ground improving. He walked up to join Dormann, whose two men were now shooting at other partisans clumsily fleeing through the reeds. 'Leave it,' Bassom told them. 'Don't waste your ammo; their time will come. We need to get out of here. The mortars are getting more accurate.' A third mortar round punched into the stream, splashing water high into the air. 'Let's get out of here quick,' ordered Bassom, his command muffled in his ringing ears.

Bassom led Dormann's group back down into the reeds, mindful of the need to retrieve the weapons container. Another flare burst above, and they all froze as it began its effortless descent.

A series of rippling snaps and the whizz of tracer buffeted Bassom, causing him to lose his footing and collapse down onto the container. Screams and near misses filled the air around him. Sparks flicked off the bridge superstructure. His men began to shoot along the stream, calling out to each other. He felt among the reeds for his

MP 40, cursing himself for not having slung it across his body. By chance he found the canvas radio rucksack, full of water bottles, and hauled it onto his back. As he adjusted its position, he knelt on something solid just below the water. As more bullets ripped through, he was once again reunited with his sub-machine gun.

Dormann and his two men had headed up the bank again, towards the bridge span. In the reeds the soldier nearest Bassom was reloading his rifle. 'Help me with this container,' Bassom roared to him over the din of the firefight, reinforcing his order by gripping the remnants of the rigging lines attached to the container. 'Withdraw, now!' Bassom shouted, hoping the order would be passed through his men.

A mortar round landed somewhere in the reeds, another on the open ground close to the bridge. The double concussion made Bassom feel he had been punched in the chest. He fought to keep his lungs pumping. Judging by the weight of the container, he was going to need every ounce of breath.

The man alongside Bassom grabbed the rigging lines of the container. The captain could see most of his men falling back across the open ground towards the olive trees. Hopefully, the grove would provide safety, at least for now. Bassom and the man with him dragged the container through the reeds and onto firmer ground. As the latest flare began to fade out, bright tracer screamed high over their heads. The fading flare had blotted out Bassom's night vision, drifting red blobs moving across his eyes.

'Let's go, soldier. Just keep moving. Don't stop, just keep going.' As they moved over the open ground with the container, the soldier with Bassom cursed under his breath. Bassom felt reassured as the rippling fire of his MG 34 teams began. He heard his men calling out to each other again, happy they were trying to regain control of the situation. But he knew a few of the shouts were his men being hit, each cry of pain making him wince. As Bassom and his comrade approached the olive grove with the container, mortar rounds fell all around them, the impacts unseen in the darkness, but the concussion from each round battering them.

The Australian Bren-gun team opened up with short chugging bursts. 'Enemy on the bridge,' came a scream.

Hallmark spun round. 'Push up,' he barked at the men following him. 'Move, move!' But as they continued forward, the Bren fire stopped. The Australians were coming under heavy fire, pinned down in the reeds, tracer screaming around them.

Bentley's men established a firing line atop one of the banks of the stream, firing at muzzle flashes in the reeds below the bridge. A mortar round landed on the open ground, another in the reeds.

Bentley edged forward to join the line, but Hallmark grabbed him by the arm. 'It's not your job to fight, sir,' Hallmark said into his ear. 'Stay back slightly. You can't read the battle if you are too involved.' Bentley nodded his understanding. He had a decent enough view of the firefight, thanks largely to the flares coming from the Australians on the hill.

Bentley watched the Germans begin to withdraw across the open ground, while Hallmark scrambled up and down the firing line, encouraging an increased rate of fire. He also told the men to change position between shots to give the Germans reason to think they were being attacked by a much larger force. 'They're falling back. Don't let them get back to the olive grove.'

Bentley joined Hallmark. 'Shall we pursue them?'

Hallmark shook his head. 'The mortar fire has switched to the open ground. So we should sit tight here. No sense in getting our blokes hit.'

Bentley risked standing up. He spotted two German paratroopers, dragging what appeared to be a drop container, and remembered Hallmark talking about a container earlier.

The flare light began to fade out. Exchanges of rifle and machine-gun fire ceased as everything became consumed by darkness once more. 'Watch and shoot, fellas, watch and shoot,' Hallmark roared, meaning only shoot at clearly identified targets. Apart from saving ammunition, it also permitted a brief pause to plan the next move. Bentley mentioned his sight of the container. 'Fuck's sake,' cursed Hallmark. 'I bloody knew they would come back for it. Didn't I say that, sir?'

'Yes, you did say so. Shame Colonel Austin wasn't interested.'

Hallmark spat into the darkness. 'Everyone OK?' he shouted. 'Do we have any casualties?'

After a while it emerged that, incredibly, there were no British or Australian casualties. Relief washed over Bentley. Strongly believing they had hit many of the retreating enemy, he felt elated at the success of the ambush.

Hallmark spent some time checking each soldier's ammunition, before returning to Bentley. 'If it's OK with you, sir, I recommend we sit tight here until first light, only then rejoining the Australians on the high ground. The boys have plenty of ammo.'

The politely phrased recommendation from Hallmark came as an unexpected surprise to Bentley, a welcome departure from his usual approach. Instead of feeling like Hallmark's apprentice, Bentley suddenly felt empowered at a time when he knew that robust leadership was in great demand. He nodded his consent to Hallmark. 'Very well, Corporal. Good call. First light it is. As the Australians on the high ground are watching over us, there's no need for all the men to be awake.'

Even in the darkness, Bentley could see some kind of a smile on Hallmark's face. 'Very good, sir.'

13

Standing in the darkness of the courtyard at the farm, Martin Bassom felt hollow. After the patrol to the stream for water and the weapons container, Sergeant Dormann and five other men were unaccounted for. Dormann had been a friendly and very capable NCO. All the men who had been lost were good German boys. Bassom looked at the crude and recently dug graveyard in the paddock, quietly praying that Dormann and the other missing men would emerge from the olive grove and allow him the chance to reprimand them for falling behind. But Bassom knew it was not to be. He heard Werner's boots approaching him from behind. 'The container. Good catch there, sir.' He sounded almost sincere.

Bassom didn't bother turning round.

'Two additional MG 34s, plenty of ammunition. Hence the weight of the bloody thing. There's a radio in pretty good condition. Corporal Stolz is already getting it up and running. Hopefully, we might talk to someone on the airfield.'

Bassom closed his eyes, having forgotten about the airfield, his primary objective. As loyal to the mission as he was, he couldn't help but second-guess what his masters might task him with next, should he be able to contact someone in authority on the new radio. In one patrol action he had lost six men, one a strong NCO. He was left with a career-minded Nazi in Werner and a beaten-up group of parachutists. To make the situation all the more difficult, there were prisoners to contend with too.

'I have made contact with other units, sir,' Stolz called out excitedly from the farmhouse.

'Really?' Bassom exclaimed. So the first radio *had* been faulty. He stomped back into the kitchen, grabbing the radio handset from the grinning Stolz.

'Yes, sir,' elaborated Stolz. 'Colonel Veck is on the airfield. He is fighting to stay there, but he's on it.'

Men began cramming into the kitchen, hopeful for good news. Werner arrived. 'Haven't you men got things to be getting on with?' he demanded, and they made themselves scarce.

Bassom put the handset to his ear, angling it so Stolz and Werner would hear both sides of the conversation. 'Hello, Foxtrot One One Bravo. This is Alpha Zero Bravo . . . Over.'

Werner, Stolz and Bassom listened for a response. After a few seconds the headset crackled into life. Straight away, Bassom recognized Veck's voice. 'Bassom, you need to speak straight and clear. The British are listening in. Our mission is no secret any more, so let's just get on with the war. Where are you? What's your fighting strength? Over.'

Eyebrows raised, Bassom looked at the handset and then at Werner. Not normally lost for words, Werner merely shrugged. Stolz spread a map out on the table.

'Bassom, talk to me, son,' called Veck.

Bassom was flustered, but after the excursion to the stream he was pretty confident he knew exactly where he was on the map, not that he could reveal their precise location or fighting strength over what sounded to be an insecure radio connection. He had just twenty-four men fit to fight. 'Roger that. Reference the high ground to the south-east of the airfield. We are just south of the stream in the olive grove. We still have reasonable strength. Over.'

'Wait, out.' Veck's reply was curt. Intermittent sound began to emerge from the handset. Now and again Veck was inadvertently pressing 'Send' on his handset. He could be heard shouting at his men, who by the sound of it were under fire. Werner stepped into the open doorway, cocking an ear to the darkened sky. He could hear gunfire, and it was coming from the direction of the airfield. The handset crackled into life once more. 'Bassom. At first light I need you on that high ground. The enemy occupy the airfield tower and the Greek barracks, but they will not be able to stay where they are if we can dominate that feature. Do you read me?'

'Yes, sir.' Bassom thought the proposed hill assault was difficult enough, but it sounded as though Veck had plans beyond that.

'Good,' Veck continued. 'I have priority call on Stuka

strikes until noon. Where do you want them? Make them count. Over.'

Bassom had no idea of enemy strength on the hill. For all he knew, there could be a thousand men up there, and he had no idea of the enemy's precise positions. But Stuka strikes might well give his men a fighting chance of taking the hill. 'I want them to hit the eastern slope of the high ground, the side that dominates my position. The slope goes down as far as the bridge across the stream. The first strike should give me breathing space to form up my men for the assault. If we can push the enemy over the summit to the reverse slope and pin them down there, I will be able to overlook them, the airfield and the barracks. Over.'

'Wait, out,' said Veck once more. Bassom had visions of the colonel poring over his own map, trying to identify the desired target area for the airstrike. 'Happy with that, Bassom. You will have Stuka strikes from first light until noon.'

'Thank you, sir.' Bassom was grateful but had forgotten something.

'Just make sure you have the means to mark your progress to our pilots,' Veck added. 'I don't want you getting too close to the strikes.'

Bassom looked up at the ceiling. He had no idea how to mark the forward line of his men during the assault.

As if he had awaited this moment all his life, Werner let out a sinister grin. He opened his smock and pulled out a bright red and black Nazi flag. Bassom couldn't help but roll his eyes. He wasn't surprised to find Werner practically wearing the flag despite the humidity. 'Roger that, sir,' Bassom said. 'We have a marker, a red and black party flag. Do you have any more information for us?'

Veck replied with enthusiasm, perhaps liking the reference to the Nazi Party. 'Roger. Friendly forces have cleared Maleme airfield in the west, and reinforcements are flying in every hour. Other friendly units closer to our objective have now consolidated and are pushing enemy units away from key and vital terrain. Roger so far?'

The taking of Maleme airfield was excellent news. The British could not survive on Crete for long in the face of continuing reinforcement of German forces and supplies of additional weapons, equipment and ammunition. It was also good to know that elsewhere fellow parachutists had survived their drops and were beginning to get organized. Key terrain was what German forces aimed to occupy, and vital terrain was ground they needed to have. Overall, the invasion of Crete was starting to look a little better. 'That's great news, sir,' acknowledged Bassom. 'How are you getting on?'

Werner frowned. Bassom wondered if he was being too informal, but what harm could it do to ask how the boss was getting on? Positive news would be welcomed by Bassom's men. The handset crackled back into life. 'We are OK, young man. Holding on. We pretty much have the airfield, but the British keep probing us with fighting patrols and illuminating us with flares, so we can't move around. Bastards. But we are fine. Thank you for asking, Bassom. Take the high ground. Out.'

Bassom gave the handset back to Stolz. 'Sergeant Werner, have the men ready for battle. We go at first light. Don't forget your precious flag.'

'What about the prisoners?' Werner asked, choosing to ignore Bassom's flippant remark. 'We can't have them at our rear, unguarded.'

Bassom nodded. 'You are right, Sergeant. We can't. The wounded will guard them. Anyone who can't move quickly will stay behind. So I'm afraid you're going to have to come with us.' Veck's positivity had given him confidence.

Werner fought to keep a lid on his anger, irritated by Bassom's insinuation that he would rather guard prisoners than fight. Stolz felt it wise to go outside before things got really ugly, but Werner wasn't going to give the captain the satisfaction of hitting him. Werner reassured himself that he could report the insolent farmer's boy to the adjutant for slurs against the Nazi Party. However, judging by the look on Bassom's face, Werner wondered whether he cared.

The men hadn't been back long from the patrol. Everyone had been glad to hear Veck's news, but they now had to get ready for the hill assault. Werner, as tired as he was, fatigue beginning to fog even him, fought on by ensuring all the men had cleaned their weapons and checked over their ammunition and equipment.

Bassom also moved among the men, asking after their welfare, ensuring they had drunk some water. The warm, moist night would soon give way to another crushing hot day, but hopefully with a swarm of Stuka dive-bombers to help them. Finally, with all their preparations complete, Bassom allowed his bloodied and exhausted paratroopers the chance to grab some much-needed rest. The walking wounded, who would not be joining the hill assault, took over guarding the British prisoners.

Bassom laid his aching frame on the refreshingly cool kitchen floor, carefully resting his head against a cupboard just below the sink. He knew he was tired, as the floor seemed to be the most comfortable bed he had ever slept in. He was off to sleep the moment he closed his eyes.

'Captain, Captain.' Bassom managed to open one eye, and the dark profile of his tormentor swam into view. Werner came into focus. 'It is time, sir.'

Bassom sat up, gathering himself. A number of other men lay asleep in the room. In the low light Bassom saw Stolz load the recently acquired radio set into its canvas backpack and then struggle into the harness. Bassom reflected on the NCO. He was a good man – dependable, young, but with a sensible head on his shoulders. Bassom watched Stolz put his helmet on, then take his MP 40 in both hands as he made for the doorway. Bassom glanced back at Werner, who was looking out of the window. 'How long have I been asleep?' Bassom asked as he let out a yawn and gave a large creaking stretch.

'Couple of hours, give or take,' confirmed Werner.

Bassom noticed that Werner's voice was hushed. He didn't seem to be his usual brash self. Bassom found it rather comforting. 'Did you manage to get any sleep?'

'Not really.'

'Surely you're running on empty?'

Werner wore a deadpan look on his exhausted face. 'I can never sleep before battle. The night before Eben Emael, Corinth Canal and coming here. I just can't rest.' Bassom was surprised at the response. Sergeant Werner was human after all. The man had demonstrated that he could take life, but he clearly feared losing his own.

The men in the kitchen clambered to their feet, Werner helping Bassom get to his feet. As Bassom adjusted his jump smock and put his helmet on, his men filed into the courtyard, nodding at him. He nodded back.

MP 40 in hand, Bassom followed his men out into the courtyard. The first light of pre-dawn was in the sky. The men stood in groups, all geared up, ready to fight. The machine-gunners had their MG 34s over one shoulder. Smokers took long greedy pulls on their cigarettes, their faces glowing as the tobacco flared. The night was relentlessly warm. Bassom could feel sweat tricking down the nape of his neck.

Bassom took the lead out of the farm complex, Werner bringing up the rear. The pace which Bassom set was deliberately slow, for he didn't want any enemy forces beyond the grove to detect movement. He also wanted to preserve his men's energy for the impending fight. Eventually, when he could see the open expanse beyond the olive trees, he ordered his men to get down onto their bellies. What remained of his depleted force was broken into three groups. Lying prone on either side of him were two squads of men armed with rifles and MP 40s, along with grenades, knives and their standard-issue lightweight shovels. They would be the assault force, driving up the hill. The third group, under the command of Werner, comprised four MG 34 teams, two teams using the new machine guns from the weapons container and acting as a fire support group. The gunners were wrapped in the belt ammunition required to satisfy the appetites of the machine guns. Werner too was draped in ammunition, but he unravelled himself and crawled up to the captain. The short crawl took its toll on Werner, such was the extent of his fatigue. He arrived dripping in sweat. Both men pulled their binoculars from their smocks and began to scan the far side of the stream, the bridge and the high ground beyond.

They spotted troops on the high ground. Bassom quickly counted at least fifty men, more than twice the size of his force. Werner thought there were potentially more on the hill. Bassom glanced sideways at him. 'Have the gun teams pay particular attention to the right side.'

'OK. Check out the stream, far side. We have movement, left to right.'

Bassom observed the area with his naked eye, before putting the binoculars up to his face. Werner had indeed spotted troops moving in from the left. These had to be added to Bassom's quick and probably low estimate of fifty. 'Shall we open fire,' Werner suggested, 'and get this whole thing under way, sir?'

'No,' replied the captain, keeping his eyes fixed to his binoculars. 'We will exploit the first Stuka attack to make for the stream. We'll keep away from the bridge. They have their mortars dialled in on that. Your group will cover our crossing. Once we are on the far side, we will cover you in joining us.'

'But what about the enemy patrol out in front by the stream?'

'We'll leave them be. Probably just inspecting the area after last night's ambush. No need to give our intentions away. At least not until the Stukas are here.'

The British patrol along the bank of the stream was slow. Bentley Paine watched his men pull dead German paratroopers from the reeds. All had died in their parachute harnesses. John Hallmark was with the lead section and made it his business to have them wrapped in their chutes, making sure each one was given proper respect, each one treated with no less diligence than the one before. He had them neatly laid out in a line on the bank. Bentley waited for the grisly task to be completed and for Hallmark to lead the patrol away, before inspecting the dead himself.

Hallmark reached the bridge, spotting the body of an

almost naked German soldier. His face was shattered, his ribcage almost caved in. Lying around him were the badly shot-up bodies of Cretan men carrying spoils from enemy dead, mainly watches and rings. The Cretans had all been carrying German weapons. Hallmark felt a presence to his right, assuming it to be Bentley. 'Why do they do it?' a totally different voice said.

Hallmark snapped round to encounter a young private. 'What?'

The private was looking down at the Cretans. 'I can understand why they take the weapons, but why their personal stuff?'

Hallmark puffed out his cheeks. He shook his head, then looked across at the disfigured German. 'No idea, mate. I'm just as bewildered as you.' There was no point in putting ideas about trophy hunting and money into the young lad's head.

Hallmark spotted Bentley catching up with the patrol. He was about to call to him when someone shouted down from the bridge, 'We've got dead up here, Corporal. Shall we search them?'

'I will take a look.' Bentley's voice caused Hallmark and the private to stop. Bentley cast a quick glance at the dead German paratrooper, then moved to join the men on the bridge. Hallmark caught sight of a cut-up parachute in the reeds and thought it would do to cover the semi-naked parachutist. He lightly jabbed the young private on the shoulder. 'Give me a hand with this.'

On the bridge Bentley observed several Cretan dead

at the feet of his men. There were also three dead Germans crumpled at the far end of the bridge. They were fully equipped and free of parachutes. 'Take the dead men down to Corporal Hallmark,' Bentley ordered. 'They are blocking the way.' His men responded without hesitation, and quickly dragged the dead Cretans down the bank, where Hallmark and the young private were already wrapping the dead German paratrooper in the tatty remnants of his parachute silk.

With every passing minute the dawn grew lighter. Bassom and Werner watched through their binoculars with interest as a large enemy soldier supervised the wrapping of German dead in their parachutes. 'An honest foe, the big one,' muttered Werner.

'Indeed,' Bassom agreed. As chivalrous as the occasion was, it broke Bassom's heart to know that his regiment had been almost completely destroyed in the parachute drop. Despite Colonel Veck's positivity during the radio conversation, he couldn't help but be pessimistic regarding the fate of those who had survived the drop. He quietly prayed they were pressing forward with minimal losses.

A small group of British soldiers walked up towards the bridge span. The big British soldier moved along the bank. He looked at the stripped and mutilated body of a German paratrooper in the reeds, then began talking with a younger, smaller, more slightly built soldier. 'Built like a Spartan, the big one,' observed Werner. 'His mother must have fed him well as a pup.'

'The British are very respectful to our dead,' Bassom replied. 'The officer even inspects them once they're wrapped in their parachutes, making sure the big man has done his job properly.'

At the feet of the British soldiers on the bridge Werner caught a glimpse of olive-drab-covered bodies. 'Look at the bridge. On the road, as it comes onto the bridge span.'

Bassom found the bridge with his binoculars. His stomach turned. He lowered his binoculars, resting his heavy head on his forearms. 'I think it's Sergeant Dormann,' he murmured, 'and two of the men with him.'

'Are you sure?' replied Werner dully.

Bassom nodded. 'I'm certain one of the bodies is his. An enemy shell landed close to there just as we began to withdraw.'

Werner could feel anger swelling inside him. He wasn't upset at the fact that Dormann had fallen, he was annoyed that Dormann had allowed himself to be caught in the open, especially with two other men. He had thought better of the man. Werner glanced sideways at Bassom, who still had his head bowed and was rubbing the bridge of his nose with thumb and forefinger. Werner was professional enough not to voice his opinion about Dormann's rookie mistake but resumed looking through his binoculars, disturbed by what he saw next. 'Partisans moving towards the bridge from the west.'

The Cretans were all armed with German weapons, along with axes, meat cleavers and kitchen knives. They appeared clean and bloodless, showing no evidence of recent killing. The British soldiers had disappeared from the bridge, the officer making his way down the bank into the reeds. But he turned back, noticing the Cretans approaching. As they approached the bridge, they waved. He gave a kind of royal wave back at them, to the apparent disgust of the big British soldier, who had just finished wrapping the mutilated German paratrooper in what was left of his parachute. The British officer gave some orders to his men, who started fiddling with their weapons and equipment, apparently making preparations to move out.

To Werner's disgust, the Cretans appeared to begin looting the dead Germans on the bridge. Then suddenly they stopped, and two of them threw Dormann's body into the stream. 'What the fuck?' hissed Werner, a little louder than he should have. 'They just threw Dormann into the fucking stream.'

Binoculars raised once more, Bassom had seen it too. Anger swelled in him. He watched Werner furiously stuff his binoculars inside his smock. Bassom suspected Werner was about to do something stupid and grabbed him by the smock sleeve. 'When the assault begins, you may do your worst to the enemy, including the Cretans. But not before our Stukas arrive, is that clear?'

'I'm fucking tired of watching these vermin mutilate and loot our dead.' Werner hissed through gritted teeth, spittle flying from his mouth. Bassom could see the hatred in Werner's eyes, and it worried him. 'We wait for the Stukas, Werner. It cannot be long now.'

Werner glared at him, shoving his hand away. He fought with his smock to get his binoculars out once more, shoving them up to his eyes. Bassom watched him for a few more seconds, before peering through his own binoculars again. 'Look, here we go. The big British man is up on the bridge. He doesn't seem happy.'

'Corporal Hallmark, get back down here. Now is not the time.'

Hallmark ignored Bentley's order and advanced on the two Cretan men who had tossed the body into the water. They were at one side of the bridge, looking over the parapet at the body, which was refusing to sink. Both had cigarettes hanging from their lips, and were chuckling and coughing as they admired their handiwork. Hallmark was enraged. The two Cretans didn't see him approaching. He gripped the nearest man around the throat with both hands and squeezed hard. The man instantly dropped his German rifle and grabbed Hallmark's wrists in a futile attempt to free himself from the iron grip.

'Corporal Hallmark!' Bentley yelled desperately.

But Bentley's order fell on deaf ears. The other Cretans raised their weapons. Bentley's men rushed up onto the bridge, their weapons also raised, but instead of shooting the Cretans, they pushed, slapped and shoved them off the bridge. 'Get away, you fucking turds,' screamed Hallmark. 'We don't need you.' He had released his victim, who was staggering away clutching his throat.

Bentley joined Hallmark on the bridge, having decided

to talk to him later about the incident with the Cretans. He feared Hallmark's wrath would turn on him if he attempted to discipline him now.

To Bentley, Hallmark's profile was a mere silhouette against the low morning sun, which shimmered on the horizon. Then what appeared to be a large flock of birds began to flank Hallmark's silhouette. As it got nearer, it gave off a God-awful screaming noise. Hallmark turned. 'Get off the fucking bridge!' he roared as he jumped into the stream.

Before Bentley could fathom what was going on, the area was drowned in the piercing scream of diving Stukas, cannon fire and exploding bombs. Instinctively, he leaped into the reeds with his men. As the first Stukas pulled out of their dives, he fought to gather his senses against a high-pitched ringing in his ears. The dull throb of thrashing water caught his attention. Hallmark came staggering through the stream, grabbing him by the shoulder. 'We cannot stay here. Look!' He pointed to the forward edge of the olive grove. German paratroopers were swarming out, sprinting for the stream. Infantry machine-gun fire began to join the aerial assault. Hallmark got in Bentley's face. 'We need to get up the hill, now! Move, move.'

As entertaining as it had been to watch the big British soldier strangle the partisan, Werner knew there was work to be done. He pulled the swastika flag from his smock and handed it to Bassom, who was still lying next to him. 'Lay that out,' said Werner, 'whenever you stop. I can then move up and join you.' Bassom looked down at the red, white and black fabric and then back at Werner. Werner knew the captain didn't approve. 'Look, I know you don't like the flag. But it stops my guys from mistaking you for the enemy, not to mention the Stukas, OK?' Bassom rolled onto his left side and shoved the flag down the front of his smock. 'We have the only working radio with us,' Werner reminded him. 'You are going to need to be able to talk to the colonel.'

Werner scrambled over to the four MG 34 gun teams. He had them sited line abreast, the gunners lying prone behind their machine guns, each with an assistant to his left, responsible for the belt ammunition. Werner had ordered only two of the four teams to support the hill assault to begin with. The two spares would take care of any developments not related to the assault – counter-attacks, for example. They would also be able to step in and replace the two teams designated to support the assault, should there be any jams or overheating barrels. Precision fire would not be required for the assault. The teams were under instructions to saturate the enemy positions, preventing them from firing at the German assault force or moving to better locations. If the MG 34 gunners could kill the enemy before the assault force was upon them, all the better. But the hope was that the Stukas would do most of the work, leaving the assault force and the gun teams to take care of the shocked and shaken survivors.

Using his binoculars, Werner observed the developing free-for-all between the British and Cretans on the bridge. The British were clearly getting the upper hand in the pushing and shoving match, which pleased Werner, for as far as he was concerned, the Cretans were cockroaches and should be treated accordingly. He joined his gunners in stifling a chuckle when the large British soldier threw one of the partisans into the stream. Werner admired the English Anglo-Saxon heritage and could understand why the Führer respected such a small nation which had once controlled a large portion of the globe. Werner acknowledged their battlefield prowess and frustratingly stubborn tenacity. His father had spoken with admiration of the British, whom he had fought during the Great War all those years ago.

As the commotion on the bridge calmed down, Werner faintly heard the arrival of aircraft over his shoulder. The drone got louder, quickly morphing into a familiar scream. High-explosive cannon shells rippled among the British and partisans. The large soldier launched himself into the stream. Bombs from other Stukas straddled the enemy positions high up on the hill. The explosions flicked bodies aside like rag dolls. It was time. 'Open fire!' commanded Werner. The two designated MG 34 teams opened up, long, steady, rippling streams of belt ammunition fighting to feed the insatiable appetite of the machine guns. The tracer element ignited at the base of the rounds, helping Werner to observe them splashing among the enemy and Cretans.

Those caught in the open were like ants after a rock had been lifted, randomly scattering. At a distance of about two hundred metres, Werner couldn't count the hits, not even through his binoculars, but a number of British and Cretans fell, not getting back up. In his left peripheral vision he spotted Bassom's assault group dashing across the open ground, making for the stream at a sprint. Werner's gun teams kept the fire mercilessly pouring in among the British and Cretans. The British began retreating back up the hill, torn between fighting the infantry assault and monitoring the marauding swarm of Stukas that preyed on them from above.

With the upper slopes of the feature being pulverized by his air support, and Werner's machine-gun teams saturating the enemy, Bassom waded into the stream, his men flanking him as they fought to exploit the enemy confusion. With his lungs burning through the effort of the sprint from the olive grove, and the nervous anticipation of battle coursing through his exhausted body, Bassom found his energy quickly sapped by the water. At just over thigh deep, it might just as well have been a stream of treacle. Most of the enemy troops that had been on and around the bridge had found cover on the lower slopes, some in rock clusters not far up. Bassom and his men began firing at them. It seemed to work, keeping the enemy pinned down. Bassom had his eye on some rocks close to the stream. It wouldn't be the best cover in the world, but it was better than standing in the stream to fight. 'Come on, men!' he roared. 'Get

among the rocks! Quickly, don't stop, don't stop!' A few
of his men staggered past him.

'They're at the stream, they're at the stream,' screamed
Bentley, fighting to catch his breath as he scrambled
like a maniac up the lower slopes of the hill. 'Turn and
fight, turn and fight.'

A number of Bentley's men spun and fired at the
enemy, who were wading through the stream. Due to
panic and their heavy breathing the British shooting
was impatient and wild, their shots going high or wide.
But the German return fire was no better, their rounds
snapping past, kicking up stone and turf, rounds screaming as they glanced off the rocks. 'Get among the rocks!'
Hallmark roared. 'Move, move!' He continued shouting,
since some of his men were still out in the open firing at
the German paratroopers, who were beginning to filter
into the lowermost rock clusters.

An explosion knocked Hallmark flat, along with the
majority of his men. The wind had been knocked out of
him, his ears screaming in protest. With his head spinning, he climbed back to his feet and decided to withdraw
towards the summit, where the Australian positions were.

When Hallmark reached the first Australian positions, he was horrified at the sight of an unmanned
Vickers machine-gun emplacement. The machine gun
looked intact, but the crew was nowhere to be seen. The
command and control position, marked by a canvas
sheet, was empty too. It looked as though no Australians

remained among the summit positions. Hallmark turned, looking down the slope. Mercifully, his men seemed to have followed his lead, scrambling up the slope, even those who had briefly found cover below. Behind them, he could see German helmets bobbing. He knew his priority was to get as many of his men as possible into the positions that had been occupied by the Australians. He considered getting the Vickers into action, but his own men were between him and the Germans.

A hail of Stuka cannon fire erupted across the entire frontage of the positions around the summit. Hallmark was knocked to the rear of the Vickers position, his face and hands smarting. He hadn't been hit by shrapnel, but by rock and timber fragments. His hearing was just a muffled throb once again.

As Hallmark kept himself low on the ground, he was joined by some men, but they seemed few compared to the number he had seen scrambling up the slope. He raised his head, looking down the hill. Some of his lads were slumped lifeless on the slope. Those wounded were rolling from side to side, groaning and sobbing. As much as Hallmark wanted to go out and get them, he knew he couldn't risk it. Germans helmets were moving among the rocks just below them. He picked out a couple of the men. 'You and you,' he ordered, 'get that Vickers firing on them rocks down there. Move.'

Bentley was with a group in a rock cluster on the slope between the Germans and the Vickers gun emplacement. He had watched a Stuka strafe the Australian positions around the summit. He saw dead and dying men out in the open and, like Hallmark, thought better of trying to go to them.

With the enemy not far behind, Bentley knew he had to get his men higher. 'Fall back!' he screamed. 'Fall back!' But he wasn't too sure where they could fall back to. Not that it mattered. The men around him were busy shooting at the enemy below. He thought about grabbing some of them by their collars, but Vickers machine-gun fire interrupted him. The fire came from above and to the right, the bullets whizzing past his position. The Germans took whatever cover they could find, bullets screaming and snapping in all directions. Without prompting, Bentley's men got up and began running up the hill.

Near the top Bentley tumbled behind another cluster of rocks. As he got his bearings, he caught sight of Australian troops tending to their wounded and a soldier screaming into a radio handset for fire support. There were some who looked fit to fight, but they were hugging the rocks, trying to make themselves inconspicuous to the circling Stukas. 'Never mind the Stukas,' an irate and sweaty Australian NCO shouted. 'We've got Germans coming up the hill. Get up and fight.'

Bassom fought to make sense of the chaos developing above him. He somehow needed to get his men up into the positions around the summit. He knew some of them had been hit as they advanced across the stream, but they had all made it to the lower rock clusters, so he had initially hoped their wounds weren't too serious. But he had managed to see some of the wounded, and it had been clear that not all of them could get further up the hill. A decision was taken to leave the wounded armed with carbines, with heavier weapons such as MP 40s being given those fit to fight. At least the wounded would be able to fire at the British positions and give the assault some support.

Stukas came swinging down again, shooting up the top of the hill. The machine-gun fire pinning the Germans down stopped. Bassom started up the hill, his men following. He hoped Werner had his MG 34 teams in a position to help with what should be the final assault. As they advanced, Bassom's men fought with all the characteristics of German paratroopers: they were energetic, darting from rock to rock, snapping shots off at the positions above them. Their fighting spirit was buoyed by the Stukas' devastating cannon fire. Bassom hoped his men would carry the day. Radio on his back, firing short controlled bursts from his MP 40, Stolz followed him everywhere he went.

The Stuka attack ended, and the heavy machine-gun fire recommenced from the summit, forcing Bassom and his men to hunker down again among the rocks, pinned down, unable to fire back. Bassom and Stolz scrambled left, trying to establish precisely where the fire was coming from. Bassom peered out from behind cover and caught a muzzle flash up by the summit, along with dust kicking up.

'A machine-gun crew has survived the Stuka attacks. We need Werner to hurry up and deal with them.'

From his position away from the lines of fire, Werner enjoyed a panoramic view of the battle. His MG 34 teams were pummelling positions on the summit. Over to his left, two of the assault force were carefully making their way around a large rock formation. Fairly close by, Werner noticed an enemy position not being fired upon by his men, a machine-gun position. The gun stopped, probably for the crew to resolve a technical issue, perhaps an ammunition belt change. 'Don't just sit there, Bassom,' Werner muttered to himself. 'Get up the hill, damn you.'

Some of Hallmark's men occupying the overcrowded machine-gun position were wounded, but none of them too badly. Others were tending to them. The Vickers crew was firing down the hill. Needing to establish the situation on the summit in general, Hallmark decided to risk a dash to a large rock cluster nearby.

As Hallmark rolled behind the rocks, he made sure he kept his head down. He didn't want to give the Germans a target. If they wanted him, they would have to grow a pair of balls and get their arses into the trench with him. He realized two rather shell-shocked Australians were crouched next to him. 'Who's in command here?' he demanded.

'Captain Farrell, but he got hit when we got strafed. He's in a bad way. Sergeant Carmichael is wounded too.'

Looking around, Hallmark realized that quite a few more men were in the position. He wondered if Colonel Austin was still around. 'OK. Are you two wounded?'

'No, we are OK.'

'Right, then. Stay with these guys and engage those bastards coming up the hill. My guys on a Vickers have them pinned down in the rocks. Support them.' The two Australians nodded. He was glad to see a few more British soldiers make it to the top of the hill. He then noticed Bentley with the new British arrivals, trying to establish some semblance of order among them. A few men moved to the front of the position, beginning to fire down the hill. Bentley was growing a pair, Hallmark had to give him that. Bentley began talking to a man with his head in bandages. Hallmark guessed he was an Australian. To his astonishment, Hallmark then noticed an unmanned Vickers machine gun, set up to point down the hill. He guessed the crew had abandoned it, afraid of attracting the attention of the Stukas. He grabbed the first two men he came across, guessing again they were Australian. He ordered them to man the Vickers. They obeyed without question. 'If anything moves below us, shoot at it,' he told them. The order was simple. In theory, even a panicking man would remember it.

Bassom watched as a storm of MG 34 fire hit the British machine-gun position that had fired down the hill at his men. The fire was devastating, smashing the weapon and those manning it. Now was the time. Bassom spun round to face Stolz. 'Have all the men follow me.'

As Stolz moved away to spread the message, Bassom quickly headed for the destroyed machine-gun position. A few metres from it, Bassom pulled Werner's hot and heavy Swastika flag from his smock, and fought to unfold it. He laid it flat on the slope, pinning it down with rocks, tufts of grass, anything his hands found. Werner's MG 34 machine guns opened up again, but the fire came nowhere near the flag.

Bassom got up onto his hands and knees and peered up as high as he dared. He detected movement in the machine-gun position, then heard voices. He knew now was the time to assault the position, but as he prepared two stick grenades, he was suddenly aware of how exposed he was. He heard movement below him. Stolz was leading the remainder of the assault force up to join him. Bassom tossed the first grenade into the enemy position, quickly followed by the second. As the grenades clattered off rocks, there were panicked shouts from the enemy. The first grenade detonated, its concussion pulsing with such force that all those in the enemy position grunted, the life punched from their bodies. After the second grenade exploded, those who were by sheer chance still alive would have been greeted by a horrifying sight no soldier wants to see – enemy infantry storming into their position.

*

Hallmark had finally got to Bentley, who explained that he had been trying to establish the situation around the summit from a wounded Australian platoon commander. The platoon had been almost completely destroyed by the Stukas. The lieutenant had explained they had been withdrawing towards the summit when the Stukas hit them. They had not run away, he emphasized; they had merely been trying to trade space for time.

Tiring of the detail of Bentley's tale, Hallmark grabbed him by the shoulder. 'Sir, glad to see you are still in one piece. We need to withdraw. We must do it in two parts. Do you understand?' Bentley nodded as panicked voices sounded closeby. 'I have a Vickers gun in a position nearby. My guys will cover you. Lead the rest up to the positions on the summit. No messing about, just get the hell up there. Understood?' Bentley was silent. 'Ready, sir? Just run your arse off, up to the next position.'

Bentley nodded then pointed to a few Cretans. To their credit, the Cretans were standing shoulder to shoulder with the men facing down the hill.

Hallmark was suddenly punched in the gut by two pulses of concussion in quick succession. Grenades. As he staggered forward, trying to regain his composure, he was stunned by the sight of a few guys from his Vickers gun emplacement running towards the summit. The Germans were among the Australian positions now. He guessed the men running up the hill had got out before the two grenades went off.

Amid crates of ammunition and discarded weapons, a Bren light machine gun caught his attention.

Before the dust had settled from Bassom's stick grenades, two of his men were already scrambling into the stricken British Vickers emplacement. Those not killed by the grenade attack were shot as they attempted to either fight back or surrender. Now was not the time for prisoners of war. Bassom and Stolz followed the men into the enemy position. Bassom saw some enemy soldiers running for the summit. Knowing they must have escaped before his grenades went off, he shot at them. He had no idea if he hit them, but his priority was to make sure they kept running away.

The first two men into the enemy position were reloading as others piled in. Bassom looked at the carnage surrounding him. The enemy had been pulverized by the grenade attack. The machine-gun team was just a shattered mess. The last of Bassom's men moved into the enemy position, bringing the Swastika flag with him. He dropped it at Bassom's feet. The captain thought it didn't matter for now. As far as MG 34 fire was concerned, Werner would be aware of Bassom's position. The Stukas were a different matter, but they hadn't attacked for a while. Bassom decided he should clear all the positions around the summit as quickly as possible. The Stuka support was limited. He turned to Stolz. 'Follow me and bring the flag.'

As Stolz began to stuff the flag inside his smock, a

large figure appeared above them all, carrying a machine gun. Bassom turned in time to watch a number of his men crumple under a hail of bullets. Stolz staggered, then he fell. The left side of Bassom's head hurt like hell. He tried to point his weapon up at the lone, large figure, but it had vanished. Bassom fell among dead and dying men, his head screaming. Pain overwhelmed his body.

'Fall back now, sir,' shouted Hallmark as he lifted the heavy Bren with ease. A fresh magazine was already on the weapon. 'Go, go, go,' he reiterated urgently. He held the Bren at hip level as he advanced on the Vickers gun emplacement his men once held.

'Corporal Hallmark, come back here,' yelled Bentley, although he had to admit that Hallmark, who was already firing it in short, chugging bursts, made fighting with the Bren look effortless. Hallmark stood over the Vickers emplacement and emptied the magazine into it, then spun away, heading back to the Australian positions.

'Sergeant, we have troops moving towards the summit,' one of Werner's MG 34 machine-gunners called out.

'Hang on, let me see,' Werner acknowledged, putting binoculars to his eyes. He quickly focused on the newly identified enemy machine-gun position. With dust and debris drifting all around it, he couldn't be sure who was in there. He had noticed the Swastika flag pinned to the ground in front of the captured rock cluster, marking the progress of Bassom's assault force, but now it had been removed. He had also seen Bassom dive into the position, followed by his men, so assumed the enemy machine gun was in German hands. But he was unsure who the soldiers running up towards the summit were. He decided that he would no longer be able to fire on the enemy positions close to the summit until he received some sort of signal from Bassom, indicating his progress.

'Sir?' Bassom heard someone say to him. 'Captain, can you hear me?' The tired, sweaty and dusty face of a parachutist swam into focus. He was looking down at Bassom. 'Sir, are you able to move?'

'I . . . I think so,' managed Bassom, looking around the newly acquired machine-gun emplacement. It seemed quiet.

'You have the luck of the gods, sir.' The parachutist grinned.

Bassom frowned, which caused him to wince. 'Really?'

The paratrooper held up a helmet with a deep gouge running down the left side. Daylight was visible through the long tear. Bassom took the helmet, which he realized was his, and rubbed the long rip with his filthy fingers. Instinctively, he put his hand to his head. It was throbbing as if he had been hit with a hammer. 'The bullet didn't even give you a haircut, sir.' Bassom sat up carefully. He realized he had trouble turning his head. The parachutist knelt over him. 'The bullet ripped the helmet off your head. You're lucky your neck wasn't broken.'

Bassom gave the parachutist a questioning look. 'What happened here?'

'The British counter-attacked. Hit a few boys around you and clipped the side of your head. I'm afraid we lost Corporal Stolz. The radio set is useless too.' The loss of Stolz hit Bassom hard. Another good soldier gone, not to mention the only radio. Bassom would feel the loss of any of his men, he just happened to know Stolz better than most of them. 'It looks as though we have the positions at this level, sir,' continued the parachutist. 'The British have fallen back to the summit. They left lots of weapons and ammunition lying around, including an intact Vickers machine gun. They left some rations too. Our boys are really hungry.'

Bassom nodded, which made him wince again. 'Good work. Where is the flag?'

'We left it in Corporal Stolz's smock, sir. None of the boys want to touch him. He doesn't look good.'

'Where is he?'

'Not too far from here, with our other dead, plus those of the enemy. Some enemy dead are partisans.'

'Partisans?'

'A few of them were fighting with the British. This place was a mess, so our boys took care of the dead quickly. We also have wounded men, enemy and ours. I think one of the enemy wounded is an officer.'

Bassom pulled himself to his feet. Carefully, he put his fractured helmet back on. The left side of his head stung, and his neck creaked as he did up his chinstrap.

'I will see the officer shortly, but first we need to mark our position for the Stuka pilots and Sergeant Werner's team.'

The soldier nodded and walked away. Bassom observed that some of his men were watching the summit, while others rested and ate. Unsteady on his feet, he held on to a large rock. He noticed the wrecked Vickers machine gun had been removed. It had been good to learn that an undamaged Vickers had been recovered. His men had been trained on enemy weapons, and would soon be employing it against its former owners. The dead were neatly stacked. All were in a sorry state. Stolz was on top, his lower jaw shot away, staring sightlessly at the Cretan sky. Bassom knew he couldn't afford to dwell on the sight, but was forced to unzip Stolz's smock and pull the blood-soaked Swastika flag out. For some reason, he closed the smock as if he didn't want Stolz to get cold.

Both German and enemy wounded sat around, smoking cigarettes and nursing their wounds. In many cases, their dressings were already saturated. An enemy radio remained intact, but gave out nothing but a constant hiss. Bassom decided someone should look at it, as it might be of some use. He noticed an aloof-looking enemy soldier, his head wrapped in bandages. Perhaps he was the officer referred to by the parachutist in the Vickers gun emplacement. Bassom chanced a nod at the enemy soldier, who returned the compliment.

Bassom climbed out of the rocks, unfolded the flag

and laid it on a parapet, pinning it down with stones. Werner and the Stukas would be able to see the marker, but the irony of using a bullet-ridden flag stained with German blood wasn't lost on Bassom. The captain was glad his men were resting, knowing they would need to push on to the summit once Werner arrived and the MG 34 teams had rested a little. Until then, the presence of the flag meant the Stukas would be able to attack the summit at will.

At the summit with Bentley and the British, Australian and Cretan survivors, Hallmark surveyed the Australian positions. The scene was one of utter horror. Many of the positions were smouldering from direct Stuka bomb hits. Australian dead littered the open ground between the positions. Few of the dead were in one piece. Those not wounded were on guard with the Cretans, watching the slopes. Bentley joined Hallmark. 'What are you thinking, Corporal?'

'Hang on,' Hallmark replied. He spied two Australians carrying one of their own off the summit and down the reverse slope. He suddenly thought that was where the survivors on the summit should go. A Stuka swept in but didn't fire its cannon or drop any ordnance. It passed in a sweeping arc, pulling out of its dive effortlessly. Hallmark wondered if the pilot knew who was where. As far as the Stuka attacks were concerned, Hallmark knew time was limited. He clapped a large hand on Bentley's shoulder, pointing towards the two fast-disappearing Australians. 'We are going that way. Get ourselves down the reverse slope.'

'Who will hold the top if we fall back there?'

Hallmark grinned. 'The Germans will, sir.'

Bentley frowned. 'That is not amusing, Corporal Hallmark.'

Hallmark waved a paw. 'Sir, the Germans have air support. We don't. If we stay here, the Germans will come up the slope, but they won't until we are pretty much pounded to dust by the Stukas. The Stukas have been running in from the east only. They have strict air control measures. They won't risk flying over Heraklion or the airfield, in case of ground fire. If we were on the reverse slope, the Stukas wouldn't see us because it is only visible from the town side. And the Australians down there have disappeared, so the lower reaches of the reverse slope aren't visible from here either. Get me?'

Bentley mulled it over. He couldn't help but feel a little inadequate in Hallmark's presence. The man knew how to read a battle.

'If we go soon,' continued Hallmark, 'we'll avoid the Stukas and have time to dig in properly on the reverse slope. The Germans won't venture down from here, because they will have no idea of our numbers. They are hurt and tired, just like us. So let's get ready to go.'

Bentley wasn't sure he entirely understood but nodded his agreement.

14

Bentley Paine passed the word to move from the summit. With the Stukas still high in the sky, Bentley's shattered patrol dashed en masse down the reverse slope with the remaining Cretans and Australians, the summit abandoned except for a few badly wounded men who couldn't travel.

It wasn't long before a fighting position came into view. Its Australian occupants raised their weapons but recognized friendly forces. Upon reaching the position, numerous other crude emplacements came into view behind it, built out of various-sized boulders and sandbags. The Australians occupying them were ready to fight. The men from the summit were waved through, Bentley pointed in the direction of a makeshift headquarters position. John Hallmark followed him, gesturing to the others to spread out and reinforce the other Australian positions. The Cretans walked away, not wishing to participate further. Hallmark was pleased to see them go. He realized the Cretans were only enthusiastic when all was going well. With the Germans now on the offensive, they were concerned to save their own skins.

Hallmark and Bentley found Colonel Austin at the Australian headquarters position, built from a combination of rocks and canvas sheets. It provided protection from the sun, if nothing else. Their arrival had been in good time; a Stuka was strafing the summit. Hallmark worried about the wounded left there. A radio man had a handset to his ear, and Austin didn't look too pleased. Bentley dreaded what the colonel might have in mind for them next. 'All right, Captain,' Austin began. 'What have the Germans got coming up the hill?'

Bentley took his helmet off, allowing his scalp to breathe. Hallmark refrained from doing the same, keeping a firm grip on his newly acquired Bren gun. 'We are looking at company strength,' Bentley unknowingly grossly overestimated, 'give or take. It wasn't their numbers that caused us to fall back, it was the Stukas. Their infantry moved up pretty much unchallenged, right up until they fought their way into our positions.'

'They will no doubt move up onto the summit shortly,' remarked the colonel. 'I know I would, if I were them. Later we will exploit the darkness to keep them on the back foot. We can't allow them to settle up there.'

'No, sir,' Bentley agreed, dreading the thought of a night patrol to the summit.

'Paine,' continued Austin, 'I have already briefed up my company commanders on fighting patrols on the summit during the hours of darkness. The Stukas will have gone by then, so the German infantry will have to hold the summit on their own until first light. You and your men will remain in reserve here. You guys have been in no-man's land long enough. Time to get my boys into the fight. After what they experienced up on the summit, they will want some payback for their mates.'

Austin's words sent a wave of relief washing through Bentley. Hallmark could tell that Bentley had not played poker much, as he failed to hide his pleasure at the colonel's orders. By contrast, Hallmark didn't give any of his feelings away; seasoned soldiers could appear unfazed even when they weren't.

'Sir,' Bentley chanced, looking at the radio, 'do you think it would be out of the question for my platoon at Brigade Headquarters to be released, to come and reinforce us?'

Austin looked puzzled. 'I have no idea. Why did you leave them there?'

'We encountered enemy parachutists forming up in a copse near our headquarters buildings. They were the only parachutists nearby to survive the drop, but we couldn't risk leaving our position exposed, sir.' He thought he didn't need to explain who had given the orders back then, thinking Austin could well write him up favourably after the battle.

Austin took the handset from his radio man. 'Yankee One One Bravo. This is Alpha One One Bravo, over.'

There was silence. Austin repeated the call. Suddenly, the handset exploded. 'Any call signs, this is Brigade Headquarters. We are being overrun. Divert any spare manpower to our loca—'

Bentley was wide-eyed. Austin looked calm and

methodical. 'Hello, Brigade Headquarters, this is Colonel Austin. Tell me what's happening.' Radio protocol went out of the window as soon as someone was in trouble. Information needed to be clear and unadorned in order to save time and lives.

There was only silence. After what felt like a lifetime, Austin handed the handset to his radio man. 'The platoon commander there?' he asked Bentley.

'Mr Thatcher, Arnie Thatcher, sir. Four Platoon.'

'Well, let's hope Arnie and his boys are kicking those paratroopers out of the headquarters.'

Martin Bassom, his head and neck still smarting, allowed Sergeant Werner and his four MG 34 machine-gun teams a brief rest once they had joined him in the enemy positions on the upper slopes. As noon approached, the Stuka air support had waned, but Bassom was keen to get up to the summit before the enemy could regain the initiative and perhaps counter-attack. Werner, sweating profusely from his climb, draped in belt ammunition for the MG 34s, gulped greedily from his water bottle. His gun teams also rehydrated while stripping down the acquired British Vickers gun kit for future use.

A lightly armed but well equipped force took the lead towards the summit, just in case the British had left an ambush force behind to hamper the German ascent. The heavy Vickers was left behind, together with some other acquired weapons and ammunition.

The dead strewn all across the summit were quickly

identified as Australian. A few wounded had also been left, clearly unable to withdraw. They waved their surrender to the German paratroopers, fearful of execution.

Bassom pointed to some of his men. 'Tend to those men. Try and use their dressings and supplies.' His men treated the enemy as professionally as available supplies allowed. He was pleased to see them share cigarettes with the wounded, their former adversaries. Regardless of nationality and cause, they were all just boys. Bassom knew the British wouldn't leave men behind intentionally. This realization made the captain think the enemy were not in great shape.

Werner had already begun siting his MG 34 teams on the flanks of the crude defensive position that was slowly forming on the summit. Two teams set up facing down the slope towards the stream and the olive grove. The other two teams left their MG 34s, returning to the previously held positions to collect the acquired equipment and Vickers. No one yet wanted to even look down the reverse slope. No one knew the strength of the enemy, but everyone at the summit knew how low their own numbers were now.

Werner eventually positioned the other two MG 34 teams overlooking the reverse slope. It was, after all, the most likely direction of an enemy attack. There weren't enough men left to form a reserve force, but a few parachutists were allocated to reinforce the MG 34 teams, Bassom and Werner sitting in the middle of it all, the Swastika flag marker pinned by rocks to the ground next to them. Werner offered Bassom a tour of the new positions. Bassom accepted, keen to see how his men were. Given the circumstances, the men were all smiles, if tired. Some were a little emotional, which Werner tended to come down on. Bassom saw right through him. Werner did it to mask his own fears and doubts. Only bullies made an issue out of weakness.

Bassom ordered his men to move the enemy dead on the summit to the slope facing the olive grove and stream, worried that the sight of dead men, even enemy dead, might sap morale. He sat with Werner, watching the grisly task being completed. In the distance, they could see Heraklion airfield and the Greek barracks before it, and the town of Heraklion itself. The Stukas were now preying on the enemy troops at the barracks and the airfield. Bassom carefully peeled his helmet from his throbbing head, gingerly touching the graze along the left side of his skull. Werner told him the graze probably looked worse than it was. Content his head was not about to fall apart, Bassom relaxed a little, briefly enjoying the cool breeze that had picked up slightly during the brilliant, cloudless afternoon.

Bassom began to doze. His paratroopers savoured the contents of their water bottles and ate the enemy rations they had acquired, before beginning to nod off as well.

Bassom suddenly snapped awake with a start, throwing an apologetic glance at Werner. 'Apologies, Sergeant. My moment of bliss got the better of me.'

Bassom shuffled into a more upright sitting position, but Werner wasn't even looking at him. He remained perched on a rock, helmet on, MP 40 in both hands, watching the battle in the distance. The Stukas were no longer to be seen. 'Don't worry, sir,' replied Werner. 'The enemy will not attack for the remainder of the day. But they will try their luck in the dark, make no mistake.' He looked back at Bassom. 'By then our air cover will be back on the mainland for showers, cognac and cigars.'

Bassom knew Werner was correct. 'Sergeant, I want minimum manpower on watch until last light. All those not on watch are to sleep as much as possible. I want everyone alert through the hours of darkness. You are right. The British will come. We must be ready for them.'

Werner nodded and set off to pass the word. Bassom cursed that their only radio had been destroyed. How to let Colonel Veck know that the high ground was now in German hands? Maybe the Stuka pilots had passed on the presence of the flag to Veck, but Bassom wondered if it might be better placed on the reverse slope, where there was a chance Veck would spot it through binoculars. Bassom clambered to his feet and strode over to the dusty flag, still pinned flat to the ground. Kicking the rocks out of the way, he pulled the sorry-looking flag up by one hand, dragging it behind him as he went in search of a better place for the thing. He cared little for any of his men's opinions, Werner's especially, if they took offence at his treatment of their flag. As far as Bassom was concerned, it was just a dusty, blood-splattered rag, which only had the merit of a signal.

The flag now half-stuffed into his smock, Bassom saw

a suitable location for it on the reverse slope beyond the MG 34 teams sited there. He almost headed straight out onto the slope, before realizing fatigue was clouding his judgement. It would be foolish to expose himself to whatever the enemy might have sited below. He didn't even have his helmet on. As he slowly pushed his head out from cover, he saw the lower slopes first. He had to lean out further to see the upper slopes.

Everything looked quiet, so he decided to get on with it. He clambered around the large, north-facing rocks that had provided his cover, then quickly scoured the area for large stones to keep the flag in place. Once he had found a few good ones, he pulled the flag from his smock, fighting with it in the stiffening, dust-filled breeze. He smoothed the flag flat against a small rock face, using stones to pin it to the top. He tried to secure the bottom of the flag, but found it impossible, the breeze flicking the lower edge up and down. It wasn't ideal, but perhaps the fluttering of the flag might attract Veck's attention. It might of course also attract the attention of the enemy, but Bassom decided to risk that.

Bassom walked back to his original position between the MG 34 gun crews. Werner was waiting for him. 'Where have you been, sir?' He frowned, more fatherly than suspicious. 'Where is the flag?'

Bassom sat with him. 'We have no radio, Sergeant. I need the colonel to know we have the high ground.'

Werner was confused as to how the captain had used the flag to achieve his aim, but after Bassom explained what he had done, Werner raised his eyebrows and nodded. 'Aha. I see, sir. Good thinking.'

Bassom didn't dignify this patronizing remark with a response. 'Are the men on maximum rest now?'

Werner nodded as he stuffed some ration chocolate into his mouth. It was a little while before he responded. 'Yes, sir. I have two out of the four '34 teams on watch, and a few other boys wandering around. Everyone else has been told to sleep as much as possible. They will switch on an hourly basis until last light.'

Bassom nodded as he got comfortable enough to allow his heavy eyelids to get the better of him. Just as sleep was about to seduce him, a distant explosion sounded. As the afternoon drew to a close, the Stukas were disappearing, but one had found its mark. As Bassom dropped off, he reminded himself that the British and their Commonwealth allies gave nothing away cheaply. With no German air support throughout the night, he thought an attempt to retake the summit was a certainty.

The soundtrack of sporadic fighting faded to the back of Bassom's mind. Thoughts of his parents and his brother Karl took centre stage in a vivid kaleidoscope of images from days gone by. If it wasn't for the fact that Bassom was exhausted, he would have been overwhelmed with homesickness. To Captain Martin Bassom, home had never felt so far away.

Heraklion was smouldering in the distance behind them as Bentley and Hallmark were summoned to Colonel

Austin's position among the rocks. As Bentley arrived, he could just make out the colonel in dialogue with a sorry-looking soldier who looked almost fit to drop. The soldier seemed emotional and crestfallen. Austin patted him on the shoulder, and the dishevelled soldier took his leave, a radio operator in tow, which made Bentley think that he might well have been one of Austin's officers. Bentley found it difficult to tell who was who in the Australian contingent, as they were all a scruffy bunch. An Australian soldier acknowledged Bentley and Hallmark and nudged the colonel. Now in conversation with his radio man, Austin turned with a stern look on his face. 'In you come, Captain. You too, Corporal.'

Bentley and Hallmark clambered in beside Austin. Bentley sensed all was not well. 'Captain Clarkson,' Austin began, 'who you must have seen leaving just a moment ago, managed to get in touch with your Brigade Headquarters. They have been overrun.' Bentley and Hallmark groaned aloud. Austin nodded. 'They had to fight their way out of the buildings. Your platoon, Captain –' he stared into Bentley's eyes '– fought as hard as they could to protect the position. The Germans in the copse were not the assaulting force. A group of enemy troops managed to get around the airfield, which we still hold, and assault the buildings.' Bentley looked down. He couldn't believe it.

'Who do we have on the airfield, sir?' Hallmark asked Austin.

'A Scottish battalion, the Black Watch. They've been fighting to hang on to the control tower and hangars.

The Germans want that bloody airfield badly.' Hallmark glanced at Bentley, who seemed stunned. Austin noticed it too. He leaned in and put a hand on Bentley's shoulder. He looked up, his eyes glazed. Bentley shuddered, knowing that chance could have seen him stay with 4 Platoon at Brigade Headquarters because of his lack of experience. 'We are to withdraw into Heraklion,' said Austin. 'Tonight, apparently.'

The news snapped Bentley out of his self-pity. 'Withdraw? Really?'

'Yeah, but I can't just tell my guys to turn tail and run. I need to keep those bastards on top of the hill occupied until we are in a good enough position to break clean and get back into the town.' Bentley wondered why they couldn't just move down the reverse slope into the fields under the cover of darkness. Their current position wasn't visible from the summit, so the initial stage of any retreat would be unobservable. Bentley wondered if Austin had a dangerous personal agenda regarding the hill. 'Evacuation from the harbour is already beginning to take place,' said Austin. Bentley tried to hide another shudder. He had seen boats moving in Heraklion harbour and knew the Stukas had been bombing them. 'News from the Maleme sector,' Austin continued, 'is that the Germans have taken the airfield and are pouring in reinforcements.'

'Wow,' responded Hallmark, a little louder than he intended.

Austin stifled a grunt. 'Wow indeed. The enemy are

pushing steadily east along the coast, smashing anyone who tries to halt their advance. Their strength increases with each group of paratroopers they encounter from the original drops. If we lose Heraklion, we will be stuck on this godforsaken rock.'

Hallmark ground his teeth and puffed his chest out. 'What precisely do you want us to do, sir?'

Bentley looked at Hallmark in disbelief. Surely he wasn't going to offer a fighting patrol to the summit to cover the withdrawal? 'Corporal,' Austin replied, 'all I want your guys to do is get down to the Greek barracks and sit tight there.' Relief coursed through Bentley. 'My men will harass the enemy above us,' continued Austin, 'long enough for everyone to withdraw safely, and join you there. We'll withdraw under cover of darkness, and we'll all be at the barracks by first light. We need to have the Germans thinking that we want the summit back. By the time they come to realize what we are up to, we will be off this hill. They can have the bastard, as far as I'm concerned. But they are going to pay for it, mark my words.'

Bentley felt better at the thought of getting that bit closer to Heraklion. He didn't want to miss the ships leaving, no doubt for Egypt. He might be new to the regiment, but he would have a few choice words to say to Captain Long, the regimental adjutant. What had Long been thinking, sending Bentley on an assignment like this? Bentley could feel himself seething at the sheer incompetence of his masters.

Bentley's anger was short-lived. Hallmark nudged his

arm. There was a commotion nearby. In the worsening light, Bentley saw a number of men moving across the slope. They were Cretans and had for some reason brought their women and children with them. Hallmark rolled his eyes. He'd had enough of the locals.

Seeing both Bentley and Hallmark were distracted, Austin snapped his fingers. 'After last light, Captain, I want you to tip your hat to me and then get your arse down to the barracks. Do you understand?'

'Yes, Colonel.' Bentley nodded.

'Remember,' warned Austin, 'there are German paratroopers scattered all over the place, so ensure you're in a decent state to defend yourselves. We'll join you at the barracks by the morning, OK?'

Bentley and Hallmark nodded. Austin held out his hand. 'Good luck. I intend to see your ugly faces again.'

They both shook his hand. Hallmark flicked his head towards the Cretans. 'What of the locals, sir?'

'Now that they are here,' Austin replied, 'they can bloody well help out, can't they? If the men want to go up the hill, guns blazing, far be it for us to stop them defending their homeland, eh?'

Bentley and Hallmark clambered out of the headquarters position, peering at the rabble of Cretans. Hallmark was horrified to see that even the women and children were armed with German weapons and kitchen knives. 'For heaven's sake,' he hissed. 'Kids?'

Bentley waved a dismissive hand. 'This is their country.' Hallmark chose not to say anything. He couldn't guarantee he would hold his tongue if Bentley came out with any more nonsense. Hallmark knew he was happy with the move to the barracks, but what Bentley was forgetting was that no withdrawal was a safe option. As the colonel had pointed out, there were German paratroopers all over the place. The risk of ambush was present, no matter what direction you moved in. The German ambush in the olive grove was a perfect example. The move to the barracks would only be successfully completed once they had approached it silently and cleared the buildings.

As the sun was setting, Werner checked their positions around the summit, ensuring all the men were awake and ready to fight. Bassom watched him from his central position among the rocks, admiring his methodical approach. Politics and values aside, Bassom had to acknowledge the professionalism of the sergeant. He didn't have to like him. He just had to work with the man.

Before long Werner rejoined Bassom. The captain put his helmet on. The side of his head continued to throb somewhat. The graze carved by the bullet had seeped a little; the fluid had dried, matting with dust and his filthy hair. It would just have to be taken care of at a later date. He reflected on how lucky he had been. An inch to the left, and the bullet would have penetrated his skull, and it would have all been over. No more war, no more family, no more future. Nothing.

Werner held out some semi-melted chocolate. 'Not exactly fine dining, but better than nothing.'

Bassom accepted the chocolate and shoved it into his mouth. It tasted bitter and rough. Typical ration-pack chocolate. Not that he had much to compare it with. Chocolate had been a luxury while growing up on the dairy farm. He swallowed it reluctantly. 'Thanks. I never ate much chocolate as a child, I must confess.'

'Really?' replied Werner, looking genuinely interested.

Bassom nodded. 'We had it, but only as a treat at Christmas time.'

'I didn't taste chocolate until I joined the Hitler Youth. Even then it was rare.' An uncomfortable silence fell between them.

Bassom looked out over the panorama of rocks, trying his hardest to think of a way to divert the subject away from anything to do with current affairs and the Nazi Party. Bassom could see the domed helmets of his men in the approaching darkness. He quietly wondered what they were talking about – women, beer, leave or the lack of it? He just couldn't see himself socializing with the likes of Werner. In the meantime they waited for the sun to finally set and for the British, who would undoubtedly come.

En route to the Greek barracks in the darkness, Hallmark silently followed the rear of the battered British patrol column. In the heat and humidity, the march was slow and tiring. Every hundred metres or so, they would have to climb over a drystone wall. The walls criss-crossed the entire area between the hill and the barracks. Despite their exhaustion, they meticulously looked out for ambushes. Navigation using map or compass was not required, for the flames billowing out of the barrack buildings provided an excellent marker, although the flames impaired their night vision. The Stukas had hit the buildings hard and Hallmark was unsure whether they were fit to enter, let alone whether any Greeks were still occupying them. He was suddenly filled with dread at the prospect of the barracks already being occupied by the enemy. The patrol had no radio, so he decided to up his pace, moving forward along the column of dog-tired men to catch up with Bentley. Thankfully, just then the column staggered to a halt for a rest break, undoubtedly ordered by Bentley. As Hallmark moved among the men, he rebuked many for not resting in fighting positions, which made them easy prey for any lurking Germans.

Bentley was crouching down behind a wall, fighting the temptation to sit and close his eyes. He peered over the wall, scouring the barracks with his binoculars. The perimeter fence appeared intact. Most but not all of the buildings were on fire or badly damaged. A burning fleet of trucks sat on an open drill square among burning Nissen huts. A two-storey brick and stone structure and a single-storey wooden building were undamaged. Bentley thought the two-storey block would provide better cover for his men.

He felt someone approach him from behind. 'Is the fence still up?' Hallmark enquired. He had no binoculars of his own.

'So it would appear. I think there is a checkpoint

entrance behind the huts, on the far side of the barracks towards Heraklion.'

'Any sign of occupation?'

'I can't tell. Here, take a look.' Bentley handed his
binoculars over.

Hallmark pulled them up to his eyes and began to
scan back and forth. After a short while he handed them
back. 'I can't see any sentries about the place. As for the
big building, it doesn't appear to have anyone in or
around it. The enemy wouldn't be near the flaming
buildings, as the light would give them away. No one
needs to keep warm tonight.' Reminded of the oppres-
sive air, Bentley wiped the back of his sweat-soaked neck.
'We need to scout out the checkpoint,' advised Hallmark, 'if we are to get in there tonight. We don't want to
be caught in the open when the sun comes up. Those
bastard Stukas will be back, you can bank on that.'

'What do you recommend, Corporal?'

'Me plus three others for a scouting mission. We will
creep around to the right and see what state the checkpoint is in. We may not have seen any enemy in the
barracks, but that doesn't necessarily mean they aren't
in there.'

Hallmark picked the first three men he found, gathering them together. As he explained what he wanted
them to do, he noticed their heads were heavy, bobbing
up and down on occasion. They were trying to fight off
sleep. One by one, he slapped them on top of their helmets, snapping them out of their lethargy. 'Look sharp,'

he hissed. 'Once we have the barracks checked out, then we can all get some rest. Understood?'

They nodded, murmuring their apologies. Hallmark bit his lip. He knew they were shattered. The constant action had worn them down, as well as the relentless Cretan sun and uncomfortable nights. He felt soldiers operated better in cold climates, as it was easier to keep warm when moving about than to keep cool. A brisk night patrolling Salisbury Plain seemed worth its weight in gold.

Hallmark led the three men off in single file around the northern side of the barracks, and Bentley moved forward a little, wanting a better view of the Nissen huts. His men moved up with him. Telling them to wait, he cautiously clambered over another stone wall, finding a dead German paratrooper. The man was still in his harness, his parachute at the full extent of its rigging lines. It seemed that no one had tampered with the body. The cause of the German's death was easy to identify. All of his lower jaw and one side of his face was missing. He still had his MP 40 strapped under his harness, and his smock pockets bulged with their contents. Two stick grenades were secured under his webbing belt. It occurred to Bentley that the body may have been booby-trapped, the Germans now wise to the looting of the Cretans. He looked across the open field before him, wondering if any Germans could see him and were about to launch an ambush.

Hallmark and his three men encountered two dead German parachutists. They had died before landing.

Like the paratrooper found by Bentley, they still had all their equipment strapped to them, not looted by Cretans or stripped by their comrades for combat supplies. If the parachutists' comrades had encountered the bodies, they surely would have wrapped them in chutes. Hallmark arrived at the same conclusion as Bentley, silently summoning his three men to him. 'Leave any dead enemy be. They may be booby-trapped.'

Hallmark continued on at a slow, careful pace, his men following. Over the next stone wall and they would be directly in front of the checkpoint. Every few steps Hallmark paused. The stifled cough of a sentry or the aroma of a cigarette would be enough to confirm the presence of someone, although not necessarily a German. Even if a person appeared to be friendly, Hallmark would have to be careful. But from his current position, fifty metres from the checkpoint, the only sounds he could hear were those of sporadic battle off in the distance. He led his men forward once more to hunker down behind the final stone wall, taking the opportunity to drink some water.

Hallmark slipped off his steel helmet and placed it carefully on the rocky earth at his feet. Bareheaded, he slowly peered over the top of the wall, his Bren gun clutched in both hands. The checkpoint consisted of a lowered pole barrier and a sentry box, which appeared to be empty. Beyond the sentry box, the single-storey wooden building had been untouched by the Stukas. No lights glowed from within, indicating to the most casual observer that the place was unoccupied, but Hallmark still couldn't be sure. A little further beyond the wooden building loomed the two-storey stone and brick block – their proposed home, once he had ensured no other tenants were in there. He lowered himself back down behind the wall, relaxing his iron grip on the Bren, and waved his three men around him.

'We need to be sure the single-storey building is empty,' he hissed. He pointed to two of his men. 'I will leave the big block to you, while we go forward and check out the single-storey building, understood?' All three nodded. He gave the man who would accompany him his Bren gun, swapping it for the man's Sten. In the initial stages the man with the Bren would provide cover from the stone wall, before coming forward to join Hallmark. The big corporal pulled his helmet back on and slid over the wall.

Bentley realized that the dead German paratrooper was an officer. There could be useful information on the body. Taking a chance it was not booby-trapped, Bentley struggled in the low light to unclip the parachute harness. After fiddling with the release straps, he finally managed to loosen them enough to get access to the man's pockets. He emptied them carefully, finding a map and compass, binoculars, a flare gun, extra MP 40 magazines, cigarettes and chocolate. While feeling his way over the torso, Bentley made out a small block shape within. He slowly opened the zip of the smock and opened it wide. In an inside pocket, he found a small book. He opened it. It looked to be a diary. He had no clue what the handwritten text said, but could just about get to grips with the name written inside the front cover. Adrian Keich. He felt nothing for the man.

Suddenly, powerful hands grabbed Bentley around the throat and began to squeeze. The jawless German wheezed and rattled as he came back from the dead, struggling to ensure that if he was destined for hell, the enemy searching him was going too. Stunned, Bentley dropped the diary, fighting to release the grip of the desperate yet powerful German. Unable to pull the German's hands away, Bentley grabbed the blood-crusted neck of the dying paratrooper and squeezed as hard as he could. It was a race to the death. With elbows locked straight, Bentley put as much of his body weight behind his shoulders as he could and bore down on the German, who was now spluttering and gargling his life away, kicking and thrashing. Soon the strength in the German began to fade, the gargling and rattling growing louder. As the grip around his own throat lessened, Bentley pressed home his advantage. The German faded away, his final battle over.

Sweat poured from the tip of Bentley's nose as he recoiled at the fresh stench emitted by the paratrooper. He sat back against the stone wall, trying his hardest not to sob or vomit. He managed to fight off the nausea, but the sheer shock of the violence had him crying into his hands. His shoulders bounced as tears poured down his cheeks. He wanted to be home or, failing that, near Hallmark. Hallmark would make it all OK. For all his faults, Hallmark was his rock.

As his sweat cooled, he began to shiver. He felt so alone. But if there were Germans lurking in the shadows watching him, they would have revealed themselves and come to the aid of their comrade. As he gathered his thoughts, it suddenly dawned on him that he hadn't even called out for help. On the other side of the wall, his men would have just sat there. He dismissed this thought as a moment of weakness, his apparent self-reliance buoying his confidence. Bentley realized he did have it in him to fight. He looked at the dead German before recommencing his search.

Clambering to his feet, Bentley saw that a section of the perimeter fence had partially collapsed outwards, allowing access to the drill square. But Hallmark was already at the sentry box, which looked empty. A man with a Bren gun rushed forward to join him as two other men entered the two-storey building. Bentley thought the single-storey building might be a guardroom.

Careful not to touch the wall of the wooden building, Hallmark and the man with him listened for any sign of life within. Hallmark was in a dilemma. If he heard voices or movement within, would he announce his presence in case they were friendly troops? If there were Greek troops inside, would they even understand him? They might shoot anyway.

Hallmark approached the front door of the building,

which stood open at the top of a short flight of wooden steps. With his Sten ready, he led the way into the building, quickly realizing it was a guardroom. Half a dozen bunk beds had blankets tossed to one side. Paperwork was strewn about the large floor. Hallmark moved silently past empty rifle racks and peered through another doorway. The glare of the moon shone through high, steel-barred windows. Three doors lined the far wall, protecting what looked to be cells. Hallmark's man slid past him, methodically inspecting the cells. His shoulder shrugs indicated they were empty. They made their way back to the front door. 'This whole place is empty,' Hallmark said in a hushed voice.

'What about the bigger building?' his companion asked. 'Someone could be hiding in there.'

'No. Anyone, friend or foe, would have made themselves known by now. We haven't seen anyone. Let's get back to the lads and bring them in here for some rest.'

As they retraced their route back towards Bentley, Hallmark was distracted by flares bursting above the hill which they had evacuated the day before.

'Wake up, wake up,' hissed a voice.

A violent shove ripped Martin Bassom from a much-needed sleep. As both his vision and hearing cleared, he became aware of a blinding light in the sky and a fizzling sound. Blinking to get the red drifting blobs of the flare out of his vision, the steady drumbeat of Vickers machine-gun fire filled his ears. He focused on the dark profile of Sergeant Werner, who was hunkered down in front of him. 'What's happening?'

'The British have been probing us,' replied Werner. 'That flare was fired by one of our guys. Wait here.' As Werner scrambled out of the position in the rocks he shared with Bassom, another flare burst overhead, flooding the whole area around the summit with artificial daylight. From the proximity of the Vickers fire, Bassom realized his men were firing the captured British gun. The fire was coming from the direction of the reverse slope. Then the more soothing, rippling sound of an MG 34 joined the cacophony of violence. The machine-gun fire subsided, and was replaced by the screams of desperate men and the chatter of other weapons. A series of thuds from grenades told Bassom that his men were in close combat. He managed to catch sight of Werner just as the second flare fizzled out. A third flare instantly replaced it. More grenades thudded across the reverse slope frontage. Bassom watched his men dash from one position to another.

The third flare faded out, darkness descending. The sounds of battle gradually receded to sporadic firing, but commands continued to be shouted. Werner rejoined Bassom, gasping and fighting to regain his breathing. 'Counter-attack. The British have partisans with them, sir.'

'Right.'

'The partisans have got women and fucking kids throwing grenades at us. Bastards.'

Bassom struggled with the notion that women and children were helping the British to counter-attack. It didn't sound right after what they had witnessed through binoculars at the stream. 'How are the men?' Bassom asked.

'A few have grenade splinters. The British are trying to knock out our machine guns. They'll probably keep trying until first light.'

'We must be with the men tonight. They need to see us in the fight.'

'Agreed.' Werner nodded. 'One of our MG 34 teams has moved across to the reverse slope. There's still a team on the side facing the olive grove, should the bastards try to come round behind us.' Werner stood up. Bassom gathered up his weapons and helmet and followed him towards the reverse slope.

Bassom took cover with one of the MG 34 teams, being careful not to cramp them. Perhaps twenty metres down, he could just make out where some enemy had fallen. The wounded groaned, some writhing about in agony. The paratroopers would not waste ammunition on the fallen, even to put the wounded out of their misery. If any British or Cretans were still alive at first light, the paratroopers might go forward and tend to them.

From an unseen position lower on the slope there was the sound of another flare streaking skywards. 'Get ready, boys,' shouted Werner.

As the flare burst, bathing their position in brilliant light, Bassom was stunned at the sudden rush of soldiers and partisans sprinting up the slope, all throwing grenades and roaring at the tops of their voices. He felt grenades clatter around the summit. He fought to seek better cover in among the rocks as the grenades detonated. His head throbbed as the concussions pulsed through him. With the din of battle muffled, amid the dust clouds kicked up by the grenade assault he fought to gather himself to meet the rush of the enemy.

Just as his lungs allowed him to take a gulp of dust-heavy air, he was engulfed in a warm heavy mass. Fighting to free himself, he quickly realized it was a body, but not one wrapped in rough material and equipment. The material was softer to the touch, but warm and slick with the coppery tang of blood. Soaked in sweat, he heaved the body behind him.

With multiple flares high in the sky, Bassom was

greeted by a terrible spectacle. Numerous dead and dying littered the slope, but some enemy were still moving upwards, a few almost upon the Germans. His machine-gun teams continued blazing away, many of the dead flinching with bullet impacts, most of the living cut down at close or point-blank range. Many partisans were armed with knives, shovels, bayonets, ammunition tins – anything that could be used as a weapon.

Bassom was suddenly attacked by a wailing woman, who scratched at his face. He tried to battle his way to his feet, but tripped over the body behind him, crashing among the rocks, the screaming woman on top of him. Her hands still clawing at his face, he tried to get hold of her wrists in the fading flare light. Just as the flares gave out, a hand gripping a Luger pistol appeared. The pistol kicked once in the anonymous hand, and the woman's face shattered. She dropped like liquid onto Bassom's chest, her lungs expelling all their air in a vile belch mixed with vomit as life left her. Bassom wasn't sure if he wanted to laugh or cry. Everything was suddenly quiet as the dark profile of a soldier appeared over him, pulling the woman off, tossing her aside like a rag doll. The soldier knelt. 'What is your obsession with these Cretan bitches, sir?' Werner joked to Bassom's amazement.

Werner's rough hand grabbed the captain by the forearm and hauled him up, keeping a tight grip until he was steady on his feet. 'Thank you, Sergeant,' said Bassom.

'No problem. I would shoot them all to make sure they are dead, but there are a lot of them, and we might need the ammunition shortly.'

Bassom could only find the energy to nod.

16

John Hallmark was cautious as he approached Bentley Paine's group in the darkness, worried about friendly fire. He had no idea how long it was since he had led his reconnaissance patrol into the Greek barracks. The three men he had brought along were on his tail, but he had reservations as to their alertness.

There was clearly a battle in progress on the hill from which they had descended. Even from a distance, the flare-lit fighting sounded horrendous. Hallmark stumbled across Bentley roughly in the same position as he had left him. Bentley was on his own, slumped against a stone wall. Hallmark presumed that Bentley's contingent was not too far away, perhaps on the other side of the wall. He could smell the familiar sweet copper tang of fresh blood.

'Any news, Corporal?' Bentley asked.

Hallmark dropped alongside Bentley, removing his helmet and running his fingers through his filthy hair. 'The barracks are empty. The Greeks left in a hurry, but it appears they took what they needed to fight with.'

'Shall we go, then?' suggested Bentley, beginning to clamber to his feet.

'Are you wounded, sir?' Hallmark asked.

Bentley silently cursed Hallmark for having a nose like a rat. 'What, me?' he responded defensively. 'No. Why?'

'You smell of fresh blood, sir.'

Bentley didn't respond. Hallmark wanted to push the point but decided not to, instead getting to his feet. He had to admit that even he was fit for some sleep.

With the patrol roused out of its slumber, Hallmark took the lead as they occupied the Greek barracks, settling inside the two-storey structure. Men were assigned to different rooms, should it prove necessary to defend the place. He didn't bother planning for the Australians, preferring to wait until they arrived. With the men bedded down and snoring their heads off, Bentley and Hallmark found their way up onto the flat roof. They stood together, keeping watch. 'It's shit being in charge,' remarked Hallmark. 'Wouldn't you agree, sir?'

Bentley found the remark blunt, but nodded. 'I don't mind telling you, Corporal,' he murmured, 'I am dead on my feet.'

They fell silent, wrapped in their own thoughts. The darkness gave Bentley a feeling of security, despite their exposed position. He peered over to where he thought the sprawl of Heraklion hid in the darkness. Nothing appeared to be happening in that direction. At what he thought was the airfield a flare lit the sky, prompting a skirmish. No sooner had the flare fizzled out than the fighting calmed down.

Hallmark spent most of the time looking at the hill they

had held with the Australians. He couldn't help wonder
who was getting the upper hand. It had been some time
since flares lit up the summit, but there was nothing to say
that the Australians, or the Germans for that matter, were
not still up there. A stifled cough from Bentley reminded
him that he was not alone. Hallmark continued to be puzzled as to why Bentley had reeked of fresh blood. As far as
Hallmark was aware, Bentley had not been wounded, and
he didn't seem the type to keep an injury to himself. The
aroma was less evident now, which made Hallmark wonder
if the blood belonged to Bentley. Hallmark decided to park
the issue at the back of his mind for now. He focused on
their watch, thinking it would be a while before he suggested to Bentley that others should take over.

Martin Bassom and Sergeant Werner had resumed their
shared position at the centre of the defensive positions
around the summit. 'Werner,' suggested Bassom, who felt
tired and irritable, 'I think we need to tidy up our position prior to first light. I think it would be good for the
men. It's been a long while since the enemy last attacked.'

Werner frowned. The order was vague, and the men
were tired. 'What precisely do you have in mind, sir?'

'Leave the machine-gun teams as they are, but have the
rest of the men clear the dead from the area around
the summit. Put the bodies on the slope facing the stream.'

Bassom saw the dark profile of Werner nod, but the
dark mass raised a hand. 'And the wounded?' Werner
asked.

'Have them put next to our position, enemy wounded included.'

'Are you saying—'

'Werner, just do as you're told.'

'I see.' Werner made no attempt to hide his disapproval.

'Gather up all the dressings and medical supplies we have,' Bassom elaborated, 'and have the men do what they can. Our men will take priority. Will that be acceptable, Sergeant?'

'Yes, sir. That is acceptable.' Werner wandered away.

Bassom lay down, stretching out, removing his helmet, knowing Werner was too professional to whine to the men. That would only cause divisions in their already undermanned and badly mauled force. Apart from Werner, none of his companions were with the original unit he had dropped into Crete with. The men might not like what Werner was asking of them, but Bassom knew they would obey without question. He had been in the military long enough to observe that men in action would follow their officers, especially those who shared the same hardships. To keep his men's respect, a *Fallschirmjäger* officer had to be in the thick of the action against the enemy. Bassom knew he was pushing his luck with Werner, feeling the friction that was building between them and dreading the content of the report that he would submit to Colonel Veck and Captain Keich.

Reminded of the plight of his father in SS custody, and his brother Karl in the Grabowsee Sanatorium,

Bassom was once more overwhelmed with homesickness. A vision of his mother at home on the farm took centre stage in his battle-numbed mind, but he also hoped his father would keep his opinions to himself while in custody. The mere thought of Karl in the sanatorium sent shivers down Bassom's spine, particularly given the reputation of Grabowsee. As a teenager Bassom had heard of families sending problem sons and daughters to the place, only to be broken-hearted when the authorities informed them that their loved ones had passed away. It angered him to think that people could die in a sanatorium. He remembered his father's stories of comrades from the Great War whose minds had been shattered by their experiences in France and Belgium, and in the east against the Russians, being taken into Grabowsee, never to be seen again. Bassom gritted his teeth, guessing many had been put down like animals.

Bassom began to hear the whimpering and groaning of the wounded. The British were being laid on one side of him, partisans on the other. Wounded Germans were mercifully few in number. A few of his men began to tend the wounded using hooded torches to supplement the pre-dawn light in the sky. It looked as though the parachutists only required dressings and cigarettes for their grenade splinters. The enemy soldiers, many of them also smoking, seemed in no worse shape; a few superficial wounds, but nothing serious. On the other hand, many of the partisans were writhing in agony, some of the younger ones sobbing.

Bassom watched two of his men fighting to stop the bleeding from one woman, who hadn't made a sound. Her clothing cut to the waist, she lay bare-chested on the rough ground. The gunshot wounds riddling her torso made Bassom wince. One of his men, cursing under his breath, held out a blood-drenched hand every few seconds for fresh field dressings for her entry wounds. Once they were all covered, he flipped her over, exposing horrendous exit wounds. She had obviously been hit by machine-gun fire at close range. Bassom's stomach turned. He fought to resist the burning bile trying to exit his stomach. He sat up, then lowered himself behind some rocks and retched. He knew that he had nothing to bring up, but more importantly he couldn't afford to give Werner the satisfaction of seeing him. His stomach settling, the bile retreating, Bassom found himself glazed in sweat.

Bassom lifted his head to watch his men carrying the woman away. Despite their efforts she was now clearly dead. A teenage boy sobbed as she was taken. Bassom's men turned to the boy. Examining him, one of them called out his wounds. Two broken femurs. Gunshot wounds to the upper thighs and what appeared to be a broken cheekbone. Bassom had difficulty imagining the pain that the boy must be in. Why on earth would you bring your children out to fight? Bassom shook his head at the absurdity of it all. His men used blood-soaked dressings and bandages taken from the dead woman to strap the boy's legs. The boy screamed through gritted teeth as his legs were pulled together. Bassom rummaged about in his smock pocket. 'Here.' He threw his morphine syrette at the man who had listed the boy's injuries.

The man fumbled the syrette, but it caught between his sleeve and his torso, and he retrieved it. 'But sir, this is your morphine.'

'Just give it to him,' insisted the captain. The man nodded in the faint light and jabbed the needle into the boy's bullet-torn thigh. Bassom knew he had broken the rules – your morphine should only be used on yourself – but he couldn't bear the thought of having to sit next to the child all night, listening while he sobbed and groaned. Bassom wondered if Werner might have seen him give away his morphine, wondering if the Nazi might include it in his report. The boy continued to grit his teeth, still ravaged by pain, but Bassom knew the morphine would take effect soon enough.

Werner appeared next to Bassom, kneeling over him. 'It appears the enemy soldiers are not British.' His voice was breathless and hurried. 'They are in fact Australian.'

'Really?' Bassom wondered if the British had already withdrawn.

Werner nodded as he unscrewed his water bottle. 'Yeah, Australians. Still, no matter. Enemy troops all the same.' Bassom agreed that the nationality of the enemy mattered little. The Australians dressed like the British, and fought like them too. But given what he had witnessed through his binoculars at the stream, he doubted the British would use the Cretans in combat, something the Australians clearly had no reservations about, even allowing women and children to participate, which was unforgivable. 'Sir,' continued Werner, 'there's just enough light to see the remaining enemy withdrawing.'

Bassom was beginning to entertain the thought of sleep again, and Werner's words were just a jumble of vocal noises that had been forced into his ears, yet to form a coherent sentence in his brain. 'What?'

'The enemy, sir.'

'What about them?'

'They are withdrawing, sir.' Bassom's eyes snapped open with a fresh sense of urgency, and he sat bolt upright, only to regret the burst of energy. His head throbbed and pulsed with the sensation of a head rush. Werner waited for the captain to gather himself. 'They are making their way north towards the town, sir. Two columns, weighed down with walking and stretcher-based wounded.'

Bassom clambered to his feet, grabbing his helmet and MP 40. 'Show me.' They jogged to a position overlooking the reverse slope. There was no need for binoculars. The early dawn light allowed Bassom an uninterrupted view of the entire panorama. On the flat ground off the reverse slope there were two columns of troops, some carrying wounded. Bassom knew the latticework of stone walls dividing the fields would make the Australian retreat cumbersome. He took out his binoculars, fixing his gaze on the columns, before scanning the surrounding area. The general axis of the retreat was taking them towards the Greek barracks, which were on the way to both

Heraklion airfield and the town. Most of the buildings in the barracks complex were badly damaged, as were a number of trucks parked on a parade ground. However, a formidable two-storey structure looked fit to defend.

'What are your orders, sir?' asked Werner.

Bassom mulled the options over in his mind. He could have the men on the captured Vickers rain machine-gun bullets down on the battered, retreating enemy, although the columns were at extreme range. Or he could rally his men and set off in pursuit, denying the Australians any chance to regroup and establish a defensive posture. 'Rouse the men. We end this today. We advance now. Let's not give the enemy a chance to rest or react.'

'Yes, sir,' Werner acknowledged. 'And our prisoners?'

'Leave them here,' replied Bassom. He put on his helmet gingerly, securing the chinstrap. 'We will not waste manpower guarding them.'

'We can't have them at our backs,' Werner objected, 'not with weapons lying about.'

'You're right, and we can't take the Vickers or the other enemy weapons with us on what could well be a long pursuit. Have the Vickers dismantled, and scatter the pieces over the side of the hill. We'll take the other enemy weapons with us but ditch them in the fields at the bottom of the slope.' Werner was clearly set to protest again. Bassom raised a hand to silence him. 'We leave the enemy wounded unattended, without weapons up here. Just put it in your fucking report, Sergeant. In fact, if we survive, I will even let you shoot me personally. Save the Nazi Party the time and expense of a court martial.' They glared at each other. 'Get the men ready to move, Sergeant, while I go and fetch your precious flag.'

The German force made quick progress down the slope. Bassom watched as his men dropped the captured enemy weapons at the base of the first drystone wall; the Vickers kit had already been scattered across the hill. The rear elements of the Australian columns were just a few fields further on, the stretchers making progress slow for them.

'Why don't we take them now,' Werner asked, 'before they have seen us?'

Bassom shook his head. 'They are retreating to Heraklion; we don't need to waste ammunition on a beaten unit.' From the corner of his eye Bassom could see Werner nodding in agreement. 'Besides, there could well be fresher units to deal with on the outskirts of the town. We need to be ready for them.'

The day was slowly growing brighter. An order was passed to remain low whenever possible. The aim was to track the Australians without being seen and avoid a battle in the fields. Apart from conserving his men's strength for later, Bassom believed it wasn't chivalrous to attack an enemy with stretcher-bound casualties.

The din of aircraft began. Bassom was pleased to see his Luftwaffe colleagues out of bed and in the fight so early. The Stukas went to work, focusing on the airfield and the outskirts of the town, but ignoring the Australian columns.

Progress was painfully slow and frustrating. Bassom knew his paratroopers wanted to steamroll through the shattered Australians, who were aware of the German pursuit by now. But the Australians chose not to fight, probably because of their wounded. They reached a choke point at the back of the barracks, passing through a gap in the fence. Bassom wondered if the British were in there. Perhaps Werner had been right. Perhaps not attacking the Australians was a mistake, if it meant the Allied forces were able to consolidate.

Bassom called a halt to the advance at the last wall before the barrack fence and gave the order to prepare to attack the barracks, should they prove to be occupied. While Werner took charge of the preparations, Bassom stumbled across another dead parachutist, still in his harness. The parachutist had been looted. This was no surprise; even during the pursuit of the Australians Bassom had noticed the odd Cretan sneaking about. He knelt next to the body. There was no evidence of mutilation; the shot-away jaw and cheekbone had probably occurred during the drop, making the soldier almost unrecognizable. Some of the contents of the parachutist's smock pockets were strewn around him. Bassom had a sudden compulsion to look at the man's identity tag. Hanging from a length of para cord around the neck, the tag was of a crude oval design, made of cheap pressed metal with a perforated line running across. The perforation meant you could snap one half of the tag off, making it possible for anyone documenting the body to take one record of identity with him, but leave another on the corpse.

Bassom was stunned to discover the identity of the dead man. Captain Adrian Keich, the regimental adjutant. Bassom put half the identity disc in his pocket, before covering Keich with his parachute. He decided not to tell Werner, knowing he and Keich had been close. Besides, although in death there was sorrow, in the right hands and circumstances there was sometimes an opportunity.

Werner dashed over. He looked down at the body without recognition. 'I need to show you what the boys have found,' he said, struggling to keep his eager voice to a whisper.

Bassom followed Werner to an adjacent stone wall, behind which six men grinned at them. A weapons container was partially obscured by long grass. The container was already open. There was small-arms ammunition, lots of it, not to mention an 8-centimetre mortar kit, complete with bipod, base plate and a quantity of rounds. There weren't too many mortar bombs, but enough to make a dent in the barracks. Bassom's smile matched those of his paratroopers. 'Good work, men. Get it put together.'

'Corporal Hallmark, wake up.' Bentley's attempt to rouse Hallmark went unanswered. 'John. Wake up, John.' His Christian name brought Hallmark to his senses, and he forced an eye open. Bentley's face swam into focus. 'The Australians are outside,' informed Bentley. 'They don't appear to be stopping.'

'What? What do you mean?'

'Come and see for yourself. They look in a really bad way.'

Hallmark pulled his hulking frame up. Forgetting his weapon and helmet, he followed Bentley out onto a veranda, joining a few of his men. The early dawn light was low, but he still shielded his eyes. The Australians were below them on the drill square, the still-smouldering trucks behind them. Some stood, but most of the wounded were lying down.

'Are we going with the Aussies, John?' one of Hallmark's lads piped up.

Hallmark shook his head. 'Damned if I know, mate. I think we're just making things up as we go along at the moment.' Bentley had gone down to the square and was walking around the Australians. He stopped at a group of walking wounded, who were crudely patched up, dressings hanging off them, then looked up at the veranda and waved.

'Stay here,' Hallmark ordered no one in particular and went down to join Bentley. Just before he reached the captain, he realized one of the wounded was Colonel Austin. A grubby bandage was already losing the battle to keep the blood inside the Australian's head. Austin looked terrible, but Hallmark was pleased to see him.

Austin was giving instructions for his men to pass though the checkpoint in the direction of Heraklion, despite the Stukas swirling around the skies.

'Good morning, Colonel Austin,' began Hallmark. 'Glad to see you made it out of there.'

'Good morning, Corporal. I am sorry that some of my men are not with us any more. Our German friends laid it on us pretty thick when we tried to kick them off the summit during the night. But we can't hang about here chatting.' He peered around. 'My rear elements have reported that German patrols are right behind us. And the Stukas will probably turn their attention to this place soon enough.' Austin crouched, waving his stretcher parties towards the checkpoint, and looked sternly up at Bentley. 'Captain Paine, I need you and your men to stay here and delay the enemy, so my guys can get the wounded into town. Any questions?'

Bentley wondered what was wrong with the British tagging on to the back of the Australians, leaving the barracks to the Germans. He had no appetite for a rearguard action. It would be a no-win situation. He shook his head. 'No, Colonel. Not all of my men will be staying here. But we will buy you and your men time to move towards town.'

Hallmark kept his thoughts to himself but admired Bentley's lack of enthusiasm, intrigued as to what he had in mind. 'How did you all get in here, sir?' Hallmark asked Austin.

Austin jerked a thumb over his shoulder. 'Fence behind the trucks is down.'

Hallmark nodded and decided to offer a suggestion. 'Right, then. Why don't we put some blokes there? If the enemy notice the gap and go for it, the firefight will give your men the time they need. If the enemy don't notice the gap, they'll need to skirt the perimeter fence, which will take them a while.'

Austin's smile came out as a grimace. He winced, his eyes squinting. 'Good thinking, Corporal. Couple of Bren guns should do it.'

'Right, then.' Hallmark turned, but after no more than a few steps a dull thud echoed across the drill square. Hallmark froze, trying to register why the sound was familiar. Another thud. He had no weapon or helmet, and suddenly felt very exposed as it dawned on him what was happening. He spun around, exploding into a sprint, his lungs already burning as he roared at the men standing smoking on the veranda, 'Everyone get inside! Get inside!'

Hallmark had gone perhaps ten metres towards the wooden steps leading up to the doorway of the two-storey building when the first mortar shell hit its roof, sending bricks, roof tiles and masonry skyward. Hallmark stood transfixed as he watched the debris cartwheel in a slow-motion arc. The second mortar round landed behind him in the open. The blast pulsed through Hallmark, sending him crashing onto the steps. Rolling onto his back, he fought to draw in breath and cupped his testicles. The intense burning in his lower gut was over-whelming, as he scrambled to get to his feet. The next two mortar rounds hit the upper floor and the drill square in quick succession.

Hallmark lurched inside, glancing back at the inert

heaps of Bentley, Colonel Austin and his radio operator. He had to find a way of regaining the initiative or else they would have died for nothing. As he scrambled into the ground-floor corridor on his knees, he could make out muffled shouts from upstairs. The voices slowly became distinct in his ringing ears. 'German troops inside the fence, behind the trucks!' Hallmark's stomach turned. They couldn't become trapped in the building. They had to break out and get to Heraklion, but first the shelling had to stop. He pulled himself to his feet. 'Find that mortar team, quick!' he roared up the stairs.

Bassom's ears rang as his ad hoc mortar team fired round after round. 'Last shell,' shouted one of the mortar men. A couple of the enemy had actually been in sight on the roof of the two-storey block, but hadn't spotted them. Their work with the mortar complete, the team dashed into position beside Bassom's other men. 'Good work,' he told them. 'Get ready to follow me through the gap, everyone.'

Leaving a small reserve contingent behind with Bassom, Werner had led the majority of the German force through the gap in the barracks fence. Now Bassom tried to identify where Werner's men were, concluding they were somewhere among the smouldering trucks on the parade ground. Amid the gunfire Bassom heard Werner shouting, trying to control the firefight.

'They're behind the trucks,' came a shout from one of the offices. Hallmark went to find the voice, which was easier said than done. Incoming MG 34 fire tore through the office windows, shattering wooden shutters, shredding documents piled on shelves and desks. Paper flew all over the place, along with smashed framed pictures of past officers from the Greek regiment that had once occupied the barracks. German tracer caused some fittings, especially curtains, to catch fire. As Hallmark made his way down the corridor, he glanced in one room to find some men tearing down the curtains and stamping out a fire. His helmet now on his head, his trusted Bren now firmly back in his huge paws, he scrambled into an office taking considerable incoming fire. Its two defenders were behind a paint-chipped cast-iron radiator underneath the window frame. They grinned at him despite the barrage.

Hallmark joined his men at the radiator. 'What have you got, boys?' he roared over the loud snap of supersonic bullets smashing the room apart.

One of the soldiers leaned over to shout in Hallmark's ear, but the incoming fire suddenly eased off. 'Machine guns to the left of the trucks,' the soldier said, 'and their infantry moving among the vehicles. We can't tell if there are loads of Germans or they just keep bloody moving.'

'I think the latter,' Hallmark replied.

'Captain Paine's alive out there,' came from a room to their right. 'He's moving.'

'What?' Hallmark was unable to believe what he had heard.

'The boss,' roared the voice over fresh incoming fire. 'He's moving.'

Hallmark took a chance, raising his head just high enough to see the broken bodies in the open. Bentley was moving – a little too much for Hallmark's liking. 'Captain!' he screamed out of the window. 'Stay still!' Colonel Austin's radio operator moved, rolling onto his side despite the smashed radio on his back. Before Hallmark could warn him to lie still, a pink mist burst from his face. 'For fuck's sake,' roared Hallmark. 'They are fucking wounded, you bastards.'

As if angered by the insolence, the Germans poured heavy fire through the windows. Hallmark placed a hand on one of the men at the radiator. 'Smoke grenades, give me all you have.'

'Aim your shots through the windows, you idiots,' Werner shouted. 'Don't waste ammo.' His men continued to move from fighting position to fighting position among the burned-out vehicles. He knelt behind one particular wreck so he could observe his machine-gun teams. They were really giving it to the enemy in the two-storey building.

'Enemy troops just the other side of the trucks, Sergeant,' shouted someone. 'I think they are wounded.'

Werner got onto his belly and crawled under one of the wrecks. He spotted two enemy wounded moving about, one of whom looked to be a radio operator. Werner pulled his MP 40 into his right shoulder and lined up the iron sights with the already bloodied face of the man. The head of the radio operator burst as the MP 40 kicked slightly in Werner's shoulder. In Werner's mind, all bets were now off. He was about to move his attention to the other wounded man when, despite the increased rate of fire coming from his men, smoke grenades clattered about the place. One rolled beside Werner. Swamped by the dense smoke and fumes, he scrambled rearwards, coughing and spluttering as he spat and cursed, the fumes burning the back of his throat, his stomach turning. 'Grenades!' he struggled to shout. 'The enemy are counter-attacking.'

With the smoke grenades engulfing both the trucks and Bentley, Hallmark dashed from the building, Bren pointing in the general direction of where he had seen the German machine guns. The Bren chugging away in short controlled bursts, he dashed into the smoke. He could just make out Bentley. Hallmark slammed himself onto the ground as German grenades cartwheeled in. Tiny grenade shards punctured the dead and wounded, now Hallmark's only cover, some hitting Bentley. Hallmark felt splinters penetrate the side of his face and neck. He flicked off the empty Bren magazine, snapping on a fresh one, before leaning over to grab Bentley. As Hallmark gripped the webbing straps on Bentley's shoulders, a stick grenade clattered to the ground on his right. Still holding on to Bentley, Hallmark swung his foot at it, sending it spinning off into the smoke. As the grenade detonated, Hallmark heard a number of grunts, followed by shouts in German.

'Captain Bassom, sir,' said a sweat-soaked, panting, panicking parachutist. 'Sergeant Werner is down. Wounded, I think.'

Bassom rolled over to the parachutist. 'What happened?' He was fearful they had lost the initiative.

The parachutist pointed to one of the smouldering trucks. 'Grenade, I think, sir.'

As the smoke began to lift, Bassom saw Werner crawling slowly among his men. To his credit, Werner was still endeavouring to control the battle, which was seemingly beginning to turn against the Germans. 'Sergeant Werner?' Bassom roared above the gunfire. 'Have your men form a base of fire. My group is going to break into the two-storey building.'

'What?' came Werner's irritated if not agonized response. Bassom felt he had no choice but to move up to talk to his sergeant. The parachutist who had told him about Werner accompanied the captain. As Bassom reached Werner, he could see the damage for himself. Both his legs, along with his pelvis, had taken the brunt of the grenade blast. Two paratroopers to his left were very much dead, their blood already beginning to pool in a dark, sticky mass beneath them. A soldier was tending to Werner. He was trying his hardest to stop the bleeding from Werner's groin.

Bassom could clearly see the fear in Werner's eyes.

The sergeant was human after all. 'Stay focused,' Bassom said in an attempt to keep Werner's mind busy. 'Command your men from here as a base of fire while my group enters the two-storey building. Understood?'

Werner merely nodded. His teeth were clenched, his face glazed with the sweat of a man in excruciating pain and fearing his own death. Bassom decided not to hang around. They could talk in more detail if the battle was won and Werner was still alive. Bassom and his parachutist rejoined the reserve force, who were spread out over a rock-strewn slope. He gathered them together. 'We're assaulting the right-hand end of the two-storey building. Ensure grenades are ready to use. Understand?' His men gave him the thumbs up.

Bassom scrambled down the fence line to one of the MG 34 crews. He took comfort from Werner's shouts as he continued to command his men, badly wounded or not. Bassom took all of their grenades from the machine-gun team. 'When you see us about to enter the two-storey building, I want a heavy rate of fire into the windows on the ground floor. We will be throwing grenades in, so we can breach. As we go inside, switch your fire to the far end of the building. Do you understand?'

'Yes, sir,' shouted the team leader.

Bassom caught sight of a large British soldier dragging another up the steps into the two-storey building. The soldier had a Bren gun slung across his back. Bassom's mind's eye flashed back to the view of the stream through his binoculars. He had seen the large soldier before. He had gone out of his way to show kindness to the German dead and had confronted armed Cretan looters. Bassom also had half a mind that he had been the man who had cut down Stolz and several others in the Vickers gun emplacement, close to the summit of the hill. Not many soldiers were strong enough to use a Bren gun as if it were a toy.

'John, John, please stop,' Bentley begged Hallmark. 'It hurts so much. Please stop.'

'Shut up, you soft lad. If I was to leave you out there, you'd be dead by now.'

Hallmark grunted and sweated like a maniac as he dragged Bentley into an office that had once been occupied by a Greek colonel. It was already showing signs of battle, even though it was not directly in the line of fire. Tracer ricochets had already made the heavy curtains smoulder. A large oak desk was pockmarked. A couple of fine and expensively framed paintings of classical ruins were ruined. Chesterfield armchairs had been punctured.

A low coffee table remained untouched until Hallmark flipped it out of the way like a dustbin lid, to lay Bentley on a once-magnificent rug. With Bentley squirming at his feet, Hallmark shoved the Chesterfields against the wall, pulled the Bren from behind his back and opened the bipod legs before putting it on the floor, ensuring the weapon was pointed at the door. He fumbled through his webbing pouches for dressings to try and stop Bentley bleeding to death all over the rug. Hallmark knew he didn't have the kit or expertise to keep Bentley alive. His medical training was basic, and the captain needed blood put back into him, fast.

Bentley tried his hardest not to sob. The pain consuming him was like nothing he had experienced in his short life. Mortar splinters had punctured his lower back and upper thighs. They must have cut something vital, as blood was continuing to seep out steadily. Hallmark knew he had to do something; his dressings would have to do for now. He opened Bentley's battledress jacket, to be greeted by a blood-soaked shirt, then he noticed a small hessian bag under Bentley's right armpit.

As he did, the entire ground floor erupted in heavy incoming fire. A large glass-fronted cabinet burst open, sending assorted glassware including a decanter shattering all over Bentley and Hallmark. Flames licked at the heavy curtains. As the gunfire began to lessen, the building rippled with a series of grenade concussions.

'German troops in the building!' screamed a voice. 'They are in the bloody building.' The dreadful soundtrack of close-quarters fighting began – gunfire, grenades, screams, shouting in English and German, crying, rage.

Hallmark went for the Bren, only to have Bentley grab him by the arm and shove the hessian bag into his chest with the other hand. Hallmark looked down at the bag, then at Bentley's bloodied face. 'John, please see my family gets this. Please.' With all hell breaking loose out in the corridor and in the rooms around them,

Hallmark tried to shrug him off, needing to concentrate on fighting the enemy, but Bentley gripped him even tighter. 'Please, John. My family faces ruin. They really need this. Please.' Hallmark looked at Bentley's face, then at the bag again. 'Please,' Bentley implored.

More grenade concussions pulsed down the corridor, sending a chandelier crashing to the floor. The smoke from the burning curtains was filling the room. Hallmark pulled away from Bentley, grabbed the bottom of the curtains and ripped them from their rail, then stuffed them out of the open window as far as he could, before the heat and smoke from the burning material forced him back.

He looked down at Bentley, who had mustered enough strength to lift the bag, holding it out with an outstretched hand. 'Please, John?'

Hallmark took the bag from Bentley. He opened it and peered inside. It was full of rings, watches and gold teeth. He couldn't believe it. He had never encountered a British looter before, although he knew it occasionally went on. Hallmark's stomach turned and he stared at the almost lifeless Bentley. 'Are you for fucking real?'

'I know it's not what—'

'We might have to surrender. If they find this, we are both dead men, you fucking clown.'

'John, please. My family has lost everything. I joined the army to save them. I can't help them from a prison camp or the grave. Please.'

Hallmark was about to throw the bag at Bentley when

a stick grenade clattered into the room, landing at one end of the desk. As Hallmark dived behind the other end of the desk, he stuffed the bag into his shirt. 'Damn you, Paine,' he muttered as the grenade detonated.

Hallmark felt as if God himself had beaten him up, his lungs emptied of oxygen, his ears full of a high-pitched scream, his lower gut burning. He fought to gather his senses. He could make out muffled gunfire and the dull thud of further grenades. He thought it was the end.

As things became quieter, it became apparent to him that he had survived the grenade. Alarmingly, however, the dull clatter of boots throbbed through his punch-drunk head, along with the angry muffled tones of foreign voices. Rough hands grabbed him by the scruff of his neck and hauled him to his unresponsive feet. He fought to hold himself upright, but his legs just wouldn't respond. The rough intrusion of something thin and metallic under his left cheekbone brought him quickly to his senses. His vision focused enough in the smoke-filled room to make out two German paratroopers. They shoved him roughly against a wall. Both were helmeted, sweating, filthy, and clearly not in the mood for pleasantries.

As the smoke escaped from the shattered windows and doorway, Hallmark found himself looking at half a dozen dusty yet heavily armed German paratroopers, all standing over what had to be the body of Bentley. They glared menacingly across at Hallmark, their eyes daring him to give them an excuse to kill him where he stood. Their chests were heaving, their eyes bloodshot and exhausted. He suddenly noticed that Bentley's legs were still moving. A dark mass behind the six paratroopers was two other German soldiers trying to save Bentley's life. Hallmark knew they had a better chance than he had.

Two pistols were shoved roughly under Hallmark's chin. If he was searched, the bag digging into his right side would be found, and he and Bentley would be killed out of hand. One of the two paratroopers holding him released his grip and stepped away. As he turned, he gestured at Hallmark to raise his hands. Hallmark knew his fate was sealed and slowly raised his heavy arms, waiting for the search to begin. But then a commanding voice called out in German. All the paratroopers turned as one towards the voice; Hallmark's searchers stepped away, the group above Bentley parting.

Bassom stepped through his men. He looked down at the two men still tending to Bentley. The man looked seriously injured. Bassom looked at his exhausted yet triumphant men in turn. One by one, he put a gentle hand on their shoulders, giving them a fatherly squeeze, silently acknowledging their professional restraint. The British had lost the barracks and were beaten, and there was no need to kill any more soldiers than was needed. 'Will he live?' Bassom asked the men tending to Bentley.

One man puffed out his cheeks, shaking his head. 'He will now. Took me ages to find a vein. He's not out of the woods yet. His body just needs to accept the plasma. He needs an aid station, if anything.'

Bassom was pleased. 'Good work, men. Get him ready to be moved outside. Let's have a stretcher in here. And get the fires beaten out. We will regroup and rest here.' The paratroopers began to carry out his orders.

He fixed his gaze on the large British soldier standing against the wall behind the desk. Bassom studied him, knowing he was an honest foe, then gestured to the two paratroopers guarding him. 'Leave this one be. He will give us no trouble.' The two men looked at each other and then back at the captain. He could read what was going through their battle-numbed minds, and beat them to the punch. 'This one knows when he is beaten. Now help the others to tidy up.'

Two parachutists arrived in the room with a captured British Army canvas stretcher. Bentley was moved carefully onto it then gently taken from the room, groaning at the pain the movement caused. Bassom slowly followed the stretcher party out of the room. From the doorway he turned to look at the large British soldier, who stood with a crestfallen look across his filthy face, his hands at his side. Bassom recognized him as someone capable of controlling almost any situation, but now he seemed at a loss, like a child whose parents had vanished. Bassom smiled at him, beckoning with an inviting hand as he spoke. 'Come, please come.' Hallmark slowly followed him out of the room. The Bren had been left on the floor, but Hallmark didn't give it a glance.

The darkened corridor was heavy with smoke, but the

fires had been put out. Spent bullet casings, dropped weapons and dead men, both British and German, marked where close combat had taken place. Hallmark grew sadder and sadder as he stepped over his men, who had fought to the end. The Germans were beginning to clear the corridor; they didn't mistreat any of the dead British, placing them with their own dead.

Hallmark shielded his eyes as he emerged into the brilliant Greek sunshine. Wounded of both sides sat, stood or lay to either side of the steps. The Germans who could still bear arms were in possession of their weapons. Hallmark was pleased to see the stretcher party had placed Bentley in among the British lads who had survived the assault. Hallmark gave his boys a weak smile, fearing he had let them down, but relief washed through him when they returned grins, clearly happy to see him all in one piece. He picked his way among them, shaking hands, before finding a spot where he could sit with them and, with a bit of luck, rest.

For the remainder of the day Bassom concentrated on his men, distributing captured weapons and ammunition between them. His mission had been to advance on Heraklion airfield and capture it, but with such a reduced force it was evident the airfield was an objective too far. So he made a command decision to hold the Greek barracks. With Werner's ragged and filthy swastika flag laid out on the parade ground, he hoped the Stuka pilots circling above would realize the barracks were in German hands. He was still without a radio and had no idea how friendly forces were faring on the airfield, or anywhere else for that matter.

In the late afternoon small groups of German paratroopers began coming in. Most were wounded. They had no officers. One group of arriving paratroopers carried a working radio and had received a broken message about German troops at the barracks. Bassom deduced that the Stuka pilots must have reported the signal flag. The stray parachutists reported their misfortunes to him. All of their tales were similarly grim: murderous drops, murderous locals, vicious but justifiable reprisals, lost drop containers. He made notes of their stories; sooner rather than later someone would have to document the events on Crete.

Bassom acknowledged the badly wounded Werner, lying among his beaten-up men. Bassom knew the Nazi would still write his report. Bassom pulled Adrian Keich's dog tag from his smock, holding it in his right hand, stroking the stamped metal with his thumb. He would use this information when the time came.

The evening began to cool after another punishing day of Cretan heat. With the exception of those parachutists tasked with tending the wounded and guarding the prisoners, Bassom's force sought refuge in the building, where it was cool enough to rest in relative comfort. The Stukas had vanished. Bassom collected his non-wounded NCOs together, including those who had arrived that day. He invited them to stroll with him in the evening air, then waited until they were out of earshot of everyone.

'Any of you speak English?' He knew a few words, but not enough to communicate.

One of the NCOs nodded. 'Yes, sir. A little.'

'A little?'

'Well, it's pretty good, actually. My mother is from Pennsylvania, America.'

'Really?' Bassom was both surprised and impressed.

'Yeah.' The NCO grinned. 'My family is a little messed up. My mother's parents are Amish. They kicked her out for falling pregnant ... with me. My father came over from Germany to help set up some sort of farm machinery, or something like that, and he found himself servicing more than just the tractors in the barn. It's a little embarrassing.' He blushed as his fellow NCOs began to chuckle, their shoulders bouncing as they fought to compose themselves. Bassom tried his hardest not to laugh, but then the NCO looked directly at him. 'If you're going to laugh, sir, get on with it.'

That did it for Bassom. The valve was opened. The ability to laugh again washed through him like a huge euphoric tidal wave. As the sky grew darker, the *Fallschirmjäger* stood in a huddle, allowing their chuckles to run their course. Bassom thought the hilarity was just as well, given what he was about to do next. Once the group had calmed down, he addressed the NCO. 'Could you please fetch the big British prisoner and bring him here. You will act as translator.'

The NCO brought Hallmark to the captain. 'Tell him he is to take the wounded into town,' Bassom said. The

German NCO stared at Bassom with shock and surprise on his face. This irritated Bassom slightly, so he returned the NCO's stare, then flicked his head at Hallmark. The NCO translated the message.

Hallmark looked at the translating paratrooper and then at Bassom. After a few seconds, Hallmark turned his attention back to the translator. 'Why?'

'He wants to know why, sir,' the translator told Bassom.

Bassom rolled his eyes, fearing this might become a painful conversation. 'Tell him that we don't have the means to take care of British wounded. Our supplies are limited, and our own wounded require attention.'

The translator relayed the information to Hallmark, who slowly nodded his head. 'What about the rest of my men?' enquired Hallmark.

The translator made the request to Bassom, who shook his head. 'No, wounded only,' the captain reiterated. 'The remainder of his force will remain in our custody. I would not want to have to engage them if they were to be put back into circulation.'

The translator relayed the reply to Hallmark, but needn't have bothered. Hallmark already understood. 'You are free to make your arrangements,' added Bassom, 'and prepare your men, but please hurry. The nights are short, and our Stukas will return.'

17

Through gritted teeth Werner found the strength to pull himself into a half-sitting position as the large British prisoner got the enemy wounded to their feet. The big man and three walking wounded laid a man on a stretcher. Through morphine-numbed eyes, all Werner could see was the enemy escaping, yet nothing was done about it, even though Bassom was watching. Rage boiled over in Werner. He would give no quarter to the coward who was allowing the enemy to leave and fight another day. He would ensure Bassom's so-called war hero of a father felt the sting of Nazi vengeance, and his retarded brother was put down like a rabid dog in the Grabowsee Sanatorium. Captain Keich would receive Werner's report with satisfaction. Werner knew the adjutant had his own reservations about the farmer boy Martin Bassom and his false allegiance to the Führer.

Feeling very vulnerable, Hallmark led the wounded out of the Greek barracks. Without weapons they were defenceless against any German units they ran into in the darkness. With sporadic fighting echoing around them, all they could do was limp their way towards the burning outskirts of Heraklion. The flames ahead made movement difficult, as their night vision was ruined by the light. The pace was painfully slow.

Hallmark was not without his own injuries. His ears continued to throb from grenade detonations, and shrapnel fragments were still stuck in his face and neck. But guilt washed over him, as his injuries were minor compared to most. He also felt bad about leaving the few uninjured boys behind at the barracks. Thankfully, Bentley was the only stretcher case. Hallmark knew he would have to rest the column often and change the stretcher party frequently; the stretcher bearers needed to nurse their own wounds. Hallmark made sure he took his turn.

Bentley made no complaints about the constant bouncing. His initial German carers had done their work, and done it well. With morphine coursing through him, he was in another place, oblivious to his wounds and the events unfolding around him. In Hallmark's mind, the fact that Bentley required urgent surgical attention might well have been a key factor in the German officer's decision to release them. In combat and afterwards, the Germans had conducted themselves in a very professional manner, as had Hallmark's own men.

The Germans would probably have behaved less well had they found their dead comrades' possessions on Hallmark. His hand drifted to the bag. He felt contempt towards Bentley, who knew how he felt about looting.

Hallmark now realized what Bentley had been doing among the dead Germans on top of the hill when the British patrol first joined the Australians. It was why Bentley had insisted on inspecting Hallmark's work on the dead German paratroopers; it made sure the Cretans wouldn't get to the dead men's possessions first.

Hallmark fought the desire to toss the bag away into the darkness, but realized he pitied Bentley's family situation. Hallmark knew next to nothing about the young man on the stretcher. He had a fair idea Bentley had enjoyed a privileged upbringing, but to risk execution at the hands of the enemy so he could send home loot to make ends meet meant life was not all jolly hockey sticks and fox hunting. What on earth had gone wrong for Bentley to take such a risk? Hallmark was intrigued. He couldn't believe he was going to deliver on Bentley's request, given his own attitude to looting, but it should be easy to find Bentley's family and see they received the loot. As the column struggled on into town, Hallmark's mind wandered to other matters and he wished the German officer well.

The move through Heraklion was not without its hazards. The Stukas had caused enough damage in the narrow streets and alleyways to cause buildings to collapse, rubble blocking the direct routes down to the harbour front. With dawn not far away, and the promise of more air attacks with it, Hallmark struggled to make progress towards the harbour. Disaster was narrowly averted when some buildings towering over the men began to collapse, their lower storeys giving way under the weight of floors above. Hallmark also heard movement and whispers in among the rubble. He wondered if any of the buildings were occupied by Germans. A few of the men got very jittery about the sounds. Hallmark just told them to keep moving. The bigger danger would be moving through the British perimeter at the harbour; it would a real shame to get wiped out by their own side at this late stage.

Before long the whispers faded away, and Hallmark thought they would soon be amid British units. The column turned a corner and began to head downhill. As Hallmark entered the new street, he was welcomed by the moon breaking out of a cloud bank, its magical glare reflecting on the sea beneath it, the silhouettes of numerous ships bobbing about. It was one of the most beautiful views he had seen in a long time. After some stops and starts, the column reached the harbour, where Hallmark recognized the dark profiles of familiar British equipment down by the jetty.

Once again Bentley Paine and John Hallmark were queuing up to evacuate on an overcrowded ship.

18

Martin Bassom had travelled the hundred and fifty kilometres from the Greek barracks to Maleme airfield. He was waiting to be called into a large, hot, dusty, wind-blown tent that served as Battalion Headquarters. Days had passed since his victorious men had finally been relieved by German mountain troops.

So many good men were unaccounted for. Bassom's wounded men, Werner included, had already been flown out of Maleme, bound for hospitals in Greece. From there, they would be taken home to Germany. Not that Bassom spared much time thinking about Werner. The Nazi would live, perhaps even fight another day, but judging by the wounds he had sustained, his career as a paratrooper was probably over.

To escape the crushing heat of the day, Bassom sought shelter just inside a tent opposite the one his meeting would take place in. He took in the airfield around him. When he arrived a few days back, the place was a mess. The entire area had been littered with wrecked Junkers and gliders. It was only in the last couple of days that German bulldozers had arrived to help the Greek machines commandeered locally. The plane wrecks were now off the runways, their smashed airframes piled up like children's broken toys.

Very quickly the airfield had begun to take shape. Row upon row of canvas tents now received fresh troops flown in from the Greek mainland, Cretan dust clinging to their fresh uniforms as soon as they left the aircraft, the new arrivals initially taken to a reception tent for processing. Junkers taxied down the runways, allowing their engines to ease down with all the sense of urgency of a commercial flight. Bassom guessed it had been a different story to begin with, every plane landing through a hail of bullets. He had watched his men looking at the fresh troops. In various stages of undress, the paratroopers would shield their eyes from the sun as they took in their clean, freshly shaven comrades who would be calling Crete home for an indefinite period. Very soon the uninjured *Fallschirmjäger* still at Maleme would be returning to Germany to rearm and refit for the Führer's next big objective.

A Luftwaffe NCO pulled back the headquarters tent flap and waved Bassom in. 'The colonel will see you now, sir.'

Bassom ducked into the stifling, dark interior of the tent. Allowing a few moments for his eyes to adjust, he followed the NCO to the far side. The sides of the canvas tent were tied back in a vain attempt to allow air to circulate, but this did little to cool the interior. Clerks and staff officers, most of them Luftwaffe, sweated and smoked as they typed their reports or spoke loudly down field telephones. The NCO came to a heavy canvas flap that served as an office door, disappearing inside. Behind the material Bassom could hear muffled speech.

The flap was pulled back, revealing a colonel with a heavily bandaged head sitting at a makeshift desk made of ammunition crates and what looked like a canvas stretcher. The bandage looked fresh on, still a brilliant white, but given the dust hanging in the air it wouldn't be long before it became a shade of eggshell. A fan worked at full speed but did nothing more than push hot air around the small space. Bassom ducked through the threshold, ensuring his service cap remained on his head. With his damaged helmet tucked under his left armpit, he snapped to attention, delivering a crisp academy salute rather than a Nazi one.

Colonel Veck nodded. 'Thank you, Captain, thank you. I would stand to return your compliments, but this diving eagle has had a wing clipped, shall we say. Please sit down.' He gestured for Bassom to take one of the folding canvas chairs in a corner.

Bassom removed his cap, before pulling his selected chair forward to sit directly in front of the colonel. The NCO took his leave, pulling the flap back into place. Veck gave Bassom a friendly smile. 'How are you, Captain?'

'I'm fine. A little rough around the edges, but in good shape, all things considered.'

'How is your company?'

'Ready to go home, sir, if I'm perfectly honest.' This

was an evasion. Apart from Werner, Bassom couldn't remember seeing anyone he knew at the Greek barracks or Maleme airfield. Although Bassom wasn't in the mood to sugar-coat anything, he knew the real reason he was sitting in front of Veck. At the moment they were just getting the military bit out of the way.

'What was the final casualty state for your company, Captain?'

Bassom looked him straight in the eye. 'Thirty-five dead, seventy wounded, fifteen missing.'

The colonel rattled the numbers about in his head. He put pencil to paper to try to assist with his maths. Then he dropped the pencil, looking up at Bassom, wide-eyed. 'Are you saying that apart from yourself you have sustained 100 per cent casualties, Captain Bassom?'

Bassom closed his eyes slowly, opening them only to look at his interlocked hands in his lap. 'Yes, sir. The men I brought to Maleme are not my original company.'

Veck slumped back in his chair, clearly shocked. Bassom could see his eyes had glazed over, tears not far away. Veck was a tough bastard, Bassom knew, but he also valued the lives of his paratroopers. Bassom had no idea how the other companies in the battalion had fared, but now was not the time to enquire. Veck composed himself and nodded. 'Our boys are ready to go home.'

There was an uncomfortable silence as both men sat reflecting on all that had been asked of them over the last week or so. It was Veck rummaging through papers that broke the silence. He held up a few sheets of paper, leaned forward and looked squarely at Bassom. 'You know what this is, don't you?'

Bassom nodded. It was obviously Werner's report on him.

'It is quiet comprehensive, I must say,' Veck began. 'It clearly indicates there is no love lost between Sergeant Werner and you.'

Bassom feigned surprise. 'Really? I found Sergeant Werner to be most professional in the execution of his duties. Without him at my side, things would have been much more challenging.'

Veck frowned. 'Captain Bassom, Sergeant Werner has accused you of allowing the enemy, partisan and uniformed alike, to escape custody. He also mentions your continued antipathy to the Nazi Party.'

'Sergeant Werner has his own agenda, it would seem. Not all NCOs get on with their officers and obey orders regardless.'

'So you don't deny allowing enemy soldiers to return to their own lines?'

'No, Colonel, I do not.'

'Why would you allow the enemy to escape?'

'I allowed disarmed, wounded enemy personnel to withdraw into Heraklion. I had limited manpower and limited medical supplies. As commander, I made the battlefield decision to hold unwounded enemy troops in custody while their wounded comrades returned to their own medical facilities.'

Seemingly satisfied, the colonel skimmed through

the report and found another section of note. 'Werner also reports that you ordered the execution of several Cretan locals. Is this also true?'

'Yes, it is.'

'It says you ordered Werner to carry out the executions. Is that correct?'

'Yes, it is.'

'Why?'

'We ambushed the partisans, who were advancing to attack us. While searching those we captured, we found them to be in possession of personal effects belonging to German paratroopers. After coming across several men mutilated while still in their parachute harnesses, my men looked to me to even the score. I had Sergeant Werner carry out the executions, which he did with relish.'

'Werner shot them all?'

'Yes, Colonel. It would appear our sergeant has quite a liking for it. He is not someone I would take home to meet my mother, but in these situations he is certainly the right man for the job. He even shot Cretan wounded in revenge for their looting.'

Veck puffed out his cheeks, sitting back in his chair once more. The bandage wrapped around his head appeared to irritate him. He tossed the report across his makeshift desk. 'Captain Keich is to submit a report to the SS police commissioner upon returning to Germany. I need you onside for this, Bassom. Keich is a Nazi. He will do what the party dictates, not listen to mitigating circumstances. I want you and your family

out of the shit as much as you do. I can't have this political drama playing out while I try and lead my regiment
on operations. Lord only knows where they will be sending us next.'

'Why is Keich so vital, sir?'

'He is our Nazi Party liaison officer. Damned if I know
why we need one. Any party business or incidents that
involve the SS or the Gestapo go through his office.'

'Who takes care of that in his absence?'

Veck eyed him curiously. 'Why do you care?'

Bassom leaned forward. 'If I may, Colonel.' From his
smock the captain pulled Adrian Keich's dog tag half,
placing it on the desk.

Veck picked the tag up, taking the time to read
and absorb the details stamped on it. After a quiet minute or so, he placed it gently on the desk. 'You've seen
him?'

'Yes.'

'Where?'

'Close to the Greek barracks.'

'What state was he in?'

'Killed in the drop, still in his chute when I found
him.'

'Had the locals got to him first?'

'No,' Bassom lied. 'He still had all his equipment and
weapons. I stripped him of combat supplies and ammunition and had the boys wrap him in his chute.'

Silence fell between them once more, more comfortable this time. Veck picked up the dog tag in one hand,

Werner's report in the other. He eyed both items, before putting them back down on the desk, focusing again on Bassom.

'Captain Bassom. Return to your men. They should be flying out of here soon. You need to be on that flight. You still have a letter of apology to write.' He picked up Werner's report again. 'I will take care of this report, Captain. I will ensure it is, how shall we say, edited. You will kiss the SS commissioner's arse, whatever it takes to get your father released. You can then go and fetch your brother. Are we clear?'

Bassom stood up, stunned at Veck's offer to help with the report. Veck had broken his original undertaking to contact the SS commissioner before the report had been written, even though there was a whole telephone contact team in the headquarters tent. But not much time had passed, so Bassom's father and brother were probably still OK. And it was obvious Veck had been through a lot of late. He got to his feet, wincing. 'Do we have an understanding, Captain Bassom? If you haven't kissed enough arses by the time I get back to Germany, I assure you I will go out of my way to kick yours.'

Still numb from the unexpected turn of events in his favour, Bassom found it in him to snap to attention and produce another crisp academy salute for the colonel. 'Yes, sir. Thank you so much.'

Veck nodded. 'Right, then. Get out before I change my mind. Dismissed.' Bassom walked to the flap. As he lifted it, Veck spoke again: 'I need you ready to go, once you return from leave, Captain. I fear the Führer will have need of us again soon enough.'

Bassom made his way back to his men. He knew their rest would be brief, but whatever the Führer had in store for them, it would just have to be dealt with.

For now, all Martin Bassom could think about was the farm, his parents and his brother Karl.

Author's Note

Bentley Paine, John Hallmark, Martin Bassom and Julius Werner are all fictional characters. Their actions and exploits during this story are fictional and should be regarded as such. However, the battle in which these characters are set was very real.

The German invasion of Crete, codenamed Operation Mercury, was primarily an airborne operation. Buoyed by the audacious success of the *Fallschirmjäger* missions in Poland and the Low Countries, Hitler was eager to deploy his new-found weapon against the British and Commonwealth forces in the Balkans region.

Allied forces were squeezed out of Greece in the first half of 1941, the large majority evacuating to Crete. Battered though they were, Hitler felt it unwise to allow them the time or the space to regroup. He needed them dealt with, so he could feel secure about his southern flank for the coming invasion of the Soviet Union, codenamed Operation Barbarossa. Hitler pressed his airborne planners to produce a compressed timetable for an invasion of Crete, aware that to delay the start of Barbarossa later than June could have his armies caught in the vast open interior of the Soviet Union, short of the ultimate prize of Moscow, when the first snows of the winter arrived. Additionally, he had plans for the *Fallschirmjäger* to be involved in the early stages of Barbarossa. So the Crete operation needed to be swift, bold, and over before June.

The planners got to work with only three weeks to get everything in place for Operation Mercury. Confident that a quick success on Crete would convince Hitler to use the island as a springboard for skirmishes into the Middle East, they also planned for the garrisoning of the island after the operation. But Hitler wasn't involved in the planning of the Crete operation as much as he should have been and, like his planners, he overestimated the ability of the *Fallschirmjäger* to defeat a supposedly disjointed and badly mauled enemy. In fact, the British and Commonwealth forces on Crete had learned many lessons from the Greece debacle, in particular from the German airborne assault on Corinth, and were therefore much more robust, organized and well-informed, the recent breaking of the German Enigma code helping preparations to meet the expected invasion. Consequently, the Crete operation resulted in the almost complete destruction of the German paratrooper force, their losses horrendous.

Fallschirmjäger losses were exacerbated by the fact that the Crete operation was conducted in daylight and by phasing the parachute drops. Hitler restricted the number of aircraft for the operation, as he wanted planes held back for Barbarossa. Many aircraft consequently had to fly two round trips, to deliver two waves of paratroopers over their targets. The first wave was tasked with seizing Maleme airfield, but was greeted with murderous fire from Allied units hiding in the farms and olive groves overlooking the airstrip. Many paratroopers were killed before they landed, and most of the remainder were killed or wounded before they had a chance to get out of their harnesses and locate the drop containers that held their heavier weapons. Other Allied units waiting along the northern Crete coast were informed about the initial assault on Maleme airfield, so were lying in wait for the second wave of German parachutists.

The severely depleted *Fallschirmjäger* units were scattered across the northern side of the island, but regrouped and doggedly pressed on with their objectives. They quickly discovered that Cretan civilians were taking matters into their own hands. Many paratroopers who survived the drops were found in their harnesses, mutilated and looted. It was the first time invading German forces had faced mass resistance from civilians, and reprisals were swift, with many civilians executed.

Despite the disastrous drop at Maleme airfield, the German paratroopers managed to take the airstrip, pushing Allied units back far enough to permit follow-on reinforcement flights to land. Many German transport aircraft subsequently arriving were hit by enemy fire, yet the planes constantly flew in. German mountain troops and Italian marines poured into Maleme, and went straight into action alongside the parachutists. Despite throwing everything at the ever-increasing Axis presence at Maleme, Allied forces were eventually forced to withdraw. German commanders pushed home their advantage, scheduling all reinforcement flights through Maleme and abandoning plans to use other airfields. Retreating Allied units were pushed along the coast, eventually forcing the Allies to evacuate by sea to Palestine and Egypt. The island would remain occupied for the rest of the war, the locals unswervingly and violently hostile towards the Axis troops.

By 1 June 1941 the Battle of Crete was over. Germany was once again victorious, but at a very high cost. In the eleven days it took to secure the island, the German parachute force was almost completely destroyed. Hitler felt Crete was a hollow victory. He would continue to use the *Fallschirmjäger* as light infantry units on all fronts, but believed the days of parachute operations were over.

Over for Germany, perhaps.

But the Allies had other plans.